Coralie drew a deep sigh as she stepped from the train to the platform and followed the crowd up the stairs. She needed something outside herself to help her face the unpleasantness awaiting her at home, but she didn't even know what it was she needed. It was no use! Suddenly it all came over her how hopeless and forlorn she was, and most unexpectedly two great tears burst forth from her lovely eyes and splashed down her cheeks. Then she was startled by a touch on her arm, and as she turned, she found herself looking into the face of Bruce Carbury, her brother's wonderful friend!

"Please excuse me," he said gently. "I happened to see you just as those two tears rolled down, and I'd greatly like to be counted friend enough to help if there is anything I can do."

Tyndale House books by Grace Livingston Hill.
Check with your area bookstore for these best-sellers.

Grace Livingston Hill

THE SEVENTH HOUR

LIVING BOOKS ®
Tyndale House Publishers, Inc.
Wheaton, Illinois

This Tyndale House book
by Grace Livingston Hill
contains the complete text
of the original hardcover edition.
NOT ONE WORD
HAS BEEN OMITTED.

Printing History
J. B. Lippincott edition published 1939
Tyndale House edition/1992

Living Books is a registered trademark of Tyndale
House Publishers, Inc.

Library of Congress Catalog Card Number 91-66148
ISBN 0-8423-5884-6

99 98 97 96 95 94 93 92
10 9   8   7   6   5   4   3   2   1

I

DANA Barron settled himself in his pullman chair, tossed his hat up into the rack overhead, and closed his eyes wearily. The day was the culmination of a fortnight of anxiety and pain and sorrow, and the errand on which he was bound promised anything but pleasure.

He was two years out of college and supposed to be working hard in a publisher's office, learning the business. But it was not business that was absorbing his thoughts as he sat with closed eyes being whirled away from the environment that had been his since childhood. He was thinking of the quiet safety and strong kind guidance of the past years, in spite of all the hard work and discipline in self-control, patience, unselfishness, that had been a part of every day. It was all changed now. A new era of life had begun for him, and old things were swept away. He was thinking most of all of those last days of his father's life. How close they had come to one another, making up for all the reticence of the years! That last talk they had had together, in which they were no longer father and young son, but equals with a common interest.

"Son, I haven't ever talked with you much about the circumstances of your life. Somehow I couldn't. I hoped you'd understand some day. And I tried to make up in every way I knew how for what you've lacked in having no mother."

"You have, father!"

He felt the throb of deep love and pity in his own heart again as he remembered he had said those words. He was glad he had spoken so. The light that came into his father's eyes when he said it was something to remember! Poor Dad! How he must have suffered! And always so patient, so strong, so tender! Such a good sport! So young and companionable, even amid the hardest of his work! Even with uncertainty and loneliness around him, death menacing in the future. Even when he knew he had come to the end and had but a few more weeks to stay!

Some people were coming through the train from the direction of the diner. One sat down across the aisle, but most of them drifted up to the other end of the car and found seats.

Dana did not look up. He wasn't interested in his fellow-passengers.

Then suddenly a familiar voice boomed out joyously. The man across the aisle stood before him and was clapping him boisterously on the shoulder, patting his knee.

"My word! If it isn't Dana Barron! What are you doing here? Oh, boy! But I'm glad to see you! Isn't this great!"

Dana came to life at once, his own eyes filled with a glad light.

"Bruce Carbury, is it really you? I thought you were on your way to South Africa or China or some end of the earth somewhere. How does it happen you are here?"

Dana moved over and made room for him, and Bruce dropped down delightedly as if it were two years ago.

"Well, I didn't go, you see! I couldn't seem to make my plans work. You know how they do, plans, sometimes? It was like that. They didn't, so I didn't. And so I'm here. But where are you going? Just a few miles up the road, or have we time to talk?"

"All the time there is," said Dana with a half sigh. "At least all the way across the continent. New York, if you're going that far."

"Oh boy! Tell the glad news again! I *am!* That's just where I'm going. I'm on my way to be tried out for a job that I've heard of. If it works out I hope to be on easy street some day, or at least in the next block to it. I've got a pull with a pretty high-up man and it almost looks as if I might make it, unless he takes a dislike to my red hair, or my frankness of speech. But you, Dana, what are you going there for? The same errand? Say, how about a partnership? If they dislike my red hair I'll tell them I have a peach of a fella with hair like a morning sunrise. How's that? They pays their money and they takes their choice. But I thought you had a swell job. Weren't you training in a publisher's outfit? Didn't that pan out all right?"

"Oh, yes. It's all right. I'm hard at work right now for them. Only I'm off for a few days. I'm not hunting a job."

"Just going for your health?" questioned his friend, studying him quizzically. "But you look fairly healthy."

A shadow crossed Dana's face. His gaze fell for an instant, thoughtfully, his straight brows drew in a troubled line.

Then he lifted his eyes to his friend's face again, and there was a kind of appeal in them, as if he dreaded putting into words what he was about to say.

"I'm going to see my mother, Bruce!" He tried to make his voice sound natural, as if it were a simple statement he was making.

But the other looked his utter astonishment.

"Your—*mother!*" he said staring in bewilderment. "Why, but I thought your mother was dead. I thought she died long ago when you were a little chap, only a baby."

Dana's face was very grave and tired-looking as he answered.

"Did I ever tell you that, Bruce?"

Carbury summoned a dazed thoughtfulness.

"Why, I don't know whether you ever did or not, kid. Maybe I just assumed it. But I'm sure you never denied it. I guess maybe we weren't talking much about mothers just then. I know mine was terribly ill when I came to college and I didn't know whether I should ever see her again. As a matter of fact she died early in my first college year, just before I got to know you well. I don't suppose I said much about her when I got back from the funeral. My loss was too new. I couldn't bear to talk about it. I just dropped back into the old life and tried to forget."

"I remember!" said Dana, and pressed his lips together as if the memory brought back something of pain of his own.

"Well, but I don't understand, old man. Did she die, and did your father marry again? Or what?"

"No, he didn't marry again," said Dana. "It was just *what.*"

"Do you mean—" Carbury was perplexed. "Were

they divorced—or—! Listen, Dana, tell me about it if you want to. If you'd rather not, just shut up. I won't ever say another thing about it. It won't change our relations, no matter what it is."

A brilliant smile broke over Dana's face, lighting up his eyes, and bringing out the gold in his close-cropped curly hair.

"I know, Bruce. Of course. Thank you! I've always known you were like that. Of course I want to tell you. Though there isn't much to tell. My mother just went off and left us, that's all. When I was a little kid. I haven't seen her since. I guess I was ashamed, that's why I never told you."

"But that's nothing for you to be ashamed of. The shame is hers, I should say."

"But she was *my* mother, you know, and other fellows had mothers who *stayed*. No matter what, they *stayed*. And I guess I was ashamed for my father, too. My wonderful father! To leave such a father as that! He was a prince, Bruce! I couldn't bear to have him shamed— my dad! The finest and most honorable I'll ever meet."

"I remember him. He came to commencement. He had hair and eyes just like yours. I remember thinking he seemed more like your elder brother than your father."

"He was," said Dana gravely. "He was both. And mother too! My mother went away when I was two and a half, so I scarcely remember anything connected with her. She went away when my sister was born. She went away from the hospital and took the baby with her. I have never seen my sister!"

Bruce listened in growing wonder.

"And yet you are going *to see* your mother?" he asked, amazed. "I shouldn't think you would want to see her."

5

"I don't!" said Dana. "It would not be my pleasure ever to look upon her. But it was my father's wish that I should go. He wanted me to see her once at least. He wanted me to judge for myself. It seemed as if, at the last, he wanted to make sure that I would find out if in any wise he had been unjust in his judgment of her. If there was anything else that he might have done. I think perhaps he wanted me to make sure she had not suffered in any way. Perhaps he hoped that through the years she might have come to be sorry for what she did, and yet was too self-willed to say so."

"Then there was no divorce?"

"Yes, there was a divorce a few years ago. Father would not ask for it. He did not believe in divorces. But he did not oppose her asking. He made it as easy as he could for her."

"And she has married again, I suppose?"

"Yes, she married again, but it did not last long. The man departed for he soon discovered that practically all the money he was evidently after, automatically transferred itself to my sister when her mother married again. Father put it into a trust fund for her till her coming of age."

"But Dana, isn't it going to be a terribly hard thing for you to do, to go and see them under the circumstances?"

"It is. The hardest thing I ever did."

"Then why do you go? Surely you could make your father understand how you feel."

"He knew how I would feel when he asked me to go. It was my father's dying request, and I promised, Bruce."

"Your father has *gone?* Oh, Dana, I didn't know. Excuse me!"

"Yes, he died about two weeks ago, after an extended

illness. I feel it was the culmination of all he had suffered."

"Man! I'm terribly sorry for you. I know what your father was to you in college. I remember him as one of the finest gentlemen I ever met. In fact I remember wishing I could have had a father like him. You know I never knew my own father. I was only an infant when he died. But Dana, I dread this experience for you. Why do you go right away when you must be feeling so sad? Won't it only make your grief the greater?"

"Perhaps," said Dana with a sad little smile. "But it is something my father left for me to do. It is something which he could not very well do for himself. Something that could not, in the nature of the case, be done while he was alive. It was something that had to be wholly impersonal, yet done by one who was a part of the whole thing."

Bruce gave him a puzzled look.

"I don't know that I fully understand just what it is that you have to do. I'm afraid my blind instinct would be to keep just as far away from this thing as possible."

"So would mine," said Dana with a faraway look. "If I consulted my feelings only I would never go near them. But you see this is a matter that affects more than this earthly life. It has to do in a way with eternity. It was a responsibility that was laid upon my father's heart, and he could not get away from it until he had told me about it, and I promised to do it for him."

"You mean?" asked his friend with kindling eyes that glowed even through the perplexity in his face.

"I mean that dad came to know the Lord in a rather wonderful way in the last few years, and he felt that somehow he had failed in not knowing Him sooner. He felt greatly burdened for my mother and sister. And yet, because of the peculiar circumstances, he could not go to them and present the matter, for it would be so greatly misunderstood that it would practically undo all he would want to do. Especially if the other husband was still involved in the picture. I do not know that he is. I have to find that out. Gossip has not been busy our way."

"But say, my friend, wouldn't this be a case where a friend might help? I'd be glad to do anything in my power. Would you like me to make some investigations for you? I could do that through—well, through someone—and you wouldn't need to appear in the matter at all. And then if the circumstances are going to be uncomfortable you could give it all up—at least for the present."

Dana shook his head.

"Thank you, no," he said gratefully. "I must go. You know I shall not be going alone. God will be with me. If it hadn't been for that I couldn't have gone. If my father hadn't known that God was real to me, and that I would feel His presence and guidance, he would not have asked me to go. It is just something that has to be done, and it is my job. I thank you from my heart for your offer of help, but at present I don't see anything that you can do. I'll ask you when there is."

"I only thought it might make things easier for you if you just knew all the circumstances before you went."

"It doesn't have to be made easier for me, does it?" Dana gave his friend a bewildering smile. "And I'm not sure it would if I knew any more circumstances than I do now. I'm afraid I should lose my nerve and run away to hide. I already know too much for my own comfort."

"But Dana, just what is it you are going to do? Go and preach the gospel to your reluctant family?"

"Not preach," said Dana decidedly. "Practise, perhaps. Just go and see, and let the Lord open the way if He will. If not, I can go back home again."

Bruce winked the mist away from his eyes.

"You're being rather wonderful about this, Dana, do you know it? I always thought you were wonderful, but now I know it."

"Oh, no," said Dana decidedly, "I've just been finding out what a coward I am. But I'm finding out, too, what a wonderful God I have."

"Yes, that's true too," said Bruce with fervor. "Well suppose you tell me what your plans are. Are you going to your mother's house to live while you are in the east? Is she expecting you? Or would there be a chance for us to bunk together for a time?"

Dana's brilliant smile beamed out.

"That would be great!" he said. "No, I'm not going to force myself on them, and my mother does not know I am coming. I would rather have some habitation to hail from, even if it is only a fourth floor hall bedroom. That's about all I can afford just now anyway."

"Then we'll bunk together!" said Bruce delightedly. "I have a room engaged in a fairly decent neighborhood. Nothing grand of course, and you'll share it with me, as my guest! Yes. That's understood, for I had the room before I knew you were in this part of the world, and you know that any spot on earth is brighter for me if you are in it. It was that way for four years in college and it'll stay that way with me all my life."

"Look out there, brother, that's a pretty big proposition you're taking on, for life!"

"I mean it!" said Bruce. "It's not a new resolve. It's a vow I registered in college when I saw you deliberately step back from honors you might have had and let a younger fellow who was struggling hard take them. I've registered it a number of times since when I've seen you do other things as selflessly, with a look in your face as if you'd been crowned. I didn't know what it all meant at first, but afterward when you led me to know your Lord I understood. I know. You would disclaim it. You're too modest to take praise. Just call it love if that will make you more comfortable. But I know, yes, I understand, it isn't you yourself, it's your Lord who is living in you, shining through the flesh. But it's very notable, and it was through that look in your face that I first understood the Christ who was willing to be my Saviour."

The look on Dana's face grew beautiful with love for his friend.

"I appreciate that, Bruce. That's the best thing you could have said, that you saw Him in me!"

"Well, it's true!" said the other with emphasis. "And now, fella, you've got to let me help all I can. I suspect you've got some hard days coming if you go through with this thing. You've got to understand that we're one in this. Whenever there's anything I can do, you'll tell me. And when there isn't I can always pray!"

"All right, old man! I'll remember that. I'm sure it wasn't just for nothing that you happened in on this journey."

They were silent awhile watching the changing tints of a marvelous sunset that was spread across the sky. Then presently Bruce spoke again out of the query of his thoughts.

"Are you planning to stay east for awhile, Dana? And if so what's to become of your business? You were getting on pretty well, weren't you?"

"Yes," said Dana, "and I liked it. But I'm holding all that in abeyance. I had a little talk with my firm. I told them I had business to transact for my father, and I didn't know how long it would take me. Would they let me go that way and return later if I found I could come back in a reasonable time? They were grand. They told me to stay as long as I needed to, and then they gave me a letter to friends of theirs in the east in the same business. I may possibly get a temporary job with them if I find I must stay long enough to make it worth while."

"That's wise. And what about your girl? Margery, wasn't that her name? Or is there a girl?"

"There isn't!" said Dana with a wry smile.

"A thousand pardons, old man!" said Bruce. "But when I left your parts it looked to me pretty well settled."

"Yes?" said Dana. "Well, I almost thought so myself at one time. But vacation came on, and then dad got sick and I was naturally with him a good deal. She went away on a trip for several months and before she came back she wrote me that she was engaged to a fellow she used to know before she moved out our way. So, that's that!"

"Well, say, fella, you certainly have been getting the hard knocks! Or—wasn't this a hard knock? Somehow Dana, I never was quite satisfied with her for you."

"Oh, I know! And I guess it was all for the best. There were a lot of things we didn't agree on. And dad didn't care for her either. She had a hard streak sometimes. But she was young. Perhaps she would have changed."

"They don't! Not usually! Not till they get hard knocks themselves!" said Bruce with a conviction that sounded like experience.

"You know so much about it!" grinned Dana. "However, that's the way it is, and I'm not fretting. Now, suppose we forget me for awhile and talk about you.

Haven't you found a girl that suits your royal highness yet?"

"Haven't had time. Haven't ever seen one I'd go around the corner after. And of course I'm not a good-looker like you so they don't run after me."

"Where do you get that, Bruce? You've always been my ideal of manly beauty. Big and vital. Lots of character in your face, strong features that mean business, you know, and all that red hair and brown eyes. You don't suppose I admire my own golden locks, do you?"

"Girls do," said Bruce with conviction. "But your hair's not gold, it's deeper. There's something about it that makes it noticeable anywhere."

"Don't I know it? Don't I hate it? As a kid I used to wish I could dye it to some common drab shade like other kids. It isn't pleasant to be singled out and commented upon. But honestly, Bruce, I don't know where I could find a finer looking man than you are, and it's time you got rid of that obsession. Only I wouldn't want the wrong girl to get her eyes on you. You're too fine for that."

"Well, so far as I'm concerned it wouldn't do any good if she did. I've got to get a few shekels put away before I ever start to think about girls. But when I do, *if* I do, I have an idea I'm going to have a hard time finding one I want. As far as I've seen they don't want to do anything but smoke and drink, and play around. I don't want a wife that doesn't take life in earnest. I'd rather go all my days alone than be tied to one of these painted-up creatures without any eyebrows. They may have brains, but they don't look it."

"Here too!" said Dana earnestly. "They tell me there used to be girls with earnest purpose, and womanly instincts, but so far life hasn't shown me any. In fact I don't even know many older women I would care to have married if I were getting on in years. I don't like the way they dress nor act. I couldn't imagine a little child being mothered or grandmothered by many of them. They're all bridge and smoke and cocktails. However I don't know many of them and that's a fact, and those I do know I don't know intimately. I only know them from afar. This getting married seems to be taking a big chance, and I for one have had enough of that kind of chance in my life without taking any on my own account. I'd have to know a girl pretty well before I ever fell for her."

"People don't usually plan for any kind of a fall," said Bruce dryly. "As far as I can judge in a matter that I haven't had much opportunity to observe at close range, when you fall you fall, and have to take the consequences. The best thing is to keep away from pitfalls. Personally, I shall be inclined to be very suspicious of any kind of a fall. However, there were some nice girls in college when we were there. There was Harriet Hanby. She was smart as a whip!"

"Too dowdy!" objected Dana.

"Oh, well, she probably didn't have the money to dress as well as some of the rest, but she was smart."

"A girl can wash her face clean, and keep her hands trim and tidy, even if she hasn't much money. She can keep her hair from stringing all around her face, and she can put on her clothes straight. Why, that girl couldn't even put on a sweater straight. She always wore one as if it were a dishrag."

"Yes, maybe so," said Bruce. "But there was Allison Brewer. Whatever became of her?"

"Married. She married that Herriot fellow. That insolent highflier who acted as if he was a millionaire, and owed every fellow in college. That's the way those pretty little girls go. Haven't an ounce of sense."

"H'm! Yes, I know. And Carolyn Ostermoor went the same way. Married that Crayton gink who drinks like a fish. Well, life is queer. Anyway I'm not taking chances at present. Whatever became of Olive Willing?"

They talked far into the night, and then reminding themselves that they had all of next day together and another night before they reached New York, they turned in, each glad that the other was resting just across the aisle. It seemed like old days at college, with their beds across the room from one another.

They had been exceptional friends, these two, through the four college years, members of the same fraternity, both notable football players, both students and in earnest. More than most college fellows they had like tastes and aims. Their parting at the close of college had been a wrench.

Dana felt a degree of comfort in his loneliness as he drifted off to sleep. Life wouldn't be altogether desolate for the next few days, even if they proved to be more difficult than he anticipated, if Bruce was in the offing somewhere.

The next day was one long quiet rejoicing to them both.

They reviewed the past two years more in detail than could be told in the first few minutes, and then they talked of life as they had found it since college, of their deepest convictions regarding principles and aims. Shyly they touched upon their own growth in the things of the spirit, but more definitely than they had ever done before. They were each greatly thankful that the other was what he was.

They sat toward evening side by side, quiet for the

moment, gazing out at the sunset sky lighted in rose and gold, fading so quickly into violet and green and purple, yet touched now and again with the vivid gold of the sun's last effort for the day. At last Bruce spoke.

"Well this has been a great day. I shall never forget it. Our first whole day with absolutely nothing to do but enjoy each other. I hope our future will hold many more such times of leisure even in the midst of our life work. But at least we have this, and it is a fitting memory with which to crown our college days."

"Yes!" said Dana fervently, a touch of sadness in his voice. "It's been great! And we'll always know we have each other even though the coming years may separate us by hundreds of miles. You can't ever know how much it has meant to me, especially just at this time. I was lonely, Bruce. Dead lonely! I don't seem to be able just yet to talk about what dad's been to me these last two years. He was a wonderful man! I don't feel as if he was dead, either. Just gone on ahead! I wish you had known him better."

"So do I!" said his friend earnestly. "But you know, in a way I did know him better than you understood. I knew him through you. I began to see you were different from a good many of the fellows about us, and studying it I decided it was because you had a most unusual father. I found that you decided most questions in the light of what your father would do if he were in your place. And every time he came to see you I watched him, and wished I had a father like that living. Well, I'm glad I knew him. He left his impress on my young life too, and I'm glad."

A look of most unusual affection and understanding for two grown men to give one another was the only answer that passed between the two. Then after another silence Bruce said, in a brisk tone, as if the sadness in their thoughts were growing almost too tender for self-control:

"Well, now, Dana, about tomorrow. I don't know what your plans are, but we're due to reach New York at eight o'clock. We can eat breakfast on the train of course, and then I thought we'd better take a taxi straight to my room. You see I have an appointment at ten o'clock, so I won't have much time to waste getting settled. But you can park your baggage there, and be free to come or go at your will. I probably won't be back until around five o'clock, and perhaps you'll know more about your plans when I get back, and of course I'll be able to tell you more about my own. If we both stay east for a time we can look around and see if there are more comfortable quarters than the place I got at random through writing to my friend. But in the meantime it will likely be comfortable enough for us till we know just what we are going to do. Will that suit you, or have you any other suggestion?"

"Suits me perfectly," said Dana with a warm smile. "Only don't carry around the idea that I'm going to sponge on you! It might get such a hold on you that I would have to bat you over the head to get rid of it."

The next morning, according to plan, the two parted at the pleasant downtown rooming house in a plain district, Bruce going to his prospective job, and Dana left alone again, with his big problem on his hands. Going to take a message to a mother and sister he did not know, from a father who had gone away from this world forever!

2

CORINNE Barron in flashily embroidered satin pajamas of barbaric colors lounged on an extremely modernesque couch of white velvet in a bleak pagan living room of her mother's ornate apartment, reading a movie magazine.

Her full name was Corinne Coralie. And when her mother had married Dinsmore Collette some years after her divorce from Jerrold Barron, Corinne, still a little girl, took her stepfather's name, leaving out the Coralie, which she felt to be superfluous, and writing it Corinne Collette. But when that stepfather took himself away from them without the usual formalities, the girl was strongly tempted to discard his name and go back to her own father's name. If her mother had not objected so furiously she would have done so. But Lisa reasoned that there would be no other name for her to take except Barron, and Lisa did not care to bring the name of Barron into the picture again. So she was known as Corinne Collette.

The room in which she was sitting was so modern that it was fairly uninviting. There were some things about it that were almost repulsive! There was no air of home or good cheer or comfort about it. The draperies were black velvet, the decorations were fauns and satyrs with a few black devils and dragons here and there. Above her head on a low broad set of squarely graduated shelves that passed for a bookcase, sported a heathen god, with a look on his evil face that boded no good to his followers. There were vast unoccupied spaces. There was one huge impressionistic picture on a wide wall. It looked like a violently angry patchwork quilt in a frame. Here and there were cupboard-like cocktail tables bearing oddly unornamental triangles of silver or blood red that were intended for ash trays.

There was nothing attractive or lovely in the room except the girl. She was very lovely in form and feature, with a patrician loveliness that the expression of her face, however, did not bear out. It was as if the little soul that looked out from her wide beautiful eyes had been starved in its infancy until malnutrition had set in and warped her whole life. The selfish twist of her pettish little painted lips that were too red belied anything pleasant there might have been about her. The long curling lashes were too heavy with mascara, and her nice straight young brows had been plucked and falsely arched, till she might have been the daughter of one of the satyrs that posed about as an ornament.

A queer freakish clock bellowed forth an abrupt chime, and Corinne flung her magazine from her impatiently. It landed near a little black and orange satyr and together they toppled from the straight unpleasant shelf on which it had stood and crashed to the hearth below in front of a distorted grate where burned a sullen fire, the only attempt at homelikeness in the place. The idol's head broke off and lolled to one side; a missing eye presently discovered itself leering alone at the farther end of the hearth. But the girl gazed apathetically and didn't care. The satyr was not a favorite god anyway.

Somewhere in the distance a bell gave forth a flute-like sound, and the girl sat up sharply, gazing fleetingly at the clock to make sure of the counts it had just uttered. Eleven o'clock? Now who could be calling at that unearthly hour? Nobody, of course, unless it might be a credit man from some shop. What a bore! Why didn't Lisa pay for things when she bought them? It was poisonous to have tradesmen constantly coming to beg for money. Tradesmen were so insistent. What business did tradesmen have bothering them in the morning before they had fairly begun the day! Well, he could just go away again, that was all. For Lisa wasn't up yet, of course, and she wasn't going to waken her. Not for any tradesman! If she had to be called, Bella could call her. She wouldn't.

Then the maid entered with a card.

"Miss Corinne, there's a gentleman to see your mamma! What shall I do about it?"

"A gentleman! At this hour? Did he say he had an appointment?"

"No, Miss Corinne."

"Well, he's just a tradesman, of course, then."

"No, Miss Corinne, I think not. He's a gentleman. No one I know, but I'm sure he's a gentleman. He sent his card."

She held out the card and Corinne rose impatiently and reached for it. From where she stood a scant city ray of brief sunshine touched her wonderful hair to red gold and brought out its glory, lit up the delicacy of her vivid young face, and made it almost seem lovely in spite of its disfiguring embellishments. She was lithe and fragile-looking even in the costly ungainliness of the garments she was wearing. She stood there studying the card in astonishment, the sun lingering upon the riot of her hair, bringing out its natural waves.

Barron! Could that possibly be—! No! It couldn't! He wouldn't *dare!* Lisa had fixed all that so he wouldn't dare to come! It must be someone of the same name. Curiously they had never met others of that name.

But stay! That was not her father's name. He was Jerrold Barron. This was Dana. That was the name they had given her brother! Curiously enough she had always thought of him as a child! Yet he would be a man by this time, of course. A gentleman! So that the maid would recognize the fact!

With a curious feeling of resentment she flung her head back and gave the command:

"Let him come in."

And as Dana Barron entered the room the sun reached its zenith for that room and flung its full brightness upon the girl as she stood in her arrogant beauty, facing the brother whom she had never seen before.

Dana entered and paused at the door, his gaze full upon her. He stopped, startled at her beauty, and at her resemblance to their father. He had not expected this.

The maid lingered with curious glances cast at both of them, marveling at the likeness between them.

Corinne had flung up her haughty young chin proudly and faced him as she might have faced a menace, and so they stood and surveyed one another a long startled moment before the girl spoke.

"You wanted to see Lisa?" she said scornfully. "Well, she isn't up yet, and I'm not going to waken her."

"Oh, of course not," said Dana quickly, regaining his normal poise and courtesy instantly. "I'm sorry!"

The girl eyed him disdainfully.

"Who are you anyway, and why should you come here?"

Dana smiled at her disarmingly.

"I might ask that of you perhaps," he said, "although," he added with a sudden twinkle in his eyes, "with that hair and those eyes I haven't really much doubt but you are your father's daughter and—*my* father's daughter too."

Corinne gave a little gasp and a little quick closing and opening of her eyes as if the sight of the look on his face was almost too much for her.

Then her face grew hard as if she were refusing to accept the conviction that was growing within her.

"What are you here for?" she asked insolently. "What do you want of my mother?"

"I have a message for—*our* mother!"

She gave that little inarticulate gasp again.

"A message? What kind of a message?"

"The message is for her, first." His face had suddenly grown very grave and responsible-looking. He looked older than when he had first come in. She studied his face sharply, wonderingly.

"And suppose I don't choose to let you see her? She won't come out to see you unless she knows what the message is about, and who it is from. I doubt if she will come if she knows who you seem to think you are. Why should you presume to claim her attention?"

"The message is not from me," Dana said sternly, "it is from my father! *Your* father! It is important!"

"How do I know that?"

"I think you know it." Dana was looking straight into her great wide wild eyes, and his steady glance seemed to have a power over her which she could not shake off.

"I understood that he was not to communicate with my mother, ever, while he lived."

"Yes. But death came in and set him free from that promise. My father died. It was his dying request that I should bring this message to her. Now, do you understand why you must tell her I am here?"

There was a little stir behind Dana, a soft thick curtain flung aside, and someone stood there. There was a great silence in the room suddenly, a defiant silence upon the part of the girl. Then a voice, hard, cynical, severe, spoke, behind the young man; and the girl, wide-eyed, was watching someone across his shoulder.

"What is all this about, Corinne?" The voice went sharply against Dana's consciousness. "Who is this presumptuous person you are daring to discuss me with?"

Dana whirled about and faced her.

She was tiny and fragile, with a face like a hard tight little flower. There was an imperiousness about her that matched her daughter's expression, though there was an artificiality over it all that was not in the daughter's.

Dana saw it at a glance and something in his heart that had been growing all the years, and that he had tried to hold in abeyance of late, until this visit, suddenly congealed and asserted itself stronger than ever. Was this his mother? How had his wonderful father ever fallen for her?

Oh, she was beautiful! There was no denying that, of course. But it was a beauty like a lovely painting that gave nothing but form and color, with no soul behind it. His father as he knew him would have seen that at once. But he remembered that his father had been very young, only nineteen, when he met and wooed and won his ruthless bride. It had taken the years of sorrow, perhaps, to give Jerrold Barron the discernment that

22

would have saved him from making such a mistaken marriage.

All this, his perception of the mother, and his excuse for his beloved father's mistake, flashed through Dana's mind, like facts that had been there always, only he had not understood them. It was the answer to the question that had been recurring to his mind through childhood. Why had God ever let such a man make a mistake like that? As if one should ask "Why did God ever allow Eve and Adam to eat the fruit?" And in a flash he saw. It had been the means through which God had brought knowledge and beauty and fineness to his father's character. It was the answer to "Why is pain?" and a line from an old hymn that his father used to sing ran through him like a ray of sunshine.

> . . . I only design,
> Thy dross to consume
> And thy gold to refine!

And God had wrought through pain and disappointment the beauty of soul that had made his father so fine! All in that instant he saw it. Then he spoke, with a gentleness upon him that was not his own, but rather the look his father might have worn.

"I am Dana Barron! And you are—? My mother? Is it so?"

Lisa's baby complexion left no space for lines in her face. Only her eyes gave forth nature's unvarnished truth, and they were hard and glittering. Her delicately penciled vivid mouth was one thin straight line. No smile lurked there. No welcoming light in the whole lovely flowerlike face. Just an alien face that did not know him.

"Indeed!" said Lisa, studying the face before her. "I might have thought you were Jerrold Barron if you hadn't told me. And what was the message you were discussing when I came in? What right did you have to come here, anyway?"

Dana studied her face calmly, a stern look upon his own, regarding the unloveliness he saw as well as the loveliness. His voice was full of assurance and gravity when he answered.

"The right that death gives!" he said solemnly, and Lisa paused and looked at him for a startled instant.

"He is dead?" she said awesomely. "Do you mean that Jerrold Barron is dead?"

Dana bowed silently, and stood respectfully awaiting her word. And as she looked at him he was so like his father, that courteous attitude of respect, that steady controlled expression, his glance withdrawn to leave her free to think her own thoughts without observation, the way his bright hair waved crisply away from his forehead, that she was taken back to the days when Jerrold Barron was courting her, when for a little while her butterfly nature was caught and carried away by his strength and beauty, till another, less strong, but full of deviltry enticed her.

"You are very like him," she said with a sudden softening of her voice, a passing hunger in her eyes.

"You could give me no praise that would please me better," said Dana, still aloof.

"He was sweet!" said Lisa, with a touch of tenderness in her voice that may have misled her wonderful lover before he married her.

"He was wonderful!" said the son.

"Yes," said Lisa thoughtfully, "I suppose he was. But

you see, *I wasn't!* I guess that was the trouble." Was there almost a wistfulness in her voice?

Corinne stood by astonished, seeing a new Lisa, and not understanding. She was familiar with her mother's paramours, and her reaction to them, but she had never seen this look in her mother's eyes before, this look of respect and honor, of something deeper than just amusement, bewitchment. Corinne stared at her mother, and gave a little gasp, and the look in her wide young eyes grew almost wistful. Was there yet another kind of Lisa?

Then Dana's voice broke the solemn quiet.

"Then why did you marry him?"

Lisa looked at her son as if she had suddenly been called to stand before a court of justice. Was that fear that flitted across the pupils of her eyes?

Then a light careless laugh drifted to her lips, as if she would take refuge in gaiety.

"Just because he was wonderful and I wanted to try out everything!" she trilled.

Dana was still for a moment, his eyes downcast, perplexed. Then he lifted that clear compelling gaze once more and looked his mother full in the face, speaking in a voice of desperate sorrow.

"Then—why—did you then—*leave* us?"

The woman dropped her errant gaze from his eyes with a kind of light shame upon her, and when she raised her eyes again a change had come upon her face, and a hardness had returned to her voice.

"Because I was by nature a butterfly. I was born that way! I could not bear confinement to duties." She lifted her chin arrogantly, almost as if she gloried in her shame. "It was not my fault!" The last words were spoken almost merrily as if a sprite were dancing in her eyes and voice.

"Would you have excused *your* mother if she ha⁻

done to you what you have done to your son,—and to—your daughter?"

Dana's eyes went swiftly toward his sullen wondering sister standing aloof by the window.

"What have I done to my daughter?" spoke Lisa sharply. "I'm sure I took her with me. What more could I have done?"

"Was that the best that you could have done?" accused Dana solemnly, "to take her from a father such as she had, a father you have just acknowledged to be wonderful, and put her in the way of becoming what you say you are—a butterfly?"

"Oh, *that!*" laughed Lisa carelessly. "But why shouldn't she be a butterfly if she chose? Jerrold had *you,* and it is all too evident that he has made you like himself. I fancy Corinne has been happy enough. Ask her if she has missed anything."

Lisa stood there mocking him, the smile upon her painted lips like a mask upon a ghastly face that was hiding its grief with a grin.

Dana looked swiftly toward the unknown sister.

She stood in the embrasure of the window looking with almost hostile eyes toward her mother. And then she met Dana's question and her own eyes fell.

"Oh!" she said. "Oh! I don't know! I'm not so keen on butterflies. I—never knew—a *father!*"

And suddenly her voice broke into a half sob, and she dropped down on a low satin stool embroidered in dragons, burying her bright pretty face in her young hands, and a tear rolled down between her fingers and dropped with a splash upon the hardwood floor.

Then angrily Lisa spoke!

"Oh, for goodness' sake! Tears! Get out of my presence! You know I never let you cry, Corinne! And especially about a thing like this! Crying for something you've never known! How absurd! Go to your room, Corinne!"

Corinne did not stir, but her mother turned to Dana.

"Now, I hope you see what trouble you've made! Was that what Jerrold Barron sent you here for, to make trouble for me? Where is that message you were supposed to have brought? Are you going to tell it to me or not? I have no more time to waste."

Dana's eyes came back to Lisa's face.

"The message is in a letter my father sent," he said quietly, putting his hand in his pocket and taking out an envelope. "I did not seek to bring you trouble, though you never seem to have thought of the trouble you made for my father and me. All through the years I have been trying to reconcile my ideal of a lovely woman, a wife and mother, with one who could abandon as wonderful a husband as my father must have been, and a little trusting child. It has been hard for me to believe you could actually have done it intentionally. But now I see it has been so. Here is the letter!"

He held the envelope out to her and Lisa with a strange look in her face, clutched it, and darted an angry flash of her eyes at him.

"That is all I care to hear from you at present!" she said sharply, and turning left the room.

Dana stood watching the door where she had vanished as if he thought she might return presently. And over on the low stool near the window Corinne sat weeping. The room was very still except for the quick little breath of a sob she gave now and then. And after a time Dana became aware of that sound and turned toward her. It was almost as if he were in a strange land

and could not get used to the sights and sounds, could not take them all in at once.

The girl was sitting bowed over with her face in her hands, a picture of utter dejection. Somehow her attitude did not fit those brilliant pagan garments she was wearing. She would have been more fitting in the attire of a gamin of the street. She looked so little and pitiful with her bright hair in confusion catching the light from the window, that Dana's heart was suddenly stirred for her. A little sister! His own! And she was sorrowing! Yet while he took in the picture something warned him. Perhaps it was not real sorrow.

He studied her an instant, then he spoke.

"Why are you crying?" he asked, and there was both bewilderment and gentleness in his tone.

She lifted her head and her face was streaked with tears. Her make-up was a wreck. Lipstick and mascara mingled curiously. He looked at her aghast, and then turned his eyes away as if it were a sight not decorous for him to see.

But his glance went back as she spoke with a pitiful little wail in her voice, a kind of desperate anger.

"Because it is so terrible!" she said, and shuddered. "One's mother! One's father! You here and we don't know one another! I hate it all. I never had a father! I needed one!" Her face dropped into her lifted hands again.

Suddenly Dana went over and stood above her. He laid his hand on the bright head with a caressing touch.

"Little sister—I'm sorry that I had to bring this pain to you!"

The small shoulders that had been shaking with almost angry tears grew very still, and then she lifted her face and looked at him curiously. Next in a hard little voice she asked as a child might have asked:

"Why should you care?"

A great gentleness came into his face, and then he suddenly smiled.

"I don't know," he said, "but I do. Perhaps because you are my sister! Perhaps because I know my father would care!"

A hungry look came into the girl's eyes.

"Would he, do you think? For after all it wasn't my fault. I never knew him. Why do you think he would have cared?"

"Because I knew my father. I'd like to tell you about him. But—we can't talk here!" He gave a quick look about the alien room, then glanced down at her again. "But I've got to tell you about father. Go and wash your face and take off those heathenish clothes. You look terrible! Get something plain and decent on and we'll go out and take a walk in the park or somewhere. Then I can tell you what a father you had!"

Corinne had never been told before that she looked terrible. She caught her breath and stifled a small cry of protest. For an instant anger struggled with her desire to hear what he had to say, and she got up slowly, rubbing the tears away from her eyes. She walked over to a grotesque mirror built in angles on the wall and studied herself for an instant. Then she turned back to Dana with a half-shamed smile.

"It is pretty terrible, isn't it?" she admitted, and turning she caught up a pack of cigarettes from the table near the couch where she had been sitting, and held it out toward him.

"Have one," she said with a show of boldness. "I'll be all right when I get a smoke!"

Dana shook his head.

"No, thank you, I don't smoke!"

She gave him another astonished stare.

"Not smoke?" Then she turned swiftly and left the room.

He wondered as he stood tensely by the window staring out unseeingly, whether she meant to come back at all. She hadn't said she would. How long should he stay and wait for her? Would his mother return perhaps and order him away? Perhaps he should go at once and save her the trouble.

But no, he could not do that. He had offered to take his sister out. He must wait and see if she would come.

He would have been surprised if he could have known how Corinne was hurrying. She, who was unaccustomed to doing the simplest things for herself, did not ring for her maid, but went at her own reconstruction with locked door. Her maid would have been surprised too if she could have seen how swiftly and skillfully she went about it, removing the make-up and finishing with a good washing in hot water and soap. She was clean at least, and looked strange indeed to her own eyes as she looked in the glass. Maybe that ridiculous new brother would discover how silly she looked now, without make-up!

She chose a little street suit, the plainest she had, bright deep blue with a hat to match and a scarf of white. To her own eyes she had a nun-like severity.

Then with another dissatisfied look at herself in the mirror she went slowly back to the living room.

3

BRUCE Carbury was on his way to the interview which meant much to his future. He had expected to be nervous, and to spend the last few minutes in planning just what he would say when he arrived in the presence of the august personage who had consented to consider him for a job in the well known concern of which he was the head. But as he made his way to the place of meeting he found his thoughts going in an entirely different direction. He could not keep his mind from straying toward Dana Barron's troubles. Poor Dana! He was such a wonderful fellow, and to think he had such ghastly sorrow in his life!

True he had had a prince of a father, but his life had been blighted too! It seemed as if it would have been kinder in the father not to have put such a burden upon the son as to require him to go and see a mother like that! And a sister like that! What a shame!

Of course there might be something about the whole thing he did not understand, but from what Dana had told him, he could not see that there was anything required of Dana toward a mother who had deserted him when he was a mere baby.

And a sister, too! How complicated the whole thing was. It did seem as if it would be much better for Dana just to stay as far away from them both as he could, and forget them. What good could possibly come of any contact, however brief? Could it be that the father had planned this meeting with his mother so that he himself would be justified in Dana's eyes?

Well, it was all a mystery. But he would try to get to the bottom of it all tonight. He wasn't sure that Dana meant to go to them today. He hadn't said so definitely. Very likely he would only scout around, see what kind of a place they lived in and get his bearings first. And then tonight, if he could get Dana to tell him more about it, he certainly would advise him to stay away from them altogether. Think what a drag they might be to him if they were the selfish type, and they must be, of course. Dana with a worldly sister! She would be a continual disgrace to him perhaps! It would be so much better for Dana to keep away from them.

Of course it might be difficult to persuade Dana, for he had such an overpowering admiration for his dead father, and such devotion to his slightest wish. But he would try to suggest to him that likely his father now, from his heavenly standpoint, would not want Dana burdened that way. It must have been a morbid wish from a sick heart that prompted him to ask Dana to do this unspeakably awful thing of going to hunt up a mother who had abandoned him without a word, and had never since seemed to regret her act!

By the time Bruce Carbury had reached his destination, he had thoroughly settled it with himself that he was the one divinely appointed to look after Dana

Barron's affairs and prevent him from getting into a mix-up with a thoroughly undesirable family.

As he entered the great bronze door of the building upon which his own hopes had pinned themselves he gave a thought to that possible sister. She would be younger than Dana, and modern of course, a modern of the moderns. A shame and distress to Dana. No, a thousand times, no! Dana must be saved from such a family! The sister would have all the modern follies. She would drink and smoke. She would dance her nights away in night clubs. She would suck the very life-blood from such a young man as Dana! Somehow he must save Dana from the hurts and dangers and sorrows that would come from such a contact. Dana was too fine to have his whole life spoiled. If need be he would go with Dana himself and find a way to protect him from any menace that might result from this contact! Even if it meant taking time from his own work, and endangering the loss of his own position he must help Dana in any way he could.

As he entered the elevator and shot upward to the fifteenth floor, he gave a thought to the possibility of getting Dana to go back to his western job after a mere call on his family and let it go at that. Dana was his beloved friend. He must be protected.

Then the elevator stopped at the fifteenth floor and Bruce Carbury had enough of his own affairs to think about without worrying about Dana's.

About that time the long distance wires were busy between the western publishing house where Dana had been working for the past two years, and a certain publishing house in New York.

"Is this Mr. Burney?" called the voice of Dana's chief. "Hello, Burney, this is Randolph. Yes, Randolph of the

Universal. Say, I had a letter from Hatfield of Chicago today, saying he heard that Maynard was leaving you to go into business for himself. Is that right? You don't say so! Well, that's going to be a disappointment for you people, isn't it? Yes, I thought you depended upon him a good deal. I remember what you said about him. Well, Burney, have you got his place filled? No? You don't say! Was it as sudden as that? Well, Burney, I've got a suggestion for you. What's that? Me? No, I'm fixed for life here, I guess. But we've got a young fellow who's been working with us for a couple of years, and he's A number one. He's suddenly had to go east on some family business that may keep him a little while. What's that? No, we don't want to get rid of him! We hate to see him go, and we've told him his place is here ready for him when he returns. But we think a lot of him and want to see him prosper while he is away. We want him to make good contacts in New York, and he's promised to go in and see you. I gave him a letter of introduction to you. I hope he'll present it soon. But when this letter of Hatfield's came today it occurred to me that you might just happen to want to put your finger on someone who is thoroughly dependable to help you out in a pinch till you fill Maynard's place. So I just thought I'd take a chance and call you up. You can't make a mistake taking our man temporarily. What's that? How long is he going to be there? Well, he wasn't just sure. It might turn out to be weeks, or even months, though he hoped he would be able to get back to us in a short time. But he'll likely know soon just what he's up against in settling this family affair. What? Oh, what's his name? Why, Barron, Dana Barron. B-a-r-r-o-n! That's right. No, I don't know his address yet myself, but he'll likely come in. He always keeps his promises and he promised.

How are you? And the wife? Yes, we're all fine. Well, best wishes. Good-bye."

Mr. Burney hung up his receiver with satisfaction and leaned back in his chair, remarking to Valerie Shannon, his confidential secretary:

"There! That sounds good. The first ray of light since Maynard left us. A friend of mine is suggesting a good man to help us out for a few days till we find the right substitute. Anything he suggests is always good."

Valerie Shannon was small and slender. She had big blue eyes and blue-black hair that hadn't quite forgotten its childhood way of curling around her face, even though it was old-fashionedly long, and done in a classic knot in her neck. She was the daughter of a dear friend of Mr. Burney's. She was not quite through college when she entered the employ of Mr. Burney, but had proved herself most efficient even in the brief year and a half she had been with him.

"Yes?" said Valerie, lifting pleasant eyes to her employer. "That sounds good."

"We really need somebody very much, you know," added Mr. Burney. "It will make quite a difference in your work, too. You have been taking on more than you should do in a day, staying overtime night after night."

"Oh, it's all right," said Valerie pleasantly.

"Now, where were we? What was that last sentence I dictated, Miss Shannon?"

"You were saying that you wished to bring out Mr. Tempest's new novel not later than next spring."

"Oh, yes. 'I am enclosing the contract of terms as agreed upon in our last talk—'"

Valerie Shannon's swift pencil flew along the paper and the routine of the morning went on.

But Dana Barron was standing by the front window of his mother's apartment on Park Avenue, looking with unseeing eyes at the people who passed, not thinking at all of the letter of introduction he was carrying in his pocket, though when he started out that morning he had quite expected that he would have been through his interview with his family, and ready to call on Mr. Burney before noon.

Then his sister entered the room, and he gave a quick startled look at her. She did not look the same. And yet she was still very lovely. She was startlingly like their father! That was what he noticed first.

A look of relief came into his eyes as he studied her.

"That's better!" he said. "Shall we go?"

She walked haughtily ahead of him to the door, a stormy look in her eyes, and a petulance in the set of her lips. If she hadn't been so intrigued to see what would happen next she might have let them have their way. She usually did when stormy eyes and petulance came together.

Out on the street her quick eyes noted his courteous way, his graceful walk as he fell into step with her, and she was surprised. She had somehow come to think that her relatives from whom she was separated were from the wild and woolly west and had not had advantages. Yet there was nothing about this brother of which she need be ashamed. She gave a quick review of all her mother had ever told her about him, and about her father, and suddenly realized that it was more from what she had not said than from what she had said about them that she had judged them.

Dana meanwhile was looking down at her with a swift comprehensive glance, thinking how startlingly like her father she was now that her face was free from paint.

"Where shall we go?" he asked. "Have you some favorite place?"

"You mean you want to get something to drink? I could have given you that before we came out."

"Drink?" said Dana looking at her in astonishment. "Why should I want something to drink? Isn't there a park somewhere near, where we could sit down for a few minutes and talk?"

Corinne gave him another startled look in which there was a tinge of amusement.

"Oh, yes, the park. It isn't far away. I used to be taken there when I was a child. I haven't been much since. Around that corner."

They walked together almost in silence through the crowds on Fifth Avenue, and more than one in the throng turned to look at the two so much alike, and yet not alike, but neither were conscious of the interested glances.

Corinne was studying her brother, with furtive side-long glances. Noting the quiet gravity of his expression, wondering what he was thinking about, half afraid of the coming interview. He would likely make her angry. She was pretty sure of that. The very set of his lips and chin showed that he felt himself so sure about everything. Yet wasn't that the set of her own chin? No, more pettish, more determined to have her own way perhaps. She had always felt that was the one thing to fight for in this world, one's own way. Let people see that they couldn't trifle with you.

Yet here she was meekly walking to the park with an utterly unknown brother, allowing him to walk in silence!

He was so very different from the young men with whom she companioned. He wasn't apparently paying the slightest attention to her. She felt affronted, and yet she couldn't do anything about it, not just now, anyway. Not if she wanted to hear what he had to say. And she very much did. She hadn't been so intrigued with anything since she was a child, as she was now to find out about this brother and her unknown father. Of course if she didn't like her brother after she had satisfied her curiosity, she could cast him off, probably would. But there was no point in antagonizing him until she found out all she wanted to know.

So they turned into the park, and the girl led the way down a path where she knew there were benches. Not that she had been in the habit of sitting in the park since her childhood days, but she remembered well the places that had charmed her when she was very young. There would be pleasant growing things about, hemlock, and perhaps a holly tree or two, things that didn't mind the brisk coolness of the autumn day, and there would not be many people walking that way, not at that hour of the day. That would be good. If she wanted to lose her temper and stamp her foot at this paragon of a brother she could do so without running the risk of being watched by the common herd of passers-by.

So they came at last to the bench the girl had in mind, sheltered across the back by a dense growth of hemlock, the grass sloping down in front to where two swans faced them judicially from the edge of the water.

4

"THIS is perfect!" said Dana brushing away a little whirl of leaves that had fallen on the seat and motioning to his sister to sit down. He took the other end of the bench and sat silently in thought for a moment. Then he looked up and smiled.

"There is so much that I want to tell you about our father that I scarcely know where to begin. But perhaps I'd better start at the beginning. I was only two-and-a-half, you know, when it all happened, and naturally I don't remember everything."

The sister lifted wondering eyes. This was all so different from anything that had ever happened to her before that she scarcely knew what to expect. She put on an almost sullen indifferent front and sat with her hands in two tiny pockets of her short coat, staring at her pretty shoes. He had smiled at her for a start, but she didn't mean to encourage him in the least. She was holding her attitude in abeyance.

"It goes back to a day when father came home with a desolated look on his face and found me howling. I had got beyond mere weeping and complaint. I had been left alone with an unsympathetic cook who was getting ready to depart also. I was frightened and forlorn and thought the world had come to an awful end. I was very young of course, but I can remember that. I can remember father's arms around me, drawing me close to his big woolly overcoat, and snuggling me up. He had just found out that he had lost his family, and that he and I were left alone. Even my nurse was gone, though neither of us cared much for her. She wasn't very comforting. And I somehow knew, little as I was, that father was feeling just the way I did. But he promptly put away his own grief and concentrated on mine. He put his face down to mine and kissed the tears away. He took his own soft white handkerchief out of his pocket and wiped my hot little face, and hugged me close. And sometimes his lips would come down to my ear and touch it tenderly, and whisper my name, 'Dear little Dana! Daddy's little boy! You needn't cry any more. Daddy will take care of you!' He held me that way and patted me softly till I fell asleep. And a long time afterward when it was quite dark in the room and I woke up, I was still in his arms, hugged close, and he was sitting there with his head back on the chair, and his eyes closed, but his arms were warm and close about me.

"I don't remember ever having had such tenderness before. Or perhaps my need had made his comfort seem different. I had mostly been tended by a gay young nurse who had no love to spare for me from her own loves.

"Presently father got up, but he kept me in his arms while he went about lighting the rooms. The cook was gone. There wasn't anybody left in the house but father and me. It wasn't a large house, but it sounded awfully empty. Queer. I haven't forgotten that! We went out to the kitchen, I walking with father, holding to his hand.

We got milk and things from the refrigerator. I had a chicken drumstick to chew on. There was custard. It didn't matter, but it was good. We ate supper together, and then father let me help with the dishes. I had a towel and dried them. Father got me to laughing. After all the tears, there was laughter! Tears in his heart and mine too, but he could laugh for my sake!"

Corinne had forgotten to look sullen. Her eyes were filled with sudden tears and she brushed them fiercely away. The woman in her was thinking of that little hungry lonesome boy who was being comforted. She had never heretofore thought of anybody but herself and what she wanted and needed.

"He got a plain oldish Scotch woman in after a few days' hunting. She cooked for us and kept the house clean, and she looked after me and saw that I came to no harm, but my father hurried home from the office to me every day as soon as he could get away from business. If there was a chance to run home at lunch time he did so. And every time I would be at the window, or the gate—we had a little white gate that I could swing on and take hold of the pickets—and always he would wave to me, and call out 'Hello, fella! Been a good soldier today?'

"Always he made a game out of the life we had to live. We were soldiers being brave. It meant a lot to me. Sometimes I think—I hope—it helped him to live out the lonely days too.

"The first day I went to school stands out. He took me there himself! He had made a story of it for days beforehand that I might get accustomed to it, and be ready to meet the new life. He told me what I would have to meet. People who didn't love me the way he did, but with whom I must get along pleasantly even if

I didn't like them all. But never must I compromise with what was wrong. I must remember that I was a soldier. I must remember that God was watching what kind of a soldier I was being. There might even be times when I would have to fight, but I must be sure I was always fighting for the right, not just to have my own way, for there would always be God.

"It was when I was ten that he first told me I had a little sister. We had been watching out the window as some people went by, and they had a little girl with them. She had gold curls flying down her back, and she was a pretty little thing. She was laughing and calling out to her mother and father; and dad—sort of caught his breath, as if it hurt him, and then he said, 'I never told you you had a little sister, son, did I?' I remember the look on his face as I looked up in wonder and began to ask questions. I could see—that he—loved you very much! I seemed to see down into his heart that day as I'd never seen before! I began to realize all at once that he was a man, with a life of his own, not just the father of me, made to comfort me and care for me. I began to see that he had a great big sorrow in his life, but he never let it get the better of him. And years later, just before he left me, something he said about God made me see that the secret of his strong beautiful life was that he had an abiding consciousness that there was always God, just as he had taught me when I was a little child, only he spoke of Him now as 'the Lord Jesus.'"

It was very still there behind the hemlocks, with only the stirrings of the swans to disturb them. The city's roar seemed far away, and they two were shut in a little quiet place, where suddenly the sister felt that God had arrived. God had never been in her life before, except as a name seldom mentioned, and meaning little. Now He stood there, an unknown One looking at her. She gripped her young hands together and gave a little shiver. Then Dana took up the story again.

"We talked about you sometimes, father and I, when we were all alone and quite quiet. Father let me imagine what we would do and say if you should come to stay with us. How happy we would be. Where we would take you. What we would get for you—that was a little joke we had together, because by that time we hadn't any money to get anything but the barest necessities. But we played we had for your sake. Father made a game of it and I would come home some nights and say: 'Dad, I found such a pretty wrist watch I think my sister would like. Shall we get it for her?' and always he would enter into the game and be as eager over it as I was. Sometimes he would say, 'Let's save it for Christmas for her.' And then he would go on planning how we would trim the tree and hang up our stockings, and how the watch would be in the very toe of your little stocking!"

Dana paused and turned his face away from his sister. Something in his memory overcame his own control, and he struggled with the mist in his own eyes. He did not look at his sister or he would have seen that her tears were pouring down her face and dripping from her chin. Unaccustomed tears. Not angry tears.

"If he had had the money to get the kind he liked I believe that he would have sent it to you last Christmas. He talked a great deal then about what he would like to do for you if he were able."

"Money?" said the girl suddenly. "But I thought that he was fabulously wealthy! Lisa always said so. She told me when I was very little that my father had slews of money."

Dana suddenly turned and looked at his sister and saw

that she was weeping. His own lashes were wet. He gave a sad little smile.

"No," he said. "He used to have plenty, but when— our mother went away, he turned all his inheritance into a fund for her and you. Even then he had barely enough to cover the sum she had asked. He had nothing left but the business, and when the depression came on, that went down and down, and we had hard work to make both ends meet, till I got out of college and got a job that paid a small salary, which was a lucky thing, for dad was down and out and needed a lot of things himself by then."

Dana's voice was low and sad as he said this, as if his memories were very sorrowful.

"But dad was more wonderful than ever then. He never murmured once, and always had a smile."

"Oh!" moaned the sister with a real sob in her breath, "I didn't know! How very mean we have been! Oh, we oughtn't to have had a thing!"

"No! I'm sorry I told you that!" said Dana with quick contrition. "I didn't realize how that would sound to you! How should I make you understand? We were glad to do that for you and my mother! Glad it was possible!"

"That doesn't sound reasonable," scorned Corinne, "to be glad to go without things for the sake of people who had run away from you! That isn't natural!"

"It's love!" said Dana gently. "And that was my father! Love! He was the personification of love! But don't misunderstand me. He was a strong man, a real man, nothing sissy about him. But he was great enough to love even over great odds. He hated sin and wrong in every form, and he would fight it to the death, and did in many ways. But he could love. And how he loved you! And he had loved your mother, too. But he loved you most tenderly. He called you Coralie always. He liked that name best. He said the other name, Corinne, meant one of a group of humming-birds, with long lance-like bills and very brilliant coloration, and he liked best the thought of the soft shell-pink of Coralie."

"Oh!" said Corinne. "I wish I were like that! But I'm Corinne, I know I am!"

Dana turned toward her earnestly.

"Look here, little sister," he said, reaching out his hand and taking one of hers gently, "I've always called you Coralie, and I'm going to keep on doing so, may I?"

Coralie choked and nodded, and her fingers curled themselves in a wild quick grasp about her brother's hand. Then suddenly she flung his hand away and sprang to her feet.

"Oh!" she said wringing her hands and flinging them out desperately, "I don't know how I'm ever going to forget all this!"

Dana looked at her wistfully.

"Do you have to forget it?" he asked sadly.

"Why, of course!" she said angrily. "How could I go on living and remember what you went through for us? How could I ever go on going to the silly parties and flirting and dancing and getting drunk, and sleeping it off, and then doing it all over again? How could I, and know that all the time I had been growing up and doing that, you and my father had been going without things so we might have more party dresses and jewels and cars and servants and wine and flowers. Oh, it makes me sick! Certainly I must forget! Good-bye! I'm going home!"

She flung away from him and darted out among the shrubbery and down the path toward the open way where walked the throngs. Then suddenly she stopped, looking back toward him where he still sat watching her sadly, and dashed back to him again.

"Where do you stay?" she asked, breathless. "I can't let you go off like this into nowhere. Where do you live? Tell me quick!"

With a strange half-smile on his lips Dana wrote out the address for her. She took the card and read it.

"Down there?" she exclaimed in horror. "Why that's nowhere to live! I can give you a lot of addresses that would be a lot better than that. That's away downtown."

"Thank you," he said, "I'm very well satisfied. And I have a friend, my old college roommate with me. We're quite pleasantly located, so don't worry. It's perfectly respectable."

"Respectable? Oh! Well, I wasn't thinking about that. I was thinking of it socially."

"Socially?" Dana grinned. "Well, I wasn't expecting to go out socially. That's out of my line."

The girl looked at him with a puzzled pucker in her young brow.

"You're so different!" she said at last. Then her brow cleared. "But you're rather nice in spite of it! Good-bye!" and she was gone.

Dana sat there for some time, thinking over the interview, seeing once more the startling face of his young sister, remembering the strange remarks she had made. And yet, there had been a latent sweetness about her in spite of it all, now that the paint was washed away, and the bold look was gone. Oh, if she had been left behind also, as he had been, and had been brought up by their father, perhaps she would have been sweet and lovely. She certainly would have been lovely.

He pondered carefully the question of whether there

was anything he possibly could do for her now. That had been the real point of his mission he knew, as far as his father's wishes were concerned. The father had been obsessed during his last days lest he should have somehow managed to get control of his little girl when she was a baby and bring her up as he had known her mother would never do. He was filled with the realization of the eternity to which he was going, and the sense that maybe he had not done right by giving up the child without an attempt to get her, a feeling that he was responsible for her and should take some means even yet, to teach her the meaning of life and death, of sin and salvation.

But the more he thought it over, the more Dana felt that he could do nothing. Perhaps he had already fulfilled whatever there was in his father's mind by just bringing that letter to his mother and by telling his sister what a wonderful father she had. Perhaps he might as well go home tonight and get back to work.

Yet his mind was not easy. He had a feeling that if he should go at this stage of things he would always think perhaps he should have stayed. At least a few days longer.

What had his sister wanted with his address? Would there be a note from her tomorrow, or in a few days, that would settle the matter for him, and give him freedom to go?

As he thought of his mother he had a strange desolate feeling that he had done all he could, and that she would never accept him, or be influenced by anything he said. But he realized that this contact with her had cleared up a matter once for all for him, and that was whether his father had been mistaken in his judgment of his mother. Perhaps he had never realized before that at times all his life after he was old enough to reason at all, he had had moments when that thought clamored at his consciousness and insisted upon being heard. And always he had put it by as something that was disloyal to the father whom he all but worshipped. But now he realized that it had been a relief to him when his father asked him to go and see his mother and take the letter to her. Had the keen tender mind of his father sensed that his son would wonder about the mother who had been so seldom mentioned between them? Or had he planned some means to see that she too knew the way of salvation? Anyway, for whatever reason, Jerrold Barron had so far been able to impress his son with the burden that was upon his own soul, that he had given up everything else and come half across the continent on this mission. And now that he was here it seemed so utterly hopeless. A sister like that! A doll! No, worse than a doll! An utter worldling who didn't want to be anything else.

He had known before he came of course that it would be so. Yet he had come! And now he was here what could he do? As well go home and get to work. Work out his own life and find a way to work for his Lord. Make a place in life that was his own.

Could he ever do that? With his father gone could he go back to that town, and that apartment where he and his father had lived together, taking their meals together downstairs in a cosy little restaurant? Could he go back and sit at the same table and eat alone? Lonely days and long evenings with nobody to talk to. Margery? No, Margery and he were done. Not that they had ever been really engaged. It was just a tacit friendship that had lasted from their high school days, through college, and a few months afterward, and then their ways had parted so definitely that it seemed useless ever to try to patch things up.

He had come home from college expecting sometime soon, when he got a good job, to ask Margery to marry him. And then had come the growing anxiety about his father, and his own absorption in him to the exclusion of other things. He hadn't gone very often to see Margery. He had stayed a great deal with his father, feeling that his illness would soon be over and he could get back to normal living.

But his father had got no better. He had only grown frailer and more dependent upon him. And when his father urged him to go out for an evening, and he yielded to please him, Margery seemed to have so many other interests, foreign to his own ways, that he had felt they were growing apart. She told him that he was too serious, that he was getting to be a regular grind. She wanted to go into the world, the world that neither of them had been brought up to care for. College had made a great difference in Margery.

One day he had made a business of trying to find out just where she did stand on a lot of questions upon which they used to agree, basic questions that seemed to him more important than anything else. He discovered, after serious questioning, that she had lost her faith, the faith in which she had been reared. She no longer thought the Bible was the word of God, as she used to believe. It was only a lot of traditions strung together in very beautiful language, but nevertheless only traditions. She seemed surprised to find that he still believed in it.

"That's the result of going to a 'hick' college," she said scornfully. "If you had gone to one of the great universities you would have come into contact with the kind of professors I had, and you wouldn't have come home with any such out-of-date ideas as you have. I can give you a list of books we had to read, and I can tell you from my notes a lot of things you ought to know. It would positively change all your ridiculous ideas. You need a lot of philosophy and science. I can't understand how you could have got by in any kind of college and kept your queer impossible religion. Going to church every Sunday just as you did when you were a child!"

"Well," Dana had responded indignantly, "I'm certainly thankful I didn't attend that kind of university if you think there is any possibility it would have made me willing to stay away from church. But I don't believe any college could have done that. God has meant too much to me all my life, for me to be willing to give Him up for any course of study the world can offer, and going to church is going to His house with His people to worship Him."

"Oh, well," she said loftily in the low throaty voice she had lately acquired, "just going to church in itself wouldn't be so bad if you would pick out the right kind of church. But that old-fashioned chapel where your father has always gone is simply impossible. It isn't such a bad thing to go for a little while, say an hour or two a week, into an up-to-date place of worship and let your soul get a real rest, sort of come into touch with the infinite. That isn't so bad. They say it is often beneficial to the whole system. The quiet beauty of a proper edifice where lovely lines of architecture, perfect workmanship in fittings, light falling through exquisite stained-glass windows designed by real artists, perfect music from costly instruments played by musicians of great attainments, singing by highly trained choirs of priceless voices, wise precepts spoken by eloquent men, all combine of course to soothe the weary soul and give it new strength to go on and attain greater heights. That would be a good thing for mind and body alike. But to go to that cheap little clapboard building that sadly needs a coat of paint, and sit on hard unpainted wooden benches looking at those ugly rough plastered walls, that uncovered wooden floor, the ugly square boxlike pulpit, the light falling through those horrid cheap colored glass windows, and hear that illiterate boy pounding out anathemas of hell-fire, to listen to such funny little jazzy songs to the accompaniment of a wheezy cabinet organ miserably played, that is simply unspeakable! I used to think you had a good mind and would amount to something, but that sort of practise would vitiate any mind."

"So you think my mind is vitiated, do you?" he had asked, looking steadily, thoughtfully at her, his face almost white in its intensity, his eyes their darkest blue, looking at her as he had never looked before, seeing a shallowness in her that had never been apparent to him before.

"Oh, not hopelessly, perhaps," she said, laughing lightly. "But any mind, no matter how brilliant, exposed to the kind of twaddle that you get at that chapel, must vitiate in the final analysis. The trouble with you is that you are too much under the domination of your father. You need to get out and get away from him and his influence. Just because your father has always gone to that chapel you think you must go too. How can you ever expect to be up-to-date if you continue to do just what he says? Your father is a dreamer and idealizes even that awful little chapel. There is nothing practical about him and he has no idea about getting on in the world."

"Is that so?" Dana had said sternly, meeting her cold young eyes with a look as keen as her own.

She colored a little but went boldly on.

"Well now, Dana, you know your father is no scholar, or he would not expect his son in this age of the world to accept and be satisfied with outworn dogmas and traditions, which is all in the world the Bible is. Your father is determined to hold you down to his type of religion. Any kind of religion is rather out of date, at least the kind of thing we used to call religion when we were young. Why, very few people even believe there is a God any more. Of course I don't go as far as that."

"Indeed?" said Dana coolly.

"No, I still believe there is an omnipotent force, and I still go to church. But it is a marvelous church, that new one on the avenue. Have you been in it? It is like a dream in architecture, wrought like exquisite lacework of stone. It is a rest just to look about its costly colorful interior. The windows in subdued tones, almost visibly blending with the music. They say the quartette and soloists are the highest paid singers in the city, and the organ is one of the finest in the world. The young preacher is said to be one of the most eloquent men that ever graduated at his seminary, and he's handsome as a picture. He gets a twenty thousand dollar salary. And you will pass up a place like that where you might get real refreshment for mind and body and go to that miserable little old chapel! Why, I'm so interested at this new church I'm even considering taking a class in Sunday School." Margery finished with a sparkle of enthusiasm in her eyes.

"Yes?" Dana had replied. "And what, pray, would you teach them?"

Margery colored annoyingly.

"Well, certainly not that old-fashioned gospel stuff you and I used to be so wild about when we were children. It's a thing of the past. It's absurd! We used to go on mere emotional jags every now and then! I'm done with it forever, and I wish you were too! But I know you. You're too stubborn to give anything up.

You're tied to your father's apron string. He's a regular old granny and the kind of religion he wants to hold you down to is entirely out-of-date."

Dana had stood it all, with only a calm word now and then, but when she began to cast aspersions upon his beloved father, and when she sneered at his deepest convictions and called them out-of-date and outworn, his face grew stern. And though he listened to the end of her gay tirade, for she seemed determined to see this thing through and conquer him once and for all, not once did his expression soften.

Blithely she went on, giving him glance for glance.

"You know," she said arrogantly, "the ideal Christ would never utter some of those cryptic sentences that were a part of the patter we used to quote in those old days when we thought we were such saints. But I'm quite sure if there were a Christ at all today He would be up-to-date. He would not be behind the times!"

Dana's voice was very solemn as he answered, still looking unflinchingly straight into her eyes:

"'Jesus Christ is the same yesterday, today, and forever.' I guess that'll be about all, Margery. I guess we're done. I'll say good-bye."

And that had been the last time he had called upon her. Soon after that his father had been taken worse, and he had no time to think of anything else. He had been by his bed almost constantly until the end. Two or three times Margery had called up, asking him to this and that, evidently thinking that it was about time that he saw things in a more modern light, but it happened that the nurse usually answered her call, and Dana was either out or busy with his father. On the occasions when he answered himself he would always say:

"Thank you, it is quite impossible for me to go

anywhere tonight!" That was all, and always in a grave tone.

She wrote him a pleasant little note when she heard his father was at death's door, and another when he died, and she sent flowers to the funeral. Dana never knew whether she came to it herself or not. It did not matter to him any more. Margery was a person of the past. And he was only glad that his father had known that, and had been relieved by the knowledge before he left him.

So it would not be for Margery's sake he would return to his midwestern home. He was not even sure she was there now anyway. She had written of a trip abroad, and that she was engaged.

But somehow with the element of a girl out of it, and with his father gone, it seemed a sad place to return to. He was not interested in the place any more, and no longer had the heart to cope with old associations, at least not at present.

And yet, why stay here longer? Wasn't it perfectly obvious that his mother and sister had no further need for him? His father's wishes had been carried out when he presented the letter to his mother. Surely there would be no further call for him to go and see them again.

He sat there a long time in the comparative stillness of the park away from the city, trying to think his way through to what he should do next. Of course there were a few errands. He must see that Mr. Burney. He had promised. And of course he wanted to have a day with Bruce before he left. But where was he going? Back to his job? Back to the old rooms where he and his father used to live? No, for they were rented, their few possessions in temporary storage. Well, that would all have to be decided. But he was strangely weary. The interview with his people had been even harder than he had anticipated. It was one thing to know conditions, it was even more startling to see them with your own eyes.

At last with a weary sigh he got up, and as he stood he glanced down at the bench and there close beside where he had been sitting lay a little delicate crumpled handkerchief, with a bit of brilliant embroidery in one corner, cunningly interwoven with a snarl of flowers. That was his sister's handkerchief!

He picked it up and the touch of the fine linen gave him a sense of still belonging to something, although perhaps it was nothing he could ever prize. But still this represented something he had to do. Get that little white rag back to its owner. Did that mean that God had reason for him to stay here yet awhile, perhaps do something more? No, that was foolish. He could enclose the handkerchief in an envelope and send it to her by mail. He wouldn't even have to write a word. She might remember where she had left it or she might not. What difference?

So he stuffed the handkerchief into his pocket and started drearily on his way back to the room he was occupying with Bruce Carbury. He didn't even remember that it was near lunch time and he had not eaten yet. All he wanted was to get back to a bed and lie down and sleep. Everything else could wait until he was rested.

5

VALERIE Shannon was Irish, on one side at least, and she had the great dark blue eyes and black curly hair that went with that race. But she was also Scotch on the other side and had a level-headed good sense and staunchness of faith, so that she was not influenced by the present-day carelessness of morals and ideals. She had a bevy of brothers and sisters who kept things merry. Some were in school and some were doing good honest hard work and some were married. They were all born in this country, but had been back to the old countries several times to visit, which gave them a world-sense as well as an intense love for their native land. The last time they came home they had brought the Scotch grand-mother to live with them, and her untarnished faith and her keen way of discerning the truth of a matter, and of expressing herself in no uncertain terms, helped to keep them up to their original quality.

Valerie had finished high school and two years of college, and then stopped college to take over her sister's job in the publishing house of Burney and Company when her sister Mavis got married. Valerie had proved to be even more satisfactory to the head of the firm than Mavis had been, and he promptly made her his private secretary. Valerie was only nineteen but she was "smart as a whip" her grandmother said, and her employer said the same, in other words perhaps.

Valerie was always neat and trim. Some of the other girls in the office called her "smart," but there was a womanliness about her attire that made the word smart seem too sophisticated to use in connection with her appearance. She was always sweet, gentle, and womanly wherever she was, in office or church or on the street, or even in the kitchen where on occasion she could shine with the rest of her family in concocting delicious meals.

The Shannons lived in an unfashionable street in a large old-fashioned brown stone house that years ago used to be an elegant mansion, but now because of its commercial surroundings was no longer considered desirable. But the house was large enough for their family, and the rooms were pleasant. They made the inside look like a real home even in the heart of the great city. The high ceilings and large rooms gave a spaciousness that was needed for such a large family. There were funny old-fashioned borders and frescoes on the ceilings, with cupids and roses and designs of the past. Some people scorned the house. Said it was too "Victorian." But the Shannons loved it all. Patrick climbed up on a step-ladder and colored the roses pink, and the ribbons blue, even tinting the cupids, giving them yellow hair and blue eyes.

They had no grand paintings to hang on these lofty walls, except one oil portrait of the old Scotch laird, one of their grandmother's forebears. It was the one fine heirloom she had brought with her from Scotland, and it occupied the place of honor in the living room over the white marble mantel. The heavy eyebrows, and the firm chin of the stern old man were a sort of hall-mark of the integrity of the family. Even the Irish ones were proud to have a share in it.

The other picture in the room—oh, there were photographs besides, of course—was an engraving of a thatched cottage in Ireland.

Things more modern came and went in the house, but these two pictures remained and set the pace of the house, as it were, reminding of a life set in sterner times, and a God-fearing family of high repute who had taught their children that life was not all to be lived on this earth, that even strong souls must look to Heaven for eternal bliss and not try to grasp it down here. The Shannons found much joy by the way, but it was not the chief end and aim of living.

So the children had come up sturdy souls with a mind to consider righteousness rather than selfishness, and with a will to work joyously and not fret.

That afternoon Valerie had reached home a little after five and hurried up to her room to finish a bit of sewing she was doing. For they were all thrifty children, and did for themselves as far as they could, rather than spend their hard-earned money on fol-de-rols. But what they made was always beautifully done, and well-fashioned. A pause at the window of some great store far beyond her purse, a sweep of the eye through the display, particular notice of some attractive garment or accessory, and Valerie had it photographed carefully in her mind to carry home. There was that old dress of five winters ago that she had cleaned and carefully folded away in tissue paper. That could be cut over, and there were bits of trimming in the carefully hoarded left-overs of other days that would garnish it in this new style. That was how Valerie often managed to look as if she had just purchased a whole new outfit. She never let a good adaptable model get by her without notice.

Valerie hung up her coat on its special hanger that kept it in good lines, and put her hat away in a box whose lid had been arranged to drop from cloth hinges, keeping the hat from dust. Then she changed from her neat office garb to a bright little dress with blue flowers scattered over it, corn flowers that matched her eyes. It didn't take long, and it gave her office dress a rest and kept it fresh and serviceable for a longer time. Besides, she was going out to a meeting that evening. Then she sat down to her sewing.

"Is that you, Vallie?" called her mother from across the hall. "You came in so quietly I wasn't sure."

"Yes, I'm home. I came in quietly because I hoped you were taking a nap," said the girl pulling out a rocker that was her mother's favorite and drawing her into the room. "Sit down. You don't need to do anything just now, you know you don't. I smell dinner cooking, and can't I go down and finish?"

"No," said her mother decidedly, "it's potpie tonight, and I always like to make that myself. But it isn't quite time yet. I'll sit down a few minutes. What's happened today at the office? Anything new?"

"No, not much. Of course there's extra work, ever since Mr. Maynard left. Mr. Burney does his best to keep everything going, but he isn't so young as he once was, and we really miss Mr. Maynard a lot. I worked most of my noon hour today. Mr. Burney had gone out or he wouldn't have stood for it. He doesn't believe in cutting lunch hours short. But I knew he would stay till midnight tonight if I didn't get those letters off, so I stayed.

We certainly do miss Mr. Maynard a lot. He was a hustler."

"But aren't they going to get anybody to take his place?"

"Oh, I guess so, but Mr. Burney is hard to suit. I believe he just hates to hire anybody. He is sort of sentimental, but sentiment won't get work done. A friend of his telephoned yesterday from somewhere that he had a young man coming east who was something unusual and he thought he might fit in for a few weeks while he was here on family business, just till we got hold of the right man. I think Mr. Burney is quite counting on him, but he hasn't come yet, and he may not amount to much when he does."

"There you go again, Valerie. Don't be so skeptical. Wait till you see the man. I certainly wish he'd come, or else you'd find somebody else right away. I don't like the idea of having you overwork."

"Oh, I shan't overwork," laughed Valerie. "Don't you worry. Say, mother, did Ranald come home for lunch? Had he had any word from his government examination yet?"

"Yes, he passed," said his mother with a proud little ring of triumph in her voice. "Of course he would, though, as hard as he works. He's just like your father when he gets started on something. He can't let it alone till he gets all there is out of it."

"Not like you in that a bit, of course, mother," laughed Valerie. "Seems to me you did just that little thing with housecleaning this spring, even though you knew you had two perfectly good daughters coming home early to help, and just needing the exercise."

The mother laughed with conscious happiness.

"Well, I didn't see having you use up your only leisure

washing windows and rubbing furniture and ironing curtains."

"No, you thought it would be better for us if you killed yourself off so we had to do it all," said Valerie. "Well, we'll fix you next time so you can't do that."

There was a sudden banging of the front door, and a clamor of eager young voices.

"There!" said the mother. "Turla and Leith have come. It's time for me to go down and mix up the dumplings."

"But, are they just getting home from school? So late?"

"Oh, no, they had a high school football game today."

"Oh, yes, I forgot!" said the sister. "I wonder how it came out? Leith was playing, too, wasn't he? I must go down and ask. He'll never forgive me if I don't. His first game this season."

"You won't need to go down," smiled the mother, "they are coming up here! There! There comes Kendall, too! He's finished his paper route so early. I must hurry!" and the mother hurried down the back stairs and went at her cooking. Then Turla and Leith, the twins, came pelting up the stairs eager to tell their sister about the game.

"Valerie, what do you think! Leith made a touchdown! He *did!* Wasn't that simply great?" shouted Turla arriving breathless at Valerie's open door. "And his playing all through was *swell!* Wasn't that gorgeous for his first game?"

"Indeed it was!" said Valerie, her eyes shining as she looked her joy toward the brother so tall and broad shouldered, with the rich color in his cheeks and the flaming red of his hair.

They stood, the pair of them, and drank in her

pleasure as if they could not take the whole of their glory until she had her share in it. It was what made that Shannon family so distinctive and different from the common run of people, their delight in one another, their unfailing interest each in the pursuits of the other.

They stood for several minutes at her door telling her about what this one and that one and the other one had done, and the narrow escapes they had had in the different stages of the game, and Valerie entered into all they told and exclaimed and rejoiced with them.

Then came Kendall trudging disappointedly up the stairs, rosy cheeked and weary, his hair standing every-which-way.

"Well, how'dya come out? I heard ya won. Did ya get ta play? Thought I'd get there for the last half, but Rasky held me up. I had ta do part of his route 'cause he had tha toothache, worse luck!"

"Too bad!" said Valerie sympathetically.

And then they had to tell Kendall all over again about the game.

"But where is Norah?" Valerie asked suddenly.

"She went to the birthday party around at Emmy Lou Patten's. Malcolm's getting her on his way home," explained Kendall. "Mother phoned Malcolm. There they come now!"

"Where's grandma?" called Malcolm from the foot of the stairs. "Here's that yarn she wanted. Norah, you take it up to her!"

So Norah came trudging up with the yarn, and grandma came out of her room with her knitting.

Turla was down in the kitchen helping mother, and Norah with Valerie's help slipped out of her pretty little pink party dress, into her red home dress, and went down to set the table.

The father came in soon after, and then Norah stepped out into the hall ringing the silver dinner bell. The whole family trooped down to the pleasant dining room and gathered around the long table, looking hungrily toward the great platter of lamb stew with its ample fringe and topping of dumplings. Then they all bowed their heads for the grace the father said.

It was after the plates were all helped and passed and everybody was passing butter and bread and pickles and cranberry sauce and delicate little string beans, that Valerie began to tell of her day. They all took turns telling of what had happened to them making all their experiences real family affairs.

"I saw two very interesting looking people this noon when I went for lunch," she said. "I'd like to know who they were. They were walking on the avenue together as if they were going somewhere with a purpose, but they were not talking together. They looked so much alike they must have been related, perhaps brother and sister, or even twins, though the man looked much more mature than the girl. But they both had the most gorgeous gold hair I ever saw, a sort of red-gold it was, and the same large brown eyes. Their features were very striking. If you had seen them I am sure you would recognize what I mean. I am sure they were strong characters, yet they were different. The girl looked utterly worldly, and the man had an expression that seemed almost heavenly, I mean as if he came from Heaven. I never saw a contrast like that in faces which otherwise were so identical."

"Sounds something like love at first sight," mocked young Leith with a twinkle in his Irish eyes.

"Oh, father!" said Valerie with a smile toward Leith, "has anybody told you what our Leith did? Made a touchdown! His first game of the season, too. Wasn't that great? Aren't we proud of him?"

"Now, dad, Val is just trying to turn the subject," grinned Leith.

"Well, son, we certainly are proud of you," said the father with a light in his eyes. "Tell me about it!" And then the talk drifted to football, and even grandma got interested and asked what a touchdown was, and everybody forgot about Leith's charge that Valerie had fallen in love with a stranger at first sight.

Suddenly Valerie looked at the clock and exclaimed:

"It's getting late! I am going out and I must hurry! Get the Bible, Norah!"

So little golden-haired Norah slipped down from her chair and went after the old Bible on the lower shelf of the serving table.

The father took it and opening to a quaint old marker read the evening portion, with now and then a word of comment, perhaps for the benefit of the younger children. And then they all knelt in prayer.

> *The cheerfu' supper done, wi' serious face,*
> *They round the ingle form a circle wide;*
> *The sire turns o'er, wi' patriarchal grace,*
> *The big ha' Bible, ance his father's pride;*
>
> . . . .
>
> *Then kneeling down, to Heaven's Eternal King,*
> *The saint, the father, and the husband prays:*
>
> . . . .
>
> *From scenes like these old Scotia's grandeur springs,*
> *That makes her loved at home, revered abroad.*

6

DANA awoke to find a bright light in the room, and Bruce Carbury standing over him.

"Hello, fella, what's the matter? You sick?" There was real concern in Carbury's face and he reached out a cool hand and laid it on Dana's forehead.

Dana blinked at him and then laughed.

"No, I'm not sick, Bruce, just disgusted."

"Was it as bad as that?"

"Pretty bad."

"Well, how about dinner? When did you have your lunch?"

Dana looked perplexed for a minute, and then he laughed again.

"Why, I guess I didn't. I went to sleep instead. That's so, I guess I'm hungry."

"Well, make it snappy! Let's get going. I'm hungry as a bear myself. Come on, I've found a swell place to eat! And don't let's talk about anything till we've had a leisurely dinner. You know things won't look so bleak to you then."

Dana was up at once. A dash of cold water in his face, the brush to his hair, and he was ready.

"But I want to talk about you," he said as they went down the street together. "That won't depress you, will it? You didn't get turned down, did you?"

"Why, no," said Bruce with a sudden lightening of his face, "I got the job, and it seems to be all that I could desire, so you don't need to worry about me. But good as it is, if things go wrong for you here in New York, old pal, I'm ready to throw it all up and go back to the old diggings with you. I'm not going to have you floating off by yourself."

"Thanks a lot!" said Dana with one of his sudden bright smiles. "I appreciate that all right, but of course I wouldn't let you do that! You know it!"

"But I mean it, Dana!"

"Yes, I know you do, and so do I," said Dana earnestly, "but it isn't coming to that, anyway. At least I don't seem to feel I'm going back, not at present. I don't know just why, but I don't feel 'released' yet from the job I came on to perform, though I don't know why. At present there doesn't seem to be another thing I can do. I wonder if you know what I mean?"

"Of course! I understand! Now, here's our place to eat. Let's pretend we're celebrating. I don't know just what, but we're celebrating, the way we used to do at college."

"Sure!" said Dana with a grin. "Celebrating that you've got your job! Besides, I have to go see a man tomorrow or next day, so that will be at least another day with you."

So they went cheerfully in to a good dinner, and talked about old times, and managed to put unpleasant things entirely out of thought while they were eating.

"We'll take a snappy walk before we go back to the room," said Bruce as they came out into the street again, and Carbury walked his friend down to show him the region of his new job. It was a pleasant little interlude, and it rested Dana as well as Bruce. At last they came back to the room and settled down to talk.

"Now," said Bruce, "tell me as much or as little as you want me to know. I don't need to know a thing if you'd rather not, you know."

So Dana described his call on his family that morning. He described the room to which he was ushered, and the girl who was sitting there in gaudy pajamas smoking when he went in. He made the scene very vivid, and now and again he would pause as if the telling of it hurt him.

Once Bruce gave him a sympathetic look and said gently:

"Don't, Dana! This is hurting you. It isn't necessary for you to tell me these things. I can see how hard it must have been for you."

But Dana shook his head.

"No, I'd rather tell. I've got to. You are nearer to me than anybody else on earth today. I think you have a right to know. You may be able to give me some light on what I ought to do, if there is anything I can do. God sent you to me again just as I was starting on this expedition, and I can't help thinking there was some intention in it. If you're willing to be bothered with my troubles you shall know them all as far as you will listen."

"I'll gladly listen," said the other, his face grave with deep sympathy, "and I'll help all I can. You don't need me to tell you that your confidence will be sacred in my thoughts. And none of it shall pass my lips."

"I can trust you, Bruce. I wouldn't be telling you if I couldn't."

So Dana went on with the story, even down to the

walk to the park and the conversation there. He let his friend see all the loveliness and the petulance of his sister. Bruce listened with kindling interest.

"Is she happy, Dana?"

"Happy?" said Dana looking up astonished. "How should I know? No, I don't really believe she is what I would call happy! But what difference would that make?"

"It might make a great deal," said Bruce thoughtfully. "I can't think that she is really satisfied or she would not have said what she did at the end. She wouldn't have wanted to forget. I think you are wrong to feel so utterly hopeless, Dana."

"Oh, I got the impression that she was merely made uncomfortable by thinking father had suffered to give her what she had had. It did not seem to me she had any real repentance. She gave no evidence of that."

"Not even the tears?"

"Not even the tears," said Dana solemnly. "That is—well, some people cry easily. It may not have meant much."

"Give her time, brother," said Bruce with a light of faith in his eyes. "Shall we pray about it?"

They went down upon their knees together, as they had done at times in the past when they had some great common desire, and Bruce prayed most tenderly.

"Oh Lord, you know these two better than we do. You know if in Your plan of the ages there is any way for these two to find and know Thee; to be saved, and come to know the joy of the Lord. And Lord, You know what the father of this family was, how he loved Thee, and how patiently and sweetly he suffered through the years, and how he must have prayed for them. Let not his prayers remain unanswered. You know Dana, too, who loves Thee and who longs that these two of his family shall come to be saved. So we come together to Thee tonight, bringing that promise that where two of us shall agree as touching anything that they shall ask it shall be done. So we ask if it be Thy will that Thou wilt send Thy Holy Spirit to draw them, and that Thou wilt hear our prayer for them. We ask Thee especially for that little girl who hasn't ever had the opportunity that her brother has had to know Thee. We claim her from Satan's power on the ground of the shed blood of Thy son our Saviour, on the ground of His victory over Satan. We ask it for Jesus' sake. Amen!"

Then after a pause, hesitantly, slowly, Dana prayed, more especially for his mother.

At the close the two rose in silence and Dana walked over to the window, wiping his eyes, and stood there for some time staring out across the lights of the city. Then he turned at last and looked at his friend.

"Thanks, Bruce," he said in a husky voice, "that's helped a lot. I guess the way will grow clearer, and I don't believe I'm meant to leave just yet, anyway. If for nothing else, I'd stay just to have this fellowship in prayer with you."

"Well, brother, I'm learning day by day that our God is a great God. There is nothing He cannot do, if it is His will."

The next day Dana spent in going about the city, seeing places and things he had always known about and wanted to see. He did not go yet to the publishing house to which his home firm had sent him. He wanted to be a little more clear in his mind about how long he was going to stay in New York before he called there.

So he went to the Museum, and the great Public Library, and to Grant's tomb, and the Aquarium, and finished up by strolling past a few famous publishing houses, idly studying their display windows. But when he went back to the room at last because this lonely sightseeing had wearied him beyond measure, and his soul was struggling with longing for the father who had gone, who would have been so interested to hear all about what he had seen, he found his friend had come back ahead of him.

"I've had a swell day," he reported. "The boss is grand and I'm going to like my work a lot. It only lacks one thing and that is to have you fixed comfortably somewhere. But say, who do you suppose I saw today, right on Broadway? Kirk Shannon! Do you remember him? He came down to college with the Robertson boys several times. He was up near Chicago somewhere going to college. Don't tell me you don't remember him?"

"Sure, I remember Kirk," said Dana. "He stayed over Sunday once. I thought he was a prince of a fellow."

"Well, he thought the same of you, of course. In fact he used almost those same words about you. Well, he's in charge of some kind of a mission here, and he wants us to come down tonight to the meeting. I told him we'd be there, that is, if you hadn't planned something else. Would you like to go?"

"Of course," said Dana cheerfully. "That would be great. I guess I need a mission or something to take the bad taste of the world out of my mouth."

So they went downstairs to a restaurant quite near at hand for their dinner, and then came back up to the room to make ready to go to the meeting.

"I'm glad you ran across Kirk," said Dana as he put on a clean collar and a fresh tie. "That will make me feel a lot better about leaving you alone in a strange city, in case I have to go soon. It will be nice that you have one old friend. And I liked Kirk a lot."

Bruce turned quickly, a disappointed look on his face.

"You've decided to go?" he asked sadly. "You didn't get any encouragement at that publishing house? I was counting a lot on that."

Dana turned toward him with a grin.

"Why, I didn't even go to the publishing house yet. I didn't feel I was ready. I thought I needed to know more about my future movements before I went there."

"What for, you goop?" asked Bruce with the old-time bantering tone. "If I ever saw such a dumb-bunny in my life! How can you know what you want to do until you see if they have anything to offer you, or to suggest?"

"Well, you see there's a more important matter than just a job to decide. I've got to know whether I should stay here for the sake of—" he hesitated for a word, and then finished lamely, "my relatives. That's something I couldn't tell just of myself. If that's entirely out, and I've done all I'm supposed to do in that line, it's just as well that I should be far away from here. So I didn't want to get entangled with any worldly business like a job until that was settled."

"I see," said Bruce, "but how are you going to decide that question? Are you planning to go and see them again?"

Dana shook his head.

"No, I don't see that. I've said all there was to say as an initiative. The rest is sort of up to them. I told the Lord if they made any move to come to me, if they showed the slightest interest, I'd stay till He showed me I ought to go. I said I'd wait a few days."

"But they don't know where you are, do they? They didn't even ask, did they? Or did they?"

"Yes," said Dana slowly. "My sister wanted to know where I was staying. I told her."

"They didn't ask you to come to them?"

"No," said Dana. "I wouldn't want to. I couldn't. Their life would be impossible for me. That is, unless there were some reason why the Lord wanted me there. But I'm sure now He doesn't. They wouldn't want me anyway. They would be terribly embarrassed by my presence."

"Yes, I suppose so," said Bruce. "And I can imagine it would be more than uncomfortable for you. I can't imagine duty lying in that direction, at least not under the present circumstances. Well, the Lord will show you the way, I'm sure. Now, are we ready?"

Then suddenly as if in answer to his question there came a knock at the door. It was a smart peremptory knock, as if the visitor had a right and was used to giving orders.

It was Bruce who answered it. Dana was over on the other side of the room putting on his overcoat. And Bruce stood there in the doorway, looking down in amazement at the beautiful girl who stood there so arrogantly.

She lifted her eyes with an impatient frown and stared him full in the face, her lips half parted to speak, and then she could only stare. At last she mustered voice to speak.

"Oh!" she said haughtily as if it were his fault that he was a stranger and not the one she sought. "Isn't this my brother's room? This is the number he gave me." And she looked the strange young man in the eyes and found him very pleasant to look at. Still there was resentment in her glance that he should be there instead of Dana.

Bruce looked down, marveling first of all, fairly startled, that his friend's answer to his prayer had come so soon, even while they were speaking about it. For he knew instantly who this girl must be. She was too like Dana in feature and coloring to be anybody but his sister.

Next he swept her with another glance and recognized something that Dana had not mentioned, perhaps had failed in his perturbation even to notice. The girl was startlingly beautiful.

Of course he had rather expected beauty of a sort, since she would be somewhat like Dana and he had always thought Dana the handsomest man he knew. There was a beauty of strength and of character, and a power of self-control in Dana that this girl did not have. Yet in spite of its lack she was beautiful.

Surprisingly she wore no make-up, and there was a softness of nature about her face that perhaps Dana had not seen. It held Bruce's attention in a kind of surprised wonder during that instant they took note of one another. Then he replied, studying her meanwhile:

"Yes, if Dana Barron is your brother, this is his room." Then throwing the door open wide he looked back toward Dana and announced formally, "Dana, your sister is calling."

Bruce stepped aside to let her pass in and Dana came toward her as she entered, his hat in his hand.

"Oh!" said the girl, "you were going out!" There was a tone of disappointment in her voice.

"Yes, we were going out. We had an engagement," said Dana, "but of course if there is anything I can do for you—" He hesitated and glanced at Bruce, and then back to the girl with a troubled look.

"May I present my friend, Bruce Carbury," he said. "Bruce, this is my sister, Coralie."

Bruce bowed gravely and stood waiting. Coralie gave a quick sharp look at her brother's friend, appraising him once more, deciding he was very good-looking in a grave different way from most of her friends. She wondered what the type was like.

"But I wanted to talk to you," she said with a childish pout, looking back at Dana.

"I see," said Dana. "Well, is it a matter of haste? Could I meet you later somewhere? You see this was a definite engagement. A man is expecting us."

"Oh!" said Coralie with a quick flash of jealousy, and another appraising glance at Bruce. "Well, I don't want to go home. Can't you take me with you?" Her young body stiffened almost as with anger, or fear.

The two young men gave startled looks at one another, and Dana drew a deep breath of troubled perplexity.

"I'm afraid you wouldn't be interested," he said quickly. "If you are anxious to see me at once I'll take you home, of course, right away. Bruce can carry my apologies," and he looked at Bruce again with a look that told him how much Dana wanted to go with him.

"Certainly," said Bruce quietly, "but how do you know but your sister might be interested? Why don't you take her at her word and let her try? You can always leave if she doesn't like it."

The calm quiet suggestion surprised Dana. Bruce wasn't a man who had any use for the kind of girl he knew his sister must be.

"It doesn't matter in the least whether I'm interested or not, I'm going with you!" said the young woman with a quick little movement of her foot that in a foot less lovely would have been called stamping. "I came all this way to the ends of the earth to find you, and I'm not going to let you get away from me till I choose!"

"Oh, well, that's all right then," said Dana shutting his lips in a decided way he had that made him and his sister suddenly look absurdly alike. "Shall we go?" and he reached up and snapped the light out in the room.

Bruce stepped out into the hall, and Dana stepped aside to let his sister precede him. Then Bruce spoke.

"Dana, if your sister wants to consult you about something I can wait somewhere and let you have the room to yourselves, or I can go on ahead and make your apologies. Perhaps I shouldn't have butted in."

"No!" said the girl with her pretty petulance again. "I'm going with you. Of course I can see quite well that you don't either of you want me, but just for that reason I'm going anyway! I want to see what it is that's such a thrill for you both. No, Mr. Carbury, please don't tell me where we're going. I prefer to see it first without knowing anything about it."

"All right, let her have her wish," said Dana with a sudden mirthless laugh. "Are we taking a taxi, or do we walk?"

"It's not very far," said Bruce, "only about three or four blocks."

"We'll walk of course," said Coralie. "What a thrill. I never walked in this quarter of the city before, not at night anyway, but I'll do anything once."

So they walked.

7

THE two young men walked one on either side of the girl, and she was rather intrigued to be taking such a walk. It really was a new experience for her. There were much more sordid neighborhoods than the one where they were walking, where she might have strolled along far after midnight with half-intoxicated escorts, and babbled with the rest noisily, taking it all as a part of their sophisticated condition, but this was different. Steady, quiet, plainly dressed people for the most part, going about their ordinary business, or hunting cheap amusements were thronging the way, but they were not dressed as she dressed when she went out for an evening. Suddenly she looked down at herself and then critically at the people she passed.

"I never thought," she said hesitating and glancing up daringly at her brother with a grimace, "perhaps I'm not dressed right for this affair we're going to. But you two were not wearing dinner coats."

Dana glanced down at her.

"You're quite all right," he said disinterestedly, noting the plain dark brown suit and little felt hat, with only a bright rainbow colored scarf at her neck to give a touch of color.

"Yes," said Bruce approvingly, "you look very nice. But it wouldn't matter anyway. People don't notice what you have on here."

"Oh," said Coralie. "Bohemia, I suppose?"

"Not exactly," said Bruce cryptically. Then he turned and led the way into a wide doorway and up a flight of wooden stairs to a hall.

Coralie mounted the stairs, her eyes wide with wonder, expecting some kind of a newfangled night club that started early.

Then a burst of music swelled out the opening door, and it was thus they entered the Gospel Mission where Kirk Shannon presided.

Coralie followed Bruce into the seat, and sat down wonderingly, her brother sitting next to her by the aisle. They were half way up to the platform, on the middle aisle and the room was filling up rapidly now, the music drawing people from the street. But there was nothing in the music to tell Coralie what this gathering was. It was an entirely new kind of music. Nothing in her experience carried tunes like these, nor words, though she didn't pay much attention to the words at first. She caught the phrase "thrilling my soul" and supposed that this was some new love song that she hadn't heard before. She stared about on the gathering throng and wondered. These people, many of them, wore a different look from the men and girls she knew. Some, it is true, carried despondent faces, gloom and despair, but these were not the ones who were singing. The singers had a lightness and joy about them that surpassed anything in her experience. There was one girl, with ugly longish hair pinned up, neatly, it is true, but with hairpins of assorted sizes and makes, a dress that never had fitted her, and shoes that were down at the heel. She hadn't any hat at all, and only a ragged old sweater for a wrap, yet there was a light in her eyes that made them beautiful, and a joy in her smile when she turned toward an old woman who might have been her mother, that gave Coralie a twinge of wistfulness. That girl looked happy in spite of everything. It must be there was some kind of a show here that they were all looking forward to eagerly, or there wouldn't have been so many here.

There were more songs, catchy ones that haunted her memory after they were over. Then suddenly all heads were bowed.

Not Coralie's. She sat staring around perplexedly. There were voices speaking in soft tones, here and there! What was this? Some weird rite in which they were all taking part? A strange upbringing had been hers in which prayer had had no part! She had never in her life gone to Sunday School, although she had lived all her life within the sound of church bells. She knew absolutely nothing of religion. Her mother had chosen for her, that she should come up a lovely self-centered animal, without mind or thought for anything but amusement. Therefore she did not know how to class this place to which she had insisted upon coming.

Bruce, watching her quietly, furtively, sometimes comparing her profile with the grave sweet troubled face of her brother, began to pray that God would reach her by His Spirit.

But the girl he prayed for sat with wide open eyes and stared.

And now the order changed and people were on their feet here and there, telling a bit out of their past, telling with jubilance of victory over sin, of a mysterious new life that had come. Coralie didn't understand it in the least. She listened to one and another, now and again a bright young girl, or a strong young man, all with that same ring to their voices, that same light of triumph in their eyes. And sometimes it was an old sodden sinner with a kindling of hope in faded eyes, and a testimony of joy amid failure and loss and sorrow. Coralie listened as she had never listened to anything before, and as she listened a wistfulness came to her. Could it be possible that whatever it was these people had could bring joy to a set whose greatest pleasure was to get drunk, whose boast was in breaking all known laws, and whose highest thrill resulted in empty shame the next day?

Without thinking it all out her emotions recognized a relief from what she had known, a longing to try this new something whatever it was, this something that her strange brother, and his stranger friend had taken up, that made them different from the world's folk. She had forgotten to be restless. She had forgotten to plan what she would do with these two young men when this freak of theirs was over and she could claim attention and demand a reward for attending this queer gathering.

The man who was leading the meeting was young and good-looking too. He didn't have that jaded look so many of her companions habitually had. There was a freshness and life in his voice and a light in his eyes. And now he was talking:

"I see an old friend down in the audience tonight," he declared suddenly, after they had sung another brief song. "I used to know him in college days. I visited his college for three days once and got to know him well. He had a lovely voice and he used to sing in the meetings those college fellows used to have. If they wanted the Lord to touch hearts they would get Dana Barron to sing

'No one ever cared for me like Jesus.' And though I only heard him sing it three times, once out in the moonlight beside a new-made grave of one they loved, I have never forgotten it. I am sure he hasn't forgotten how to sing it either. And though I haven't seen him in three years, and I haven't had a chance to speak with him, I'm going to ask Dana Barron to come up here now and sing that song for us. Will you come, Dana?"

Dana sat quietly watching his old friend as he talked. The old college days trooped around him tenderly. He had forgotten that this was New York, a strange city. He had forgotten his sister, his alien sister sitting by his side. When Kirk Shannon asked him to come he just answered the call as he used to answer it, and came.

And his wild young sister sat in awe and watched him.

Valerie Shannon was sitting at the piano, watching as he came down the aisle. Suddenly she knew that this was the man she had seen in the street a couple of days ago. And that was the girl who had been with him, walking down the avenue, that girl back there with whom he had been sitting!

So, this was Dana Barron! The fellow Kirk had talked so much about.

He was up on the platform now, and that sister of his, or wife, or girl, or whatever she was, was staring at him almost as if she were frightened, and most evidently wondering what was about to happen. If he was anything of a singer why should this girl be frightened?

Valerie slid softly into the opening chords of the song, and Dana's voice rolled out deeply, sweetly, tenderly.

> *"I would love to tell you what I think of Jesus*
> *Since I found in Him a friend so strong and true;*
> *I would tell you how He changed my life completely,*

> *He did something that no other friend could do.*
> *No one ever cared for me like Jesus,*
> *There's no other friend so kind as He;*
> *No one else could take the sin and darkness from me,*
> *O how much He cared for me!"*

By this time Valerie Shannon realized that she was accompanying a most unusual voice. Her fingers felt their way in perfect accord making a lovely setting for the voice, every note of which shone like a jewel from the golden run of the accompaniment.

The audience was absolutely still, breathless, listening with hearts as well as ears.

Coralie sat almost petrified with wonder, first at the beauty and resonance of her brother's voice, and then almost instantly caught and held by the words he was singing. For he seemed to be singing a bit out of his own experience and no ordinary experience either. It seemed as if he were voicing the depths of every human heart there, the longings, the dissatisfaction, the need, and then the remedy. So! He had not always been like this, so different from other men! Something, someone, had come in and changed him!

And as he sang, it seemed as though he were singing just to her, answering some of the questions she had come that night to ask. It was as if he were singing the answer to her own dissatisfaction and unhappiness. Giving her a hope that there was somewhere a solution to this problem called Life, that would make it possible to go on, that would still this horrible yearning within that everyone must have, though most were unwilling to acknowledge it.

Tenderly the soft music swelled on and died away and Dana's voice took up the story again:

"All my life was full of sin when Jesus found me,
All my heart was full of misery and woe;
Jesus placed His strong and loving arms about me,
And He led me in the way I ought to go."

Was it possible that her brother with the heavenly
look in his face knew what that feeling of misery was,
understood the things that she had felt? That his life had
been full of *sin*? She doubted that. She had never called
it sin, what she had felt. Sin was murdering somebody,
wasn't it, or stealing great sums of money? Or adultery?
She had never heard people call other things sin, things
which everybody did without thinking. Sin? Why, she
was sure Dana had never been a sinner.

"No one ever cared for me like Jesus—" sang on the
glorious voice, and everyone who heard it was con-
vinced of the reality of that friendship with Jesus about
which he was singing.

And the sister, beginning to sense what this brother
must have suffered through the years, how lonely he had
been without a mother, felt sudden compunction for the
part that she unwittingly must have played in that suffering. What a lonely little boy he must have been! Yet, he
had that wonderful father about which he had told her.
She hadn't had a father. She had had a mother—yes, if
one could call Lisa a mother. But she had felt a lack.

Coralie was really thinking. Perhaps she had never in
the whole of her life done so much thinking as she had
been forced to do during the last two days!

Again those tender notes of the piano made exquisite
interlude, while the words dug deep into each listening
soul reechoing with the soft melody.

"Every day He comes to me with new assurance,"

sang Dana taking up the story again, and the look on his face made real the words—

> *"More and more I understand His words of love;*
> *But I'll never know just why He came to save me,*
> *Till some day I see His blessed face above.*
> *No one ever cared for me like Jesus,*
> *There's no other friend so kind as He;*
> *No one else could take the sin and darkness from me,*
> *O how much He cared for me!"*

As the last notes died away there was such a stillness in that audience as Coralie at least had never experienced.

Bruce with bowed head was praying for the girl by his side, praying as it seemed he had never prayed for anyone before, and as the song finished and he lifted his head he glanced at her furtively and saw a look in her face that filled his heart with awe. It was the look of a hungry soul, hearing of food.

The message which followed that song was simple and powerful and unlike anything Coralie had ever heard, especially from the lips of a young man. She listened intently, and now and then would suddenly look up wide-eyed at Bruce with a kind of question in her glance, as if she wondered if he agreed with the startling things that were being said. It is safe to say that Coralie had never in her whole life listened so long to words about death, and hell, and Heaven and Life. But this was new and frightening and it called her entirely out of herself, to consider grave matters which she had always heretofore ignored.

Bruce watched her unobtrusively, and prayed, thanking God for the plain direct way in which Kirk Shannon was telling of salvation. Perhaps this girl of the world would never have another opportunity to hear it again, but she certainly was getting it now, and taking it in, too. Of course that might not mean that she was accepting it. Yet such things had happened before.

"And now," said Kirk after he had closed his brief message with a tender prayer, "I see another old friend down there. Bruce Carbury, come on up and help Dana and me sing something."

Bruce gave a startled look at Kirk, and then a troubled one down at the girl by his side. He couldn't go and leave that girl down here in a strange audience alone, could he?

But her face was blazing with interest.

"Go on," she said, "I want to hear you!"

"All right," he smiled. "Sorry to leave you alone." And then he strode past her and up the aisle.

How those three voices blended together! It was beautiful. It was gripping, and they sang the words as if they were speaking.

> "O listen to our wondrous story,
> Counted once among the lost;
> Yet, one came down from heaven's glory
> Saving us at awful cost!
> Who saved us from eternal loss?
> Who but God's Son upon the cross?
> What did He do? He died for you!
> Where is He now? Believe it thou,
> In heaven interceding."

The story was all new to Coralie. Any gospel heretofore that had sifted through the world to her mind was so hazy that it had meant nothing whatever to her. With the same wonder that she had watched the whole meeting she listened now as those beautiful voices brought out the full story. On to the last verse:

"Will you surrender to this Saviour?"

Then this was not something from which she was barred. She sat a little forward on her chair and it seemed to her that Bruce was looking straight at her as his deep bass blended with the other voices, and when he said, "He will save you, save *you now!*" it seemed as if he were offering her something tangible that she might take too. She caught her breath and the look in her eyes grew wistful. Not that she realized the fullness of what they were singing about. She was too utterly ignorant for that. But she was greatly touched, and vaguely yearning for something she had not known, which evidently her brother had.

When the meeting was out and while the throngs of people swarmed around her, talking eagerly, she studied their faces. Common people they were, most of them, though there were a few who were fashionably dressed. Three or four girls had highly illuminated faces. Coralie sensed that these didn't seem to belong. They had not that look of utter joy and peace the others wore, the look that marked her brother and his two friends. She wasn't at all sure now that she wanted to be like these people. There would likely be a lot to give up, and the wonder might go away at nearer intimacy. Yet what, exactly, was it that she would mind giving up? When she tried to think, she couldn't honestly put her finger on one thing she minded surrendering. Any price would be worth paying for real joy and peace.

But then, if all this they had been singing and talking about was real, why wasn't the whole world in search of it, instead of frittering away its time in nonsense that didn't really bring lasting joy?

Suddenly she looked up and there came Bruce down the aisle toward her, his eyes meeting hers. A bright smile lit up his face, an almost tender twinkle came to his eyes. He looked as he had when he sang those words, "You too shall come to know His favor." And that wistful eagerness sprang into her own eyes again.

"Sorry to have left you alone," he said in a low tone as he took his stand beside her.

"Oh, I didn't mind," she said, almost shyly. No one who knew her would have believed that Coralie could ever be shy. Then she brightened and lifted her eyes with a look of sincerity in them.

"I like to have you sing! You have a gorgeous voice!" she said.

He gave her a quick surprised look.

"I'm glad you felt that way," he said gravely. "I was afraid we were letting you in for something you wouldn't understand or enjoy. Something you might not like at all."

And then people closed in about them and began to talk to Bruce, and finally to her as if she belonged to them too. It was some minutes before Dana and Kirk and Valerie Shannon came down the aisle and were introduced to her, and they all started toward the door.

"Now," said Valerie Shannon with one of her engaging smiles, "of course you're all coming to our house for a little while. My sister made a huge pan of delicious fudge this afternoon and we can eat it and get acquainted. I've heard Kirk talk so much about Dana Barron that I must get to know you all. Will you come?"

And so they passed out into the clear cool night air and walked down the street. Bruce was walking by Coralie's side as if it were his business to care for her. Valerie Shannon was walking with Dana.

8

BACK at Lisa's apartment a party was in progress. It was because of the prospect of this that Coralie had come off by herself hunting her new-found brother, hoping that perhaps she might inveigle him into taking her to something entertaining.

Her reason for wanting to escape the party was because Lisa had invited two men that her daughter detested, and the girl was determined not to have anything further to do with them.

The older of them, Ivor Kavanaugh, was Lisa's latest admirer, a tall foreign-looking man with an offensive manner and a fondness for gambling. The younger was his nephew, Errol Hunt, a young man with baggy eyelids, and much given to drink. He had been pursuing Coralie assiduously for the past few weeks. The idea seemed to be that the uncle would marry Lisa and Errol would marry her daughter. Lisa seemed quite willing, but her daughter did not care for the arrangement. Only a few days before Lisa had come out in the open and told her daughter that such was her plan, and that it was about the best she could hope to do. Lisa had heard that both men were fabulously wealthy.

Errol Hunt was not in any sense good-looking, and he drank too much on all occasions. He was constantly taking for granted that Coralie—Corinne, he called her—belonged to him, thus driving other old friends away. He was an insolent cub, and he sometimes treated Coralie as if she were the dust under his feet. Then when he had been drinking too much, he would fawn upon her and come whining to her for companionship, like a naughty child who wanted to be petted and played with.

At first all this rather amused the girl, but now, since she had begun to see that they were using Lisa as a good way out of their gambling debts, constantly borrowing money from her, and neglecting to pay, she had rebelled. They had had a near-quarrel about it that afternoon when a lot of things had come out into the open.

"If you are going to marry Ivor, I'm done with you," she had told Lisa, and Lisa had narrowed her eyes and looked at her daughter speculatively.

"What about you marrying Ivor's nephew?" she had asked, almost like a taunt.

"Nothing doing!" said the girl with her chin in the air. "I know how to hang onto my money if you don't yours," she said. "Those two are just grafters."

"How ridiculous!" said Lisa with a cold look and a freezing voice. "Ivor is very wealthy! He has more money than you ever dreamed of having."

"Oh, yes?" said the girl disrespectfully. "How is it he has to borrow of you all the time? How is it he spends all his time gambling, if he has to borrow money to pay his gambling debts?"

"How absurd. Child, you know nothing of finance. These are debts of honor he must pay at once. He will have no trouble in paying them back when he gets this foreign exchange business straightened out. You are rather outrageous, you know, talking that way of my best friends."

"I wonder?" said the girl insolently. "I just wonder if you didn't have any better discernment when you ran away and left my father than you are showing today. You certainly didn't pick well the second time. And really, I don't see what you see in this owl-eyed ape. He flatters you, that's all. I should think you had had enough of getting married anyway. And besides you'd have to get a divorce first. You're not sure your present husband is dead. No, if you are going to pull off that stunt again I'm leaving, understand? I'll have no more fathers messing around with my bank account, and what's more I'm not lending you any more money, either, not if it's going to those two crooks."

Lisa had narrowed her eyes again, this time almost in alarm, for it wasn't but a couple of days since she had called up the bank and told the authorities that her daughter wanted several hundred dollars paid to her mother's account, and she had been daringly drawing checks upon it since. Of course she felt the girl was paying no attention to her own financial affairs. Her father had put the money in trust till the child was eighteen, and it was but recently that Coralie had been taking any account of her money. She had dreamily hoped that the girl would continue of such mind, at least until she was married.

"Take care, you young serpent," said her mother. "You may go a little too far some day in your pleasantries."

"Yes, and how about you?" snapped Coralie.

"Well, how about me? Am I accountable to you?"

"It's a pity you weren't accountable to somebody," said the daughter. "If you go and annex that big goof you'll wish you hadn't, that's all."

"Look here, young lady, you'd better take care! You may have to eat those words some day. The 'big goof' has a nephew who is richer by far than he is. You can't afford to let that slip through your fingers."

"Can't I? You watch me!" flung back the girl, and went to her room, slamming the door after her and locking it.

An hour afterward Coralie had stolen out quietly while her mother was dressing for dinner, and gone to hunt her brother, angrier than she had ever been before. She had been looking at her monthly statement which the mail had brought that afternoon, and had discovered Lisa's purloining. Item after item helped to open her eyes. Experience had taught her that when Lisa juggled her bank account she had something planned ahead, or was conducting some sort of an enterprise that she didn't want to tell her about. Sometimes it was heavy gambling. Sometimes it was some admirer who wanted to borrow money. Coralie had come to the point where she felt it was time to take a stand for her own rights. There seemed to be no one with whom she could take refuge who would not question her, and she felt in no mood for questions tonight, so she sought out the strange new brother whom she did not understand.

On the way she decided to take her money away entirely from the bank where it had been in trust during her minority, and put it where Lisa could not find it. She certainly did not intend to finance another foolish marriage for Lisa. She was old enough now to run her own affairs and she intended to do so. That was why she had been so insistent upon going with Dana.

But as the evening progressed she had gradually forgotten all about the cause for her being in this strange new environment, and had grown interested in studying everything that went on.

In between the other things which drew her attention she was greatly impressed by Bruce. Furtively she studied him when he was not aware of it, as from long practice she well knew how to do. And she could not help comparing him with Errol Hunt. Those heavy dark bags under Errol's small selfish eyes, the thick sensuous lips, were such a contrast to the clear-cut face of Bruce Carbury, whose wide dark eyes set in the lean strong face, heavy copper hair, and firm pleasant lips, all bespoke a man of intellect and courage and conviction. Not that she named those things. She simply realized that this was a face that was pleasing to her, a face that showed no selfishness, and had honesty and sincerity written all over it. When she thought of marrying Errol as her mother had suggested she shuddered from head to foot, and her eyes snapped fire. And yet, if she stayed in the life she was now living, and Lisa should be determined to go on with her present evident intentions to marry Ivor, she would have to in self-defense. Also, if things went on this way she would have no money left, and neither would her mother. And from what Dana had said there was going to be no more forthcoming from the dead father.

That was why she had sought out Dana. She wanted to get these things clearly arranged in her mind and know the truth about everything.

Just supposing that was true and her father had left no money? And supposing Lisa should lose her head and marry that man Ivor and he should somehow get control of the money Coralie's father had put in trust for her, what would she, Coralie, do? Heavens! She would have to get a job like any common working girl, and Lisa would never stand for that! She would have to leave Lisa if it came to that. She could never put herself under the control of those two, Ivor and Errol!

Coralie had been thinking this over on her way to find her brother. She hadn't any idea of telling Dana about it. She had not then got so far in trusting him that she wanted him to know her private affairs.

But the meeting had driven all these thoughts away, and as she went into the cold night air and a memory of her earlier walk came to her it seemed very far away and unreal. It was as if she had just now been dwelling for a little while on the borders of some sort of heaven, and suddenly had to come down to earth again. The rest of this evening wouldn't last long. They were going to the musician-girl's house to eat some fudge and then she would be expected to go home and take Dana with her, and where could she take Dana? Not to the apartment, for though there were rooms enough, they would be filled. There would be people there. There were always people there in the evening, unless they went out themselves. Even then there were some few who felt free to come in during their absence and smoke and visit and have drinks served them. There simply wasn't a spot where she would like to take Dana. He wouldn't understand it, and he wouldn't like it any more than he had thought she would like that meeting.

Well, the meeting had been strange and absorbing to her, but she had learned enough about her new brother to know that he would never be at home where drinking was going on. She could imagine what Ivor would be like at this hour of the evening. And that unspeakable Errol Hunt! She mustn't let them ever come in contact with her wonderful brother. They would insult him. Just their eyes upon him would be an insult. Strange that the evening had wrought that change in her that she thought Dana was wonderful, but she did.

And this young man who was walking with her, keeping pleasant step with her steps, looking down at her with dark eyes from beneath that thatch of deep red hair, he was wonderful, too!

She wouldn't feel afraid of Errol Hunt, nor Ivor, if she had this man with her. There was something strong and vital about him that made her sure he wouldn't let any harm come to her if he were by. But Errol—! She gave a little shiver as she thought of him. There was revulsion in her heart at his memory.

At that shiver Bruce laid his gloved hand over hers gently, reassuringly.

"Are you cold?" he asked anxiously. "It's rather sharp outside this evening in contrast to that room we were in, isn't it? Somehow those crowded rooms always get overheated, and then it is not so good to come out into the cold."

"Oh, I'm not cold," said Coralie, nestling her hand under the strong warm one. "I was just shivering at the thought of some things I don't like. All those people in there seemed so happy. But *I'm* not. They wouldn't look happy if they had *some* things to bear."

"Perhaps you haven't got the same reason for being happy," suggested Bruce with a gentleness in his voice.

She looked up puzzled.

"Perhaps you don't know their Lord Jesus," he went on. "You see it's that that makes them happy, not earthly circumstances. They didn't look happy because they have nice homes and rich friends, and a lot of money, nor even because they were getting their own way.

They looked happy because they have accepted the Lord Jesus Christ as their Saviour, and they know their sins are forgiven. They are living and rejoicing in eternity, not in this little space of life they are living down here."

"Oh!" she said faintly. "No, I don't know anything about that. Do you believe all that they were saying? You sang as if you did, but I thought maybe you were just singing, and didn't really mean it."

"Oh, yes, I meant it. I meant every word I sang. I accepted the Lord Jesus several years ago, when your brother led me to Him, and I've been happy ever since just because I'm saved, and because I expect to spend eternity in Heaven with my Lord, and the dear ones who love Him."

"And is it real to you all the time? Don't you ever get away from it all, and forget it, and do the way other men do?"

"I'm not perfect, if that's what you mean. But no, I don't forget it. I'm as conscious of the Lord Jesus all the time as I ever was of my friends around me. When you get to be God-conscious every hour is pervaded with Him, and when you go away you feel He would not like to have you go, you are grieved, and want Him to forgive you."

"Don't you ever drink?" asked Coralie sharply.

"No!"

"Because if you drink you couldn't be God-conscious all the time. If you were drunk you wouldn't know what you thought."

He gave her a curious pitiful look.

"If you knew and loved the Lord Jesus you wouldn't ever be drunk. You wouldn't want to lose that God-consciousness."

She studied the thought a moment.

"I don't suppose I ever really liked to get drunk and do foolish things, but then when everybody else does it what can you do?"

"Why, do differently. Why should you be a fool just because everybody around you is? But you know *every*body else doesn't do it. There are a great many people who never touch liquor."

She looked up at him thoughtfully.

"I don't believe my father ever got drunk."

"I'm sure he didn't. He was a wonderful man. I'm sure he never took liquor."

"Perhaps if I'd been brought up by him I never would have touched it either."

"I'm sure you wouldn't."

"Did you know him?"

"Yes. I knew him and admired him greatly."

"Well, I *wasn't* brought up by him, so what can I do?"

"Why you can do the way you think he would have brought you up, if you want to, can't you?"

"Goodness! What would everybody say if I should?"

"Would that matter?"

"Oh! Wouldn't it? They could make it unpleasant."

"Yes? Well, don't they make it unpleasant for you when they get drunk sometimes? Or, don't they? Perhaps you like the way they act when they are not quite themselves."

"No, I don't. Not when I haven't been drinking myself. I hate them all."

"And yet you put yourself in a class with them! That seems queer to me."

"It is funny, isn't it?" She was silent for a minute and then with a shrugging of her shoulders, and a flinging out of her free hand she said lightly:

"Oh, well, what's the use? I couldn't ever be anything

worth while when I was traveling along with the rest. It isn't in me. And I couldn't go a pace like that alone."

"But you wouldn't have to go it alone, you know. One would go with you, if you really started out on that road."

She looked up at him wonderingly.

"'One'?"

"Yes. The Lord Jesus. If you really took Him for your Saviour you know He would never leave you."

"That seems queer," she said meditatively. "But I don't think He'd like the company. No, I'd have to leave them. I'd have to go off away from them." She seemed very positive about it.

"Maybe that was what you were meant to do," he said gravely. "You know He has said that we must come out from among unbelievers. We must be separate."

She looked almost frightened at that.

"I wouldn't know how to manage," she said. "Lisa would never stand for my going. And besides, I think she's got my money all tied up so that I couldn't get it."

"Well, you know those things don't count. If you want to go God's way He will make things plain and clear for you. You may have some hard things to bear. But there is always peace and joy when you are in the way with Him. Besides, you only have to go a step at a time. The first step is to take Him for your Saviour."

She shook her head positively.

"I wouldn't know how," she said decidedly.

"The way is very plain. Any one of those young Christians you saw tonight could tell you. God's word makes it quite clear."

"Would you tell me how, sometime?" she asked after a moment of silence. "I won't promise I'll do anything about it, but I'd like to understand it."

"Yes, I will gladly tell you," he said.

They had come to a halt before the big old-fashioned house where the Shannons lived and there was no more opportunity to talk.

"All right. That's a promise. We'll fix a time and I'll ask a lot of questions."

"Well, I'm going to begin to pray for you tonight," said Bruce.

Then they went in with the rest, and found the father had built up a fire in the fireplace and the flames were crackling and snapping cheerily. The mother was there, and the children were there, having just finished their school homework. The piano was there and Valerie soon took her place at it, but to Coralie's amazement when she began to play it was not jazz. If it had been her crowd and these young people were anything like all of them they would have been in a wild whirl of dancing at once, but these young people seemed to have no such thought.

Coralie sank into a chair, after the introductions, and stared around. She stared most at the gentle-faced mother, and tried to think of Lisa being a woman like that. That sunny look of real love in her eyes! Lisa didn't have it in her. When she tried to conjure her face she could see only the hard steely glitter she wore when she found fault, as when she had railed out at her that morning Dana had come to see them, because she cried. Lisa was hard. Could Lisa ever have been a mother like that? Or was she born hard and selfish? Oh, she was beautiful of course, and that went a great way to make people selfish. But was Lisa born selfish so she couldn't help it? Or did she go to work and make herself selfish by always trying to get her own way?

She pondered this till Mr. Shannon came into the

room again with an armful of wood for the fire, and then she saw Kirk and Kendall both spring up to take it from him and make him sit down beside the fire. It gave her a glimpse of what an unselfish loving family could be, and she watched them all enviously. Then she studied the quiet pleasant-faced father, whose interest seemed to be bound up in them all. Would her father have been like that? What a pleasant life it must be to live in a home with a father and mother like that. Oh, why couldn't Lisa have been like this Shannon mother and stayed in her home and brought up her children and made life happy for them?

Turla and Leith came in presently with little frosted cakes, a platter of fudge, and a great tray of glasses of lemonade. What fun it was! Nobody asked for anything stronger, nor seemed to want it! And not a soul of all those girls and boys were smoking! It was incredible! Could it be possible that none of them ever smoked? Oh surely they must do it on the sly! Yet these young people did not look as if they ever did anything on the sly.

Norah had grown sleepy. She curled down on the floor on the other side of her mother with her head in her mother's lap and went to sleep. The mother's arm went sweetly around her. How would it have been to be little and sheltered that way? To have grown up in such an atmosphere?

They made Dana sing some more, and then they all sang, several Scotch songs the grandmother called for, for she too had drifted down the stairs and sat in her sheltered rocker near the fire. The father called for some Irish melodies. And by and by they came back to sweet old hymns again.

Only they were not old to Coralie. They were so new

she didn't even know they were hymns till she caught a word or two about the Lord and guessed it.

Before midnight they said good night. Wistfully with a backward glance Coralie went out with Bruce and Dana into the clear starlit night again.

"Lovely household, wasn't it?" said Bruce as they waited for Dana who had stepped back with Valerie for a moment to find a piece of music he had promised to learn.

"Yes," sighed Coralie, "but it isn't a bit like my household. You can't think how different it is!"

"Every household is not alike," said Bruce, wisely feeling his way. "Yours would be different of course."

"Yes, and how!" said the girl with a sigh.

"Oh, but the Lord is able to make beauty and peace abound wherever He goes," he said, smiling down at her.

"I'd like to see Him try it in ours!" said she almost fiercely. "The very devil is to pay there."

"Oh, he's everywhere, doing his best, but he isn't as strong as the Lord. Why don't you try letting Christ come into your household through you, and see what He would do? He is able to save to the uttermost, you know."

Then Dana came running down the steps and there was no further opportunity to answer. So Coralie walked along between the two, measuring her steps by theirs, listening to their quiet converse concerning a world about which she knew nothing. Now and then she caught a look on her brother's face that she knew her own face could have carried if it only had the same knowledge and feeling. And then she would steal a glance at his friend. He wore no hat, and his red hair shone coppery in the starlight. She liked the way he smiled, and the quick way he looked up in response to something Dana had said, and the way that heavy wave of red hair fell down across the whiteness of his forehead.

Then as they neared her home she thought of the sharp contrast of Errol's heavy face, small dull eyes, colorless hair, and the silly look on his drunken face. That was the way she would find him if she were to go into the rooms where they were amusing themselves now. And they would cry out upon her and want to know where she had been. If she should dare to tell them she had been to a prayer meeting how they would laugh and mock her, and refuse to believe her!

But she did not mean to go in there. She would slip into the kitchen area at the back and up the back stairs to her room. She would lock herself in and not appear at all. She could not face them. She *would* not. She wanted to keep the beautiful vision of that sweet home and family in her heart and memory. She wanted to get into her bed with the pretty starlight coming in on the crisp night air, and read the whole wonderful evening over like a book, letting it thrill her again if it could. That would prove that it was real, and not just a fantasy.

She would not turn on her light in her room. She would undress in the dark, and then she would lie down and go step by step through that evening again. She would review every look and word and action. She would study the face of that young man who had walked by her side and looked down at her as he talked. She would study it as she could not study it in reality lest he might see her doing it, and think into her thoughts and know how she had been moved by him. She wanted to think it all out. To hear her brother's voice singing those strange stirring words, and hear that other voice too, and think of that girl at the piano. How sweet and strong she looked! She would like to know that girl better, but probably there would be no further opportunity, though she had asked her to come again.

No, she did not mean to go into the orgy that Lisa was carrying on, not tonight; she meant to stay by herself.

So when they reached the apartment building she took things in her own hands.

"You're not to go up with me," she said firmly to Dana. "Lisa is having a party up there and you wouldn't fit."

She saw by the quick glance of anxiety that passed between the two that they were instantly worried about her.

"Do *you?*" asked Dana with a keen glance into her sweet young face.

"Perhaps!" said Coralie with an inscrutable look, "I don't know yet. It's all I've ever known, you know. But don't worry. I'm not going in tonight. I'm going up the back way and nobody will know I'm home. I want to get by myself and think it all over, and see where I do belong."

Then suddenly she turned to them, gave a little impish grin, and blew them a kiss on the tips of her fingers, comically.

"Couldn't we—help you?" asked Dana looking up at the lighted windows anxiously.

"Yes," said Bruce. "Let us go up with you."

"Not on your life!" said Coralie. "That would bring them all down upon me. I'm just going in this lower door, and up the back way. The butler's always ready to cover my tracks. Good night! See you again soon."

She half turned and then flashed back again.

"Oh, I forgot. Dana, Lisa wants to see you sometime. Business, I guess. She didn't say what. Morning would be best. Not earlier than eleven. That's what I came to tell you anyway."

"Oh, but you said you wanted to talk," said Dana. "We can walk back to the park, or stop in the parlor of a hotel," he suggested. "I completely forgot what I promised."

"It's all right," said the girl. "It will do another day. Tonight was perfect, and there might not be another such. Good-bye!"

She flashed around the angle of the basement door and was gone. Dana tried the door to follow her, but found she had put the night latch on and it was useless, so after lingering a little they went slowly on toward home.

9

CORALIE carried out her plan of undressing in the darkness with a locked door. Lying in her bed with the starlit windows opposite her, she stared at the square of dimness, and tried to think her life through.

Never before had she come face to face with realities as she had this evening. She had been dissatisfied and unhappy ever since she could remember. There had been nothing to tie to, nothing really to care about except herself, and mostly herself could not satisfy. It had never occurred to her that she had had any part in this unhappiness. It had all seemed to be thrust upon her by some unkind power, mostly through other people who would not do what she wanted them to do. She had fretted and fumed, but had never arrived at any solution. She had even blamed her lazy selfish mother, but it did no good. And she had never really loved anyone. Oh, a dog or a kitten perhaps, when she was little, but then they too disappointed her, for when she mauled them they died. She had never had any impression of anyone loving her. Human love had meant to her a matter of what you could get out of anyone for the least you could give.

And now this other kind of love—was it God's love?—had come into notice as something of an entirely different nature. Something intrinsically rare. Something that could make a young man look as her new brother looked, and could touch the strong, virile nature of a man like her brother's friend, Bruce Carbury. Love could be something tender and precious. She had seen it in his eyes. She had felt it in the touch of his hand when he laid it over hers for that brief instant of sympathy. It wasn't a fleshly thing, a love like that. It was of the spirit, though Coralie had never before been conscious that flesh and spirit were not one and the same. Now however she saw it dimly, and she perceived that others had seen it too.

There was that whole family of Shannons, father, mother, and all the children. They all had such love for one another. Not for anything each could get out of the other. Just for enjoying the preciousness of each other. Maybe a love like that had been what she had been longing for all her life, vaguely reaching after, thinking that perhaps it might be found somewhere. Yet the yearning was so indefinite that there had been nothing but restlessness concerning it in her mind.

She had never had much faith in married love because of what her mother had done, but seeing those two married lovers at Shannons had given her a different view entirely. It seemed that two people could go all their days, through hardships, and trials, and perplexities, and yet bear that tender relationship in spite of it all, still look at one another with that almost worship in their eyes. Ah, to be married, like that, to one who loved you so, that would be as near perfection as one could hope ever to get on this earth!

But—and she gave a little shiver—to be married to a man like Errol Hunt—! That, ah, that would be like hell!

She could dimly hear his irrational stuttering voice. She knew just how he looked when he talked like that. He was very drunk indeed!

And now he was calling her name. "Corinne! Corinne! Hey, Rinny, where are you? Why'n ya come when I call ya?"

She gave a great shudder beneath the bedclothes. Oh, if she were out there he would be offensively near her. He would be trying to put his arms around her, drawing her head down on his flabby shoulder, trying to kiss her with his thick red lips. She could almost feel the hotness of his breath in her face now, the rankness of the liquor he had drunk. Once he had attempted a caress when he was drunk and she had not had even a glass. The memory of it filled her with horror. Perhaps he had often kissed her like that when she had been drinking herself, and it had made no impression on her memory. But now she was filled with disgust at herself that she ever could have been willing to put herself into a condition where he could dare to be affectionate. Oh, how she hated him! A silly beast! That was what he was.

And it was the memory of that one time when she was herself, and hated his intimate touch on her lips, her hands, her shoulders, that had lingered with her and made her loathe the very thought and sight of him. Made her feel that she would rather die than marry him; though the thought of death was fearful to her.

Vaguely, dimly, now his voice sounded through the halls, through the very walls, and died away. Then grew louder, and came nearer. She could hear him stumbling along the hall, lurching against her door, and her heart stood still. Though the door was locked and bolted securely and she knew he could not get in, she was trembling from head to foot. She scarcely dared to breathe.

He was babbling her name, calling out to her.

"C'reen! C'reen! C'mon out I say. I wantcha! Come on out'n dance! Fa lal la! Doncha hear the music? C'mon out'n get a drink! I got a bottle a' something swell. Saved it fer you! C'mon, C'reen! Wha's tha matter? Wha's getting ya? C'mon, C'reen! I'll marry ya ef ya'll come out! We'll go get married right now!"

His voice muttered away indefinitely, and at last after pounding and rattling at the door intermittently, he groped his way back along the wall and she could hear his stumbling walk, hands on the wall.

It was some time after he had gone out of hearing before she dared to breathe freely again, and she was cold with terror. How she wished she dared steal to the telephone and call up her brother, or one of those people she had been with during the evening, and ask for help. Well she knew they would come at once, any one of them. Especially she knew that Bruce would come, and of course, Dana. They had shown a care for her well-being that she had never known before.

But she dared not do it. The crowd would hear her talking. They would know she was there and come to break in the door and stop her if they knew what she was doing.

Besides, she could not bear the shame of having Dana and Bruce know what was going on in her home. She could not have them come and find her beautiful mother drunk. Especially Dana must never see her that way. Dana, in spite of all he had borne from his mother, had somehow retained an ideal of motherhood, and it would appall him so to see his mother like that. She shrank from it for him. And she wondered at herself even while she was thinking that, for she had never cared what others suffered before. She had never been willing to bear anything to save another in any way. Yet now she wanted to save that heavenly face of her brother from bearing the imprint of horror and disgust. She had been learning what love meant, and she knew he had it. Perhaps some love for him was stealing into her own brazen little heart too. But anyhow she could not let Dana come here now and see things as they were. Somehow she must stand it and keep still till this was past. And then tomorrow she might go away somewhere and hide. Never again subject herself to such terror as this.

But where could she go? With Lisa borrowing again from her funds, making it appear that she had given consent. Lisa could sign her name in exact imitation of hers. There was no telling but her money for the quarter was gone. There would be no more for three months. Where could she go without money?

Of course she might be able to do as some others were doing, get a job. But what could she do? She had never been taught anything worth while. She couldn't even sew. Perhaps she might get a job as a social secretary, but Lisa would make a terrible fuss about that. Everybody would talk. Oh, of course, she might try to get a job as a style model. But there again Lisa would think she was an utter disgrace. She would simply have to leave town if she attempted anything like that, and even at that if Lisa ever found out where she was she would queer her at once and lose any job for her that she could possibly get. There really was nothing for her at all, unless she stayed with her mother, and it began to look very much as if *that* would mean marrying that awful beast of an Errol. And that she would never do, not even if she had to drown herself.

She lay there a long time shivering and quaking in her miserable young soul, and wondering what those Shannons would think of her if they knew what torment she was in. And what would that nice red-haired Bruce think? Wouldn't he do something about it if he knew? Yes, he would, she was sure, but she was equally sure that she would rather die than let him know. She would never want to look him in his eyes again if he knew.

Dana would do something about it too, she had confidence enough in him now to know that. But again she could never tell Dana her shame. She had got to carry it off somehow herself. Her pride would carry her through as it always had done of course, only she was heart-sick now. And moreover she had had a revelation of another way to live. She might not have liked the other way any better if she had been brought up in it, but at least it looked better at first sight. At least those people *looked* happy, and when she thought it over carefully she couldn't think of one of her friends who had a radiant look like those people. Radiant and tender, that was the way they looked.

Why hadn't she been born like other children, with the right kind of father and mother, and a home? Why couldn't she have had a grand brother like Dana, and a friend like Bruce, and lived a perfectly normal life? Why was she ever fed on wine and whiskey and allowed to grow wild?

But the night wore on and the air that came in her window was full of sounds, weird, jazzy sounds, out of a world she knew, sounds that brought pictures to her mind. All about her there were people making merry, without any real mirth in their hearts. She could hear the tunes to which they were dancing, the foolish babbling and wild mirthless screaming with which they punctuated the night. Hadn't she been a part of it often and often? She knew the silly languishing glances with which they were accompanied, and her soul was loathing it all. She seemed to be flung down at the bottom of a deep pit, into the mire of her life, with no way whatever to get out to the top where the air was pure. She struggled, caught her breath, and felt that she was stifling.

Then suddenly like a clear breath of air blowing from some eternal hills there came the echo of her brother's voice singing:

"I would love to tell you what I think of Jesus . . ."

She had that line. She was sure of it. Then the tune trailed off vaguely to another phrase or two. "No one ever cared for me like Jesus." It rang in her heart. It pierced her through and through, and touched the sore place of her own loneliness, and terror, and fright of life.

And now the song was banishing the other life about her. It had cleared the atmosphere. "Oh, how much He cared for me!" Ah! Could that possibly be for her? Was there a way out of all this?

"Oh, Jesus! Jesus! Where are you?" Such a desolate little desperate prayer, that didn't even know it was a prayer.

Dana and Bruce had walked slowly, silently for the first two or three blocks toward home, and then Dana asked sadly:

"Well, you have seen! What do you think? Is it any use? Should I have come?"

"Yes!" said Bruce with a ring to his voice. "I am glad you came. She was wonderfully stirred by your song. Stirred by the whole evening."

"Perhaps!" said Dana sadly. "But only because it was something new she had never seen before, don't you think?"

"I'm not sure," said Bruce. "I thought the Spirit of God was working."

"Well, but the effect will all be disseminated when she gets among her own crowd again." Dana had a sad despondent manner.

"She said she was not going among them tonight. We will go home and pray!"

"Yes," said Dana, "I know. God can work where we cannot see, of course. When you come to think of it, wasn't it rather wonderful she should come in on us that way just as we had been talking of her?"

"Yes. It was," said Bruce. "Perhaps that was why I felt from the first that it was God's doing. But don't begin to pull it to pieces and wonder. Just be glad we have such a wonderful God. For I think she has been greatly stirred by everything. You in the first place of course, and then the meeting, and the Shannons. They are great people, you know."

"Yes, aren't they? But what do you suppose they thought of my sister?"

"Thought she needed saving, likely. Kirk is always on the lookout for souls. Say, he's got a mighty fine family. It's no wonder he is such a fine fellow. It pays to have a good family."

"Yes indeed!" agreed Dana. "Kirk has some marvelous sisters, hasn't he? That girl that played tonight has a fine delicate touch."

"Yes. A potato could sing with an accompaniment

like that. I felt it bearing us along in that trio. My, I like to sing with you and Kirk! I almost feel as if I had a voice too!"

"Yes, you poor humble creature, it's a pity about you!" said Dana. "One of the finest bass voices I've ever had the pleasure of hearing, and yet you talk like that! Kirk's sister couldn't get over how deep it is. By the way, what was her name? I didn't catch it."

"Valerie, I think. And what did she say about *your* voice, you poor beggar?" answered Bruce.

"Why, I don't remember that she said anything special," said Dana laughing. "Well, she's a fine girl, and Kirk has plenty of people in his own household to help in his mission work. That must be wonderful. Do you know, this evening, I couldn't help wishing my father could have known that family."

"Well, he will some day! Say, it's going to be great knowing all God's family, being related to them, isn't it?"

So they talked as they walked along, and went back again to the experiences of the evening, till at last before they reached the house, Bruce told Dana of the conversation he had had with Coralie.

"Well, that's great!" said Dana eagerly. "Thank you so much for taking my poor little sister on your hands, and carrying on when I had to go up and sing. And thank you for so cheerfully taking the interruption to the pleasant evening you had planned for us tonight, and my sister spoiled. I'm afraid she may unexpectedly spoil a lot of our nice times if I remain in New York."

"That's all right with me, Dana," said the other. "I'd rather have the nice time God plans always, than any time I plan. But I mean it, I really had a good time tonight! That little sister of yours is very interesting.

You'd better get acquainted with her and find out for yourself. I know, she doesn't talk your language yet, but it's not impossible for her to learn."

"Thanks a lot, Bruce. I needed that encouragement. I was pretty down about her. And as for my mother, I don't know what to think."

"Doesn't the fact that she has sent for you, *wants* to see you, give you any hope?"

"Well, I'm afraid not, old man. You don't know how she impressed me. Just as one who was so hardened that nothing would reach her. So hardened that even the love of God wouldn't mean a thing to her. I suppose it is prejudice of the years, and what she did, that makes me feel so strongly, but somehow I caught no gleam of interest in her. She looked startled. I could see she recognized my likeness to father. But I felt that when she looked at me it was as if I was, to her, one who had risen from the dead. As if when she decided to leave father and me long ago she had killed us from her heart, and now she resented that I had come back to haunt her. I was in the nature of a 'hant,' if you know what I mean. I didn't see a single flash of real personal interest. Nor I didn't recognize a hint of any repentance that she had left father. He was something that had died long ago out of her life, and all I did was to remind her of him. Even when she once acknowledged that he was 'sweet' as she called him, you could see it wasn't a sweetness she had *missed* out of her life, or had perhaps ever cared for deeply at any time. I suppose that fact made me resent her even more than I had before I came. To have had my father's wonderful love, and not to care, that seemed unforgivable!"

Bruce was quiet for a moment and then he said thoughtfully:

"I suppose that is what we will be thinking in Heaven some day about people who treated our Lord that way."

Dana sighed deeply.

"Yes, I suppose. But you know, Bruce, it has given me such a hopeless feeling about her, and I'm afraid my sister is bound to be like her."

"I don't believe so!" said Bruce suddenly with strong emphasis. "She may be more like your father. She looks like him! And anyhow she is your sister, and we're going to pray for her! I told her we would."

"Yes," said Dana. "And of course I'll pray for my mother with all my heart, only God hasn't given me the assurance yet that she is going to change. But I guess I'm glad I came. And now, tomorrow morning, I'm going down to see that publisher and sort of clear the atmosphere of things I have to do. Then, if nothing turns up for me to work at, I can at least go down to Kirk's mission and help him out with the singing. He needs a song leader badly, he told me."

"That's the talk!" said Bruce. "Cheer up, brother! We have a great God, and He has allowed us to help in His great work."

So they went up to their room to pray for Coralie.

And as they knelt and talked to God about her, Coralie lay wondering at her strange and unwonted thoughts.

In the living room of the apartment Lisa was carrying on her wild party, forgetful that she even had a daughter, except when one or another of her guests would ask about her, and Errol Hunt would go rambling about trying to find her, taking another drink every time he failed.

Back at the Shannon house the whole family sat around the fire talking. It wasn't their custom to sit up so late and talk after a meeting, especially when most of them had to be up early the next morning. But somehow this seemed a special occasion.

While the girls and their mother went out to the kitchen to set things to rights the father and sons had sat around the fire. Norah was sound asleep on the old couch, the lamp turned low, the firelight playing shadows with her golden curls. The mother was setting the first buckwheat cakes of the season for breakfast the next morning.

"What a lovely voice that young man has," said the mother, giving a final stir to her batter and setting a plate carefully over the top of the bowl, nestling it all in a sheltered corner of the kitchen shelf.

"Which one?" asked Turla. "I thought they both had nice voices."

"Yes, they had," said Valerie, "and they blended so well. Kirk's is a nice voice too."

"Of course!" said mother. "But that Dana-man has a voice like an angel."

"Now mother-mine, when did you ever hear an angel sing? I thought you always taught me that angels don't sing, at least it isn't so recorded; they only discourse."

"Well, perhaps it's Kirk that has the angel-voice then," said the smiling mother. "But I still say the Dana-man has about the most beautiful man's singing voice I ever heard."

"It is lovely," said Valerie suddenly sobering. "I felt honored to accompany him. And he seems to have a lovely character, too. Kirk says he had a marvelous father. But mother, what did you think of his sister?"

"I should say she was a flat tire!" said Turla wiping a pile of plates deftly and swiftly.

"Say, if she didn't have dope on her eyelashes I'll eat

my hat!" said Leith, suddenly appearing in the pantry doorway with a little cake in his hand.

"Oh, my dearie!" said the mother gently, "she was just a poor little frightened lass out of her element! She didn't know what to make of it all."

"Frightened! My eye! If she was ever frightened of anything I'd be surprised. She's tough as they make 'em, mither-my-dear!"

"Tough she may be, and painted she may be, my laddie, and also a flat tire to our way of thinking, but she was that frightsomed I was just wearying to put my arms around her and mother her a bit! Valerie, you'll have to go after that wee bit lamb and bring her around the whiles, till we see if we can't comfort her a bit and make her have blithe lights in her eyes."

"I will, mother dear," said Valerie as she turned out the kitchen light. Then they all trooped back into the living room and gathered around the blinking fire again.

It was Leith who asked his father:

"Dad, what did you think of that girl? Wasn't she a queer little tough nut? She's a looker of course, but they don't come that way naturally, do they?"

"She's the perfect picture of her brother," said Turla, "and she certainly has a style to her clothes!"

"Anybody can have style to their clothes if they don't do anything but think about them," said Kendall loftily as if he knew all about it. Then they all laughed. Kendall was just beginning to grow up, and sometimes put on knowledge as a garment.

"I don't understand it," said Valerie. "That brother is unusually fine."

"He had a marvelous father," said Kirk. "I heard the fellows talking about it at college. They said he was a grand man."

"Well, if it was the father, why didn't the girl have him too? And didn't they have a mother?"

"I don't know," said Kirk. "Maybe the mother died and the girl was sent away to school or something. Maybe a worldly relative."

"However, it doesn't matter," said the father. "It's not our business. But I guess that doesn't bar us from praying for her. Kirk, you lead us tonight in our evening prayer."

And again earnest souls were upon their knees, praying for one little frightened solitary girl who lay by herself hearing the echo of a heavenly song, and wondering if there was anything real in it for her.

After the Shannon family got up from their knees and went to their rooms, there were other prayers made in that house that night in which Coralie was included. The mother prayed, and the father, and Valerie. Her brother Kirk, also, for he loved Dana. And if Dana's sister needed saving he wanted to pray for her.

And if any of them could have seen the living room where Lisa was entertaining her guests that night, those Shannons would certainly have felt that Coralie needed their prayers.

10

DANA went the next morning to see Mr. Burney.

Not that he was expecting to get anything definite. It was just that this visit was one he had promised his employer at home to make, and he wanted to get it off his mind and be ready to go back if he felt impelled to do so.

But Dana was utterly unprepared for the cordial welcome that he received.

"Well, Barron, I was about to get a dog and a gun and go out and search for you," Mr. Burney greeted him cordially. "You see, my friend Randolph telephoned me about you, said he heard that one of our men had left us, and he didn't know but it might be convenient to us to know that you were in these parts and could help us out till we found a new man. So I've just been watching the door to see you come in for the last three days. Now, sit down and let's talk. Randolph has given you a high recommendation. But tell me about yourself. I certainly shall be glad if you can help us, at least for a few days till we can look around and get on our feet again."

So they sat and talked. Mr. Burney rumpled his white

hair and looked more and more pleased, deciding that he liked Dana Barron fully as much as his friend Randolph had told him he would.

At last he touched a bell for his secretary and Valerie walked in.

Mr. Burney greeted her with a smile of satisfaction.

"Miss Shannon, this is Mr. Barron who is going to take over Mr. Maynard's department, for a little while at least. Can you take him to Mr. Maynard's office and show him what we have on hand just now? Tell him anything he needs to know. We want to get that matter of the advertising for the Christmas catalogues off as soon as possible. I guess you understand all the details."

Dana Barron stood up courteously to acknowledge the introduction, and there stood Valerie Shannon, as amazed as he was!

A flash of recognition went between them, but Mr. Burney broke in upon anything further they might have said by a question.

"Is Mr. Brownleigh out there in the office waiting for me, Miss Shannon?"

"Yes, Mr. Burney."

"Then ask the desk secretary to send him in, please."

Thus dismissed, Dana followed Valerie into another office.

"Why, Mr. Barron, I didn't know that you were coming here!" said Valerie in surprise.

"Well, neither did I, until a few minutes ago," laughed Dana. "But neither did I know that you were here," he added, smiling down at her, and thinking how very blue her eyes were.

Those blue eyes twinkled their pleasure in his courtesy, and then she drew a little cloak of distance about her. She was a business woman now, on business intent, and not on pleasure, and he was about to become somewhat of a superior in the business. There was a dignity and honor due him from her. She must not mingle friendship with work.

When Dana Barron settled himself in the desk chair in the office to which Valerie led him, he was conscious of a glow of interest in the work to which he had just committed himself temporarily, that he had not felt before Valerie entered the situation.

But if Valerie was equally pleased she did not show it. With all the ease of a well-trained business woman she proceeded to explain the business in hand, making everything very clear.

Dana listened intently, watching her speaking face, his eyes firing with understanding as she made the situation plain. Now and then he asked a keen question which showed Valerie that he understood, and had good sense about things in general. Good business heads they both had, quick of comprehension, capable, responsible. Each recognized this in the other, and did honor to such ability.

"Now," said Valerie, "I think that is all, except that Mr. Burney is very anxious to get this matter of the Christmas advertising out of the way as soon as possible. Mrs. Trent has always been Mr. Maynard's secretary, and I think she is to be yours. I'll speak to Mr. Burney and send her in right away. I suppose you'll want to get at dictation at once."

"Yes, thank you, I do," said Dana.

She gave him a little formal smile and vanished, presently returning with a small brisk gray-haired woman whom she introduced as Mrs. Trent. She left them at once and Dana settled down to his work, glad to get back to something definite.

About an hour after Dana sat down at his new desk Lisa entered her daughter's room.

"Did you get in touch with Dana?" she said to Coralie, who was seated at her desk writing a few notes, trying to clear up a lot of odds and ends that she had lazily let go for too long. Her experience of the evening before had inspired her with a longing to do something really worth while, and the only thing she could find that might be called work was to get a clutter of invitations and bills out of the way.

Coralie looked up, noted the jaded look on her mother's face, that was not wholly covered by the lavish make-up, and answered carelessly:

"I told him you wanted to see him."

"Didn't you say when?" she asked sharply.

"I told him around eleven was a good time," said the girl indifferently.

"Well, it's after half-past now," said her mother suspiciously. "Are you sure he understood?"

"He seems fairly intelligent," said the girl insolently.

"Well, I don't understand it. I don't like to be kept waiting, and I'll make him understand that when he gets here."

"I wouldn't advise you to be too particular. Not with him."

"What do you mean? He's my son, isn't he?"

"It looks that way, but that's for you to say. However if he is, he must have inherited a fair amount of your own imperiousness."

"Why should he be imperious?"

"I'm sure I don't know. Why should I? In fact, why should you be imperious yourself?"

"You're being impudent!"

"Am I? Well, I'm supposed to be your child! Why don't you call me imperious instead of impudent?"

"That's enough!"

"All right. I didn't begin this!"

"Corinne, I forbid you to talk that way any more. Go to the telephone and call Dana. Tell him I want him to come at once."

"I don't think he has a phone!"

"No phone? Why, how ridiculous! Well, then get the hotel and tell them to call him."

"He isn't in a hotel."

"Well, then, where is he?"

"In a rooming house downtown."

"Downtown? In a rooming house? How simply impossible! Surely you told him that was no place for him to stay?"

"Oh, yes, I told him. But you know, Lisa, in some ways he's very like you. He said he was very well satisfied with the place where he was, and he didn't care to move, or words to that effect."

"Well, I'll see that he moves at once!" said Lisa with her lips in a thin line and her chin in the air.

"I wonder?" said Coralie.

"What do you mean?"

"I mean that he won't move for anybody if he doesn't happen to want to, so I wouldn't advise you to tell him he must, or you may have to eat your words."

"You're very offensive!"

"Yes, so are you sometimes. There are times when I've been moved to wish that you hadn't been so beautiful, and had just been a plain woman who wanted to stay at home and take care of her children. You never did bring me up, you know, so you can't complain that I don't please you."

"Corinne! Will you be still? You have said something you'll have to live down, now."

"Well, what is there in my life that I haven't had to live down? Can you tell me?"

"Corinne, go and get that rooming house on the phone at once and tell Dana to come here immediately!"

"You'd better do it yourself, Lisa. There isn't any phone in that house at all, and I don't know how to get Dana."

"You are just trying to be helpless now. If it was one of your friends you wanted, you would get him soon enough. Well, give me the address, and if I can't find a phone there I'll send a special messenger boy after him. I declare, it seems as if you might do a little something once in a while. Where is that address?"

The girl gave it to her silently and went on with her writing. Lisa took it impatiently and went out. After about an hour she returned.

"You must have made a mistake in that address, Corinne, or else Dana was bluffing you. I sent a messenger there and he couldn't get in. He said an old man who has a shop in the basement said that everybody was out, and they didn't usually get back till night."

"So why do you think I made a mistake, Lisa?" The girl lifted cool eyes at her.

"Why, Dana would never room in a place like that, a place where no one is at home all day, and a shop in the basement!"

"Why not?"

"Why not! You absurd child! As if a Barron wouldn't go to a respectable place. I don't believe that's his address at all."

"Oh, yes it is, Lisa. I went there myself and found him!" said the girl impatiently, sealing her letter and flinging it into the letter tray ready to go.

"You went there and found him? When?"

"Last night!" said Coralie wearily, yawning.

"Last night! You mean you went to an unspeakable place like that, alone, to find Dana?"

"It wasn't at all unspeakable, Lisa. It was a perfectly quiet house on a quiet street. Plenty of people going back and forth. Decent people! I went up to Dana's room. It's a big room with two windows, on the second floor, and there is furniture enough to make it comfortable. Sort of old-fashioned, maybe, but clean and respectable, and Dana seems to like it there. He had a college friend with him! They didn't appear to be very glad to see me either. They were going somewhere!"

"Of course! Men always do! I suppose Jerrold Barron would be surprised that his paragon of a son would go out places like other young men of his age. I don't suppose you stayed long enough to find out where he went, did you?"

"Yes," said the girl. "You'd be surprised. He went to a prayer meeting."

"To church, you mean?"

"No, it wasn't in a church. It was some sort of a mission, I gathered."

"Oh! How did you know where he went? He told you anything he pleased, I suppose."

"No, he didn't tell me where he was going. I found out because I went with him."

Coralie's voice was very quiet, almost as if she were taking some kind of stand that was important.

"You went with him! Did he ask you to go?"

"No, he wasn't keen on my going, but I told him I was *going* so I *went*. And he sang. Lisa, he has the very most gorgeous voice I ever heard in my life. If he were on the opera stage the world would rave about him!"

Lisa was still for an instant. Then she said:

"Yes, Jerrold had a gorgeous voice!" and her face looked almost ashamed as she said it. Then she suddenly came back to the present.

"So, that was where you were when you knew I had guests and expected you to be present! You went with a nobody to a mission, and left the man you are going to marry to wander around using up all my good liquor to console himself!"

Her voice was very bitter and she hurled the words at her daughter as if they had been actual missiles.

"That was why I went out!" said Coralie calmly. "Because I knew those unspeakable people were going to be here, and because I am *not* going to marry Errol Hunt. I don't want to see him ever again!"

"Corinne! You little fool you! A man rich enough to give you anything you want! And ready to lay it all at your feet! And you go off your own way, and leave him to drink himself drunk all for love of you! Do you call that right?"

"Oh! I know! Didn't I hear him? You let him come slobbering at my door, pounding away and calling to me, when he didn't have sense enough to call out my name. Coming in that condition to ask me to marry him. Yelling it out so everyone in the house could hear him! Do you suppose I want to marry a man who shows his love for me by getting drunk? No! You may as well understand it now as any time, Lisa. I'm *never* going to marry Errol Hunt, and I wish you'd tell him so! I loathe him, and I never will willingly speak to him again! If there is no other way out of it I'll appeal to my brother to help me!"

Lisa stood and stared at her child aghast. She had seen her angry before, she had seen her insolent, but never had she seen this calm assured woman who knew what she wanted and meant to have her way.

Then Lisa's anger flashed up crimson.

"You'll appeal to your *brother!* What right have you to call him brother, I ask you? Did I tell you you might? Just try it if you dare and I'll have every cent of your fortune taken away from you, and have you put in charge of the court, and sent to a home for insane people! You unspeakable little outcast! Do you think I will stand for any such nonsense as that?" Suddenly Lisa came swiftly over to where Coralie stood and lifting her white, exquisitely manicured hand with its polished crimson nails, she struck her daughter sharply across her face, gashing the delicate skin of her cheek, and cutting a slash across the cupid lips. The blow was terrific, even though it was struck by a frail woman, but she was a very angry woman, and her eyes were flashing like sparks from blue steel.

Coralie stood perfectly still, as if she had seen the blow coming in time to brace herself to bear it, and she stood without flinching and took it.

Lisa drew back like an angry panther and stared at her child with hate, noting the broad rising welt where her blow had left its mark, the drops of crimson where her sharp gaudy nails had gashed, and fairly radiating hate.

"I wish—" she said, drawing in a deep breath and flashing her great eyes again, "I wish—that I had never brought you with me when I ran away!"

It was the height of her anger always when she uttered that wish, and it was not the first time she had said it. Usually those words brought the girl to terrible tears of rage and hate and recrimination.

But there were no tears on her face now as she stood there white and still and looked at her mother with a look she had never worn before. As Lisa stood panting, her hands clenched, Coralie spoke, in a low terrible voice.

"I certainly wish you never had!" she said, and her face was white and set.

Lisa stared at her wildly, as if she could not believe her ears. Her eyes were large with something almost like wonder. Then she lifted her chin and threw back her head in that arrogant way she had as if she were a dictator, and said in low sibilant tones:

"You'll take that back, young lady, or I'll make you suffer for it good and hard!"

She whirled around and stalked out of the room.

Coralie locked her door, and threw herself down upon her bed with her face in the pillow, but she did not weep. She was trembling as if in an ague chill.

AT five o'clock Dana called up his mother's house. The office had just closed and he did not wait to get back to his room. All day he had thought occasionally of his sister's casual request that he come to see their mother, and that he make it around eleven o'clock in the morning. It had not occurred to him that the message necessitated haste. The swift arrival of a job and the necessity for beginning work at once, had driven out any other ideas for a time. When he did remember it it did not seem important. Probably she just wanted to invite him to stay with her, and that he had no intention of doing.

But when he started away from the office it came to his mind again, and he went into the first telephone booth he could find. If she was at home he would go to her at once.

But he found it was not so easy as he had expected to get into touch with his mother. He found that there was a butler to deal with, and then a maid, and when he finally persuaded her to carry his message to his mother, word came back that she had expected him that morning and why hadn't he come?

He told the maid to say that he was employed in an office in the morning and was not free until five o'clock. Then she sent back word that she was busy and could not see him until the next morning at eleven.

"That is impossible," said Dana quietly. "For the present I can only come after five."

After some delay Lisa's voice came sharply over the wire. "Dana, this is ridiculous! I can't be upset this way. Give up your job then and come when I say. It's absurd for you to be having a job anyway."

Then Dana's voice had answered coldly:

"That is quite out of the question."

There followed a long pause, and Dana almost thought she had left the telephone. At last she answered impatiently.

"Oh, well, I can't be bothered this way. Come over at once if you must, and be quick about it!" and she hung up the receiver sharply.

Dana walked slowly out to the street considering. He was being made to appear as the one who desired the interview, and it was the last thing just at that moment that he wanted. But he reflected that there was a good deal of pride mingled with his wrath, and that his feelings were not to be considered. So he hailed a taxi and drove swiftly to Lisa's apartment. But even then he had to wait until a lengthy toilet was completed before she came to meet him.

In a long formal room where there was a commingling of complex simplicity, and ornate complexity, she appeared in a dress of black velvet with a sweeping train and an open back showing the delicate curves of her flesh interrupted only by a jeweled clasp.

She was startling in her beauty; the tints of her complexion were like a baby's, and her silver-gilt hair shone like a halo. For just an instant Dana was glad that he had seen her so. It seemed to justify his wonderful father for having fallen in love with her, a thing he had never been quite able to explain or excuse. But she was lovely, breath-taking in her beauty, if one did not remember the tones with which she had just spoken over the telephone.

"Well?" she said at last, breaking the silence that he did not attempt to break.

"Yes?" he asked pleasantly. "You wanted to see me?"

"Not at this hour," she complained. "I am always busy in the evening and cannot be troubled with business." She dropped down on the edge of a queer chair.

"I beg your pardon," he said, turning to go. "I understood you to say you wanted me to come at once. I will not detain you."

He picked up his hat and started toward the door.

"There you go, flying off the handle just the way your father used to do at the slightest word! I want to know what you mean by a position. Why do you need to take a position? One as well off as you must be shouldn't be keeping the poor people out of jobs."

"Well off?" asked Dana looking at her with an amused query.

"Yes, well off. Wealthy, if you like that word better. But I can't waste time. I'm having guests tonight. I sent for you to ask where your father's will is, and why I was not notified about it at once?"

"Will?" asked Dana.

"Yes. I suppose you know what that is, don't you? Where is the will? Who has taken charge of it? When is it to be probated?"

She flung the questions at him. But Dana only looked at her quietly.

"There was no will," said Dana, and his voice was almost sad.

"No will?" Lisa almost screamed, her eyes growing angry at once. "Do you mean he gave everything to you, and you had the insolence to accept it without consulting me?"

"No," said Dana, still quietly, "there was nothing left to give. Barely enough to bury him."

"Do you mean he gave you nothing?"

Lisa had risen and was standing angrily facing him, her delicate nostrils spread as if for battle, her eyes flashing furiously.

"Nothing but the little old house where you went as a bride," said Dana, facing her and holding her glance with his, steadily, condemningly, "and which you scorned and left! You did not want that, did you? He gave it to me several years ago because he loved it, and because he knew that I loved it too. It was all the home I have ever known. I have lived there all my life with my father."

A look of bewilderment spread over Lisa's face.

"But I don't understand. Why did you live there? I understood that your father was fabulously wealthy. Why did you not go to a more fitting place to live?"

Dana looked at her questioningly and then shook his head.

"No, father was never fabulously wealthy. He inherited some money when I was a small child, and he was successful in his investments, but he turned it all over to you, that is, to my sister, in trust, after you married again. He desired that you and she might never be in want. He kept only the little old house and his business. But when the depression came his business began to fail, as his health was failing, until it was all gone, and he was unable to do anything about it. If I had not been able to get a job with a small salary as soon as I came out of college, he would have suffered actual want. As it was we had some very hard times getting along. If it had not been for father's earnest request I would not have thought I could afford the journey to New York at this time to bring you his letter. That is the reason I was glad to get my present job temporarily. I cannot afford to risk losing it."

He held her attention with his look until he was done speaking, and she listened. Then her face took on a beautiful scorn as she tried to face him back.

"But you see I don't believe you!" she said haughtily. "And I shan't waste any more time talking to you. I shall have this matter investigated thoroughly by my lawyer. That's all! I don't want to talk to you any more!" and she swept from the room leaving him staring blankly at the doorway where she had disappeared.

Dana stood there looking after her for a full minute before he picked up his hat and went out.

There seemed to be no one around anywhere, so Dana let himself out into the hall, and down the elevator to the street. No one seemed even to know he was there. He went out slowly, looking about as he went, hoping to see his sister somewhere, but there wasn't even a sound of her, and no servant about to ask. Well, he was done now surely, and he had learned one thing. Never was there the least possibility that his father had been mistaken or wrong. Such a woman was heartless, and utterly wrong from the beginning. There was no mother nor wife in her. She was just a selfish soul who wanted everything she could lay her hands on, and had no love for anybody.

He recalled how harshly she had dealt with her daughcer on his last visit when she had wept. Of course she was angry then, but even anger should not have allowed her to reprimand the girl so severely before one who was really a stranger to them both. Well, he had done his duty, surely, and there could be no reason whatever for feeling he must go back to see her again. The girl, perhaps, if the way opened, but not the mother.

He was standing at the door of the apartment house as this thought came to him, and just at that instant a man in livery stepped up to him and touched him on the shoulder.

"Madam would like you to return," he said with the authority in his voice that some servants know how to assume.

Dana looked at him in astonishment.

"I am the butler," explained the man, "and madam sent me down to say she wishes to see you for a moment at once."

Dana looked at the servant thoughtfully, considering. Should he go back? His natural inclination would lead him to disregard her wish. She certainly had not been pleasant to deal with. Then there came to him a verse he had read that morning before going out: "Even Christ pleased not Himself," he paused. He had thought his duty to his earthly father discharged, but was there yet a higher obligation, a duty to his Heavenly Father?

He turned and followed the man to the elevator and up to his mother's apartment once more.

The butler led him to another room, a small reception room just off the hall, where an open fire burned, and all the chairs were stiff and formal. But he did not sit down, though Lisa waved her hand toward a straight chair she had obviously placed for him, opposite to her own, as if he were to be tried before a judge.

"I sent for you because I wish to ask you the address of your lawyer." She had a tablet and a fountain pen in her hand.

"Lawyer?" said Dana, and then smiled. "I have never had occasion to have a lawyer."

Lisa jerked her head back impatiently.

"Well, then the name and address of the man who attends to your affairs."

"When one has nothing there is no need for such a man. I usually attend to my own affairs, such as they are."

Lisa studied him thoughtfully for a moment.

"Very well," she said insolently, "if that is the attitude you intend to take we shall fight you from the start. Suppose you give me the name of your bank."

Dana gave her one steady sorrowful look and then he answered her quietly, giving the name of his home bank, and adding:

"But there is less than a hundred dollars on deposit there. I was obliged to draw out a little for carfare and board while I am here." He named the very small sum he had drawn out.

She jotted down the address and figures he had given her. Then she fixed him with her cold business-like glance again.

"You have a safety deposit box in that bank?"

"No," said Dana.

"Then where do you keep your valuable papers?"

He studied her gravely. Then he said:

"I have no valuable papers except the deed to the little house and my college diploma, if you would call that valuable. Those I always keep with me."

She considered this contemptuously.

"You expect me to believe that?" she asked with a sneer.

"Why, I don't know that I do," said Dana. "I hadn't thought about it. I am accustomed to being believed, but you needn't do so if you find it hard. I could easily prove it. My father brought me up to tell the truth. I don't see why you should think I would want to tell a falsehood about a thing like that."

"Naturally you don't want to give up what money your father left you, but I believe I am the judge of whether you will keep it or not. Your father gave me a writing a few weeks after we were married which would give me all rights in everything he left."

"Yes?" said Dana with a lifting of his brows. "Well, I'm quite sure you are welcome to the little house you once left, if you want it. But there really is nothing else. The few dollars I have left in the western bank was my own salary, deposited there by myself. Would you have a right to that, too? The salary of a deserted child?"

"Don't be nasty. It isn't necessary. Of course I don't want any such trifle as that. But what of your father's securities? Stocks and bonds and so on. Where did he keep those?"

Dana looked up with his rare smile.

"So far as I know they were all in Heaven," he said pleasantly. "He was penniless so far as earthly riches are concerned. But since you doubt my word why don't you write to our old minister, and also the doctor who attended my father? Or, in fact, anybody you used to know out in our old home. The lawyer who used to take care of father's affairs long ago has been dead a good many years. But I am quite sure any of these others will make the situation plain for you beyond a doubt."

Lisa's mouth wore a disagreeable curve as she answered.

"I fancy we shall be able to find out what I want to

know without having to consult ministers and doctors, especially those who would obviously be prejudiced."

"Then is that all you wanted of me?"

"That is all at present. But when I send for you again, that is, if I find it necessary, I wish you would come when I want you. I think you will survive even if you have to quit your job for a few hours. Personally I don't see any point to your taking a job. When we unearth a few of those buried securities I fancy you won't be so keen on jobs."

Dana looked at her with disgust. Could it be possible that a woman—just a woman, not even a wife or mother, could so far lower herself as to say such unbelievable things?

Then he turned swiftly and went out, hurrying away from the neighborhood. Not for any butler would he go back again to that presence.

Half an hour later Bruce came into their room and found him in the dark sitting by the window with his face in his hands, a look of utter dejection upon him.

He turned on the light and looked at him. Then he said:

"Say, brother, it seems to me you are in the wrong position. You ought to be on your knees, not bolt upright in despair."

Dana smiled wearily.

"Yes, I know," he said. "I was sort of knocked endwise. But at that it was no more than I expected when I came to New York."

"What's the matter? No chance of a job?"

"Oh, no, it wasn't that. I got a job and a good one. If I make good I imagine there's a chance of permanency, provided I want to stay in this part of the country. I suppose I ought to be praising God instead of being utterly dejected. The salary is twice as large as I had hoped for, too."

"Well, now, fella, what's gotcha? Thank the Lord for a good job and a good salary, and let the Lord take care of the other things that are troubling you. They'll all come out in His good time."

"I suppose so, but I can't see how."

"Do you need to see?"

"No. Of course not!" And Dana turned on his brilliant smile again. "Thanks old man. I owe a lot to you."

"And I to you, fella. And now, do you want to tell me, or shall we forget it?"

"Oh, I'd better tell you. Probably you'll help to dispel the shadow. You know all about me, you might as well know the rest."

So Dana, in as few words as possible, related the story of his visit to his mother, feeling again keenly the half hidden insults she had given.

"H'm!" said Bruce when the story was told. "Money-crazy is she? But that poor little girl! I feel sorry for *her!*"

Dana gave him a swift surprised look.

"Do you know, I hadn't thought about her at all. I suppose that attitude has done a lot of things to my sister, hasn't it?"

"Of course," said Bruce. "She must have led a terrible life, and got tremendously warped about facts. She isn't entirely to blame, you know."

"Of course not," said Dana looking at his friend sadly. "It all seems so terribly sad, Bruce, and especially that there is nothing I can do about it."

"Yes, there is something you can do," said Bruce assuredly. "You can pray. Perhaps that is why God has let it seem so absolutely hopeless to you, that you may see that of yourself you cannot do anything about it. You are shut up to Him, and His power. Perhaps He is leading you to the place where you will be even closer in touch with Him than you are, so that He can work, where you alone are helpless."

It was very still in the room while Dana thought this over. At last he looked his friend in the eyes.

"You're right, Bruce. That's just what I needed. Shall we pray now?"

And the two young men went down upon their knees together, calling upon God, pleading His promises, claiming the shed blood for sinners. The boy was praying for his mother who had deserted him, and his friend was pleading earnestly for the girl who had deeply touched his heart because of her ignorance, and unhappiness, and her hopeless situation.

After they had prayed there was a cheerful note in their voices, a rested look in their faces.

"Well, I feel that God is great enough to deal with this situation, and I'm here to do His will, if He has orders for me." said Dana as he brushed his hair and made ready to go out for the evening meal.

The answer his friend made was to burst out in a deep clear voice, singing:

> *"My faith looks up to Thee,*
> *Thou Lamb of Calvary,*
> *Saviour divine!"*

Dana joined in with his lovely voice, and the wonderful words rolled out and drifted down through the house. More than one lodger paused, looking up, listening in wonder, and turned back to blessed memories of other days.

"Now, brother," said Bruce as they finished their song

and started out, "here's where you lay down your burden and forget it until God has orders for you. He's bearing the burden now. Come on, let's go, and suppose you tell me a bit about your new job. I'm tremendously interested to hear about it."

So they went out the door and down the street to their dinner, Dana telling all about Mr. Burney, and the office, and how Valerie Shannon was Mr. Burney's private secretary.

"It all sounds good to me," said Bruce. "If you ask me I'd say the Lord has indeed been working on your behalf today, and it is evident He wants you to stay here in New York, at least for the present."

"I guess that must be true," said Dana. "And really, I suppose my state of depression over the afternoon's experience was brought on by the hurt to my own pride. You know it was anything but easy to have one's mother talk that way about money, as if I were trying to cheat her."

"Well, of course that was tough. But she never has had the natural feelings of a mother, and you can't expect them. Besides, you are no worse off than you were. And you're much better off than that poor little sister of yours, for you had a father, a wonderful father, and she has never had either mother or father."

"That's true. I wish I could do something for her to make up for what she has lost."

"You will, Dana. And I'd be glad to help too."

"That's great of you, Bruce. I know she's not the kind of girl you naturally would pick out to be interested in, even distantly, and I know you can't enjoy even an occasional evening, or hour, in such uncongenial company."

"That's all right with me, Dana," said Bruce. "I'll be thinking how my Father loves her. And at least there's this, I haven't any other girl to object to my taking a little interest in her. But, do you realize we're making plans without her consent? She may already have had enough of us. In which case you and I will be shut up to prayer entirely in the matter, and maybe that's what God intends."

"Yes, I know," said Dana. "We'll just have to wait."

12

MEANTIME Coralie had taken her departure from the city to a house party at a beautiful estate on Long Island. She was fed up with quarreling with Lisa. She was determined not to see the obnoxious Errol again, and could not brook the thought of Ivor Kavanaugh. He seemed to be under foot almost any hour of the day or evening. She could not see how Lisa could have him around. So she had accepted this invitation that in itself was not especially attractive to her, just to get out of the house and away from all that was going on there.

She had taken the precaution before she left the city, of going to the Trust Company that held her own fortune in its care, and making a request that no more money should be given to Lisa or anyone else except herself.

Their answer was to show her the signed requests from herself for all monies that had been paid out since she had reached the age when the money was to be in her own care. There they were, in writing that very strongly resembled her own! What could she do? Perhaps Lisa was expecting to pay it all back when she married her reputedly wealthy Ivor, but Lisa was most casual with money, and Coralie was pretty sure that when it was gone it was gone. There was nothing for it but to protect herself now. Of course Lisa could not touch any portion of the capital nor could she herself, but Lisa must be stopped from purloining these amounts from her account which the interest replenished quarterly. Lisa had a little of her own, enough to live simply. So she looked up from the papers and spoke boldly.

"Mr. Brewer, I didn't sign these papers. This is my mother's signature. She hasn't got used to the idea yet that I am anything but a child, and thinks she ought to control my expenditures. But isn't it true that I was to have the interest on my money to use at my own discretion when I was eighteen?"

"Oh, yes, of course," said Mr. Brewer. "I told them I could not let this money go out without your signed warrant for it, and so your mother brought these papers every time. It certainly looks like your signature, though of course it did not seem necessary to have an expert examine it."

"Yes," said Coralie sadly, "of course it wouldn't. But I shall have to ask you to take some steps so that you will not cash *any more* checks to which she has signed my name. I simply won't be tied down this way without my rightful money."

"Well, I'm very sorry that this has occurred," said Mr. Brewer. "I won't let it happen again. I will see that there will be no further mistakes."

"I'm going to change my signature anyway," said Coralie. "And I'm not going to tell my family I'm doing it. I've been signing my checks Corinne Collette. After this I shall always sign my name Coralie Barron. That is my real name anyway. Please don't give *any* more of my money to anyone else but myself. I simply will not be managed this way."

As Coralie left the bank she reflected that Lisa had done this thing sometimes without any further comment than, "Darling, I just stopped in to the bank to get money to pay Madame for those costumes you bought last month. I knew it would save you trouble!" knowing that Coralie would pay no further attention to the matter. Perhaps if Ivor Kavanaugh had not appeared on the scene Coralie would have gone on oblivious to what was happening. But her lack of belief in him and her horror of having him for a second stepfather made her see through her mother's present desire for money. It did not occur to her that it was a rather dreadful charge she was bringing against her mother in stating that she had forged her signature and taken possession of her rightful money. Coralie had never been educated in things ethical, and that phase of the matter did not disturb her as it would have disturbed a girl with the traditions of Valerie Shannon for instance. The whole thing was a matter of fighting Ivor Kavanaugh, and money was the only weapon she knew.

So she was not disturbed about what she had done as she wended her way to her house party. It had seemed to her the only thing she could do. Of course there would be a tremendous battle with Lisa when she found out that her daughter had told Mr. Brewer not to let her have any more of her money. But what was a battle more or less?

So she entered into the gaiety determinedly. She danced with the rest, and tried to put away all serious thoughts. This was life. This was happiness, of course. So she had been brought up to believe, and she would believe it. Persistently she put away the gnawing thought that this was not real happiness, that she had lived all her life this way, and it had never made her glad like the people in that meeting.

And when she could no longer put away the memory of looks and words she had heard at the meeting she recklessly drank, glass after glass, knowing that she was on the way to being very drunk, but feeling that at least her thoughts would no longer torment her.

The third day she came to herself. After a long sleep and a delicious breakfast for which she had no appetite, she looked about the elegantly appointed room with distaste, and turned sick to the soul with the thought of the life she was living.

As clearly as if he stood there at the foot of her bed she seemed to see her brother, looking at her with those keen earnest eyes, reproaching her with having somehow missed the meaning of life. Then she seemed to hear an echo of the song he had sung in the meeting that night.

Around her then trooped the members of that unique lovely family of Shannons, knit together with a beautiful love that she had never seen anywhere else. The people she was with now were all for themselves, each striving to be gayer than the other, each trying to prove that hearts did not ache nor courage fail, that there were no sordid things in the world, that all the days were rolling joyously by toward a common natural desirable end, and nobody had longings for anything better. But oh, it was not true. This was not joy. This loathsome physical lassitude, this intermittent fever of riot. What was there about it all that was desirable?

If she went on and married one of these companions who waltzed through the gay days and settled down contentedly to a continuous round of this sort of thing, how could she endure it through a normal lifetime?

Suppose she married Errol, and went to live in one of his fabulous castles abroad, and went on and on through the days? A castle might be interesting for a few months, but even that would pall in a short time. Just the old round of pleasure, with no real pleasure in it! Why did one have to live anyway? Why not just find a comfortable way out? There was so much that was sordid and useless!

She shuddered and pushed the handsome tray of food away from her. Well, at least she had escaped Ivor and Errol for a few days, and that was worth something. But tomorrow she would have to go home. The house party would be over, and everybody else would be going. And there would be Ivor and Errol once more, and the problems all to be dealt with again!

She sighed as she reached for a cigarette, and then suddenly withdrew her hand. This was only a part of it all. To dull the senses for a few more minutes! To go on with the round of wearisome entertainment. Why carry on any longer? Why not find some way out, or around, or over it all?

If only she knew how to be like Dana. Or like his friend Bruce. But it was likely too late for that. That kind of life that was so *clean* had to be started when one was very young, of course. If she tried to go that way now, she would be pulled down by the weight of all her past.

Perhaps, if she went to work, *some* kind of work, she might manage to be different.

These thoughts idly drifted through her mind as she prepared for the day. She could tell pretty well before she went downstairs just what each hour was going to bring forth. She wondered what those others would be doing? Dana and the rest? She did not wonder about Liṣa because she well knew every minutest detail of the program at home. But she tried to think out those others whose lives she knew so little.

This was Sunday, and they would likely be going to church. Would it be like that meeting she had attended? No church she had ever known was like that, of course, but then neither were the Shannons like the other people she knew. It was thinkable that they would find a church like themselves.

Well, suppose she were to try to carry out a program like theirs, how would she begin, say today? Suppose she were to go downstairs and tell them she was going to church? How they would laugh! They would tell her of their plans. Walks and rides and picnics, maybe a hunting program, billiards, cards, tennis—or was it too cold for that?—swimming in the indoor pool that the house boasted? And if she persisted in going to church they would try to send her in a car. No telling how far it was to the nearest church. Or, if she insisted on walking, there were at least three young men who would want to go with her, unless she could succeed in evading them all.

Oh, why bother? It was best just to take life as one found it and let it go at that. Perhaps when she got back to the city she could make changes, find that mission again, and find out what was the secret of those happy contented faces. Maybe it was only that they were prosy people who were easily satisfied, and took small things as a foundation for pleasure, things that would not satisfy her any better than her own present life.

Still, there was Dana. He must have inherited some of the same nature as herself. And there was that Mr. Carbury. And there were the Shannons!

Over and over again she went, always coming back to that strange meeting she had inadvertently attended.

When she finally went downstairs the morning was well gone, and there was no time to consider doing any of the erratic things her mind had suggested as possibilities.

The casual breakfast at the hour a later meal should have been served, the lazy excitable company, the carelessly informal costumes, all combined to make her feel the hedge of worldliness that was about her life. The oppression of custom, of group-habits and opinions, the hopelessness of disentangling herself from the order that she had known all her life! Why not drift with the tide?

So she took her place among the guests, tasted of the different viands, toyed with her wine glass, and finally left it by her plate with only a sip or two missing. There came a great distaste in her soul for all that she had heretofore known, a longing to get away and rest till this ache went out of her heart and she could see things more clearly.

As the day progressed she kept comparing the group about her to her brother and his friends.

They rallied her on her silence, her lack of appetite, and called to her to come and join their lightness. But as the afternoon waned and liquor flowed freely, she withdrew from the revelers about her and went and sat down by an older woman, with a sudden longing to ask an older and wiser one what was the meaning of it all, and why one had to live.

But when she had taken the chair opposite where she could watch her, she saw a look in her face that she recognized as like the look in Lisa's face, and she had to prod herself to carry out her purpose.

"Are you happy?" she asked the woman suddenly, right out of the round of laughter and forced merriment that surged about them.

"Happy?" chanted the woman. *"Happy?* Say that again, girl! I'd almost forgotten there was such a word. Happy? She wants to know if I am happy! Well, listen, young thing, I haven't been happy since the day when I was five and sat under an oak playing teaparty with acorns for cups and green leaves for plates, and my nurse came out and told me my mother had been killed in an accident."

"But you've lived a long time since then," said Coralie anxiously, "hasn't any of it brought you happiness?"

The woman looked at her almost stupidly and laughed, with a bitter ring in the end of her mirth.

"Happy? Oh, maybe a day now and then. Of course I've been married three times, but they were all alike. They loved themselves more than me, and I was left with dead hopes and no memories worth while. Happiness! Is there ever any happiness in earth? Ask the waiter to pass me another glass, won't you? I can't bear to think about it."

An ardent man who wasn't quite himself any more, took her out for a walk in the grounds at sunset, but she had not been drinking enough herself to enjoy his foolish gabble and was glad to get back into the house again. Back to the babbling, the games, the foolish talk, the aimless shouting and empty laughter. Was it always like this? How strange it was to be among all these and not be a part of them, and to have in place of her former gaiety a bitterness toward life itself! How did she get into a state like this? Was it just because she was comparatively sober?

With a sudden resolve she slipped away to her room. No one was noticing her. Even the young man who had been asking her to dance had been easily appeased by another girl.

Hidden away in her room she lay down in the dark behind her locked door and faced her situation, with a brain too weary by her round of thinking to suggest any way out of her present mental state, or her present situation. In the morning, before the others awoke she would steal away and take the early train.

To that end she arose very early, before daylight, hastily packed her belongings, wrote a blithe note of farewell and apology to her hostess, and went boldly out of the house and down the drive toward a little nestling village where a train might be supposed to be, carrying her own suitcase, a thing she had never done in her life before.

Somehow she felt like a new being as she walked briskly along the drive and down the silent road, with the shimmer of rose and gold heralding the sunrise all over the sky. There was excitement and exhilaration in the adventure of escaping without attendance, almost like that she had felt sometimes in school carrying out some escapade.

The exhilaration stayed with her almost all the way to the city, and then as the first sight of the New York skyline came into view a vision of the home she was going to struck her, and she was suddenly weak with the dread of it. All the thought of the apartment, room by room, came to her, each one drearier than the preceding one, and a little shiver went over her. She didn't want to go back. The whole place would be lit with the lightning glance of Lisa when she found out about the money. Would it have happened yet? Would Mr. Brewer have telephoned her about it Saturday after she left him? No, for Lisa would surely have called her up at the house party. So it would likely happen today, late this morning, and it was going to be an ordeal to meet, anyway she planned it. Lisa was always very cross and easily irritated on Monday, for Sunday was a heavy day at the apartment, and often continued till the small hours of the night—or morning. Lisa's nerves would be shot, and she might go to all lengths. She certainly would make it as hard for her daughter as possible, and keep at it until Coralie gave in and let her have all the money she wanted.

But she wasn't going to do that this time. It was high time she stood out against Lisa. For if Lisa kept on this way, and married Ivor, and then perhaps got sick, Coralie knew she would have to take care of her. Ivor never would. He would likely vanish. And if she didn't save the money now there wouldn't be anything.

Almost the girl thought of such a possibility with calm, because she would rather have anything than to have Ivor in the scene.

When they reached the city Coralie was still perturbed in her mind. For now she saw unpleasantness looming imminent, and she didn't know just how she was going to meet it. Should she go into a fury, as had been her habit on occasion, and try to outdo, or at least equal, Lisa in a tantrum? No, she had never got anywhere doing that. Lisa was at her best under such circumstances and eventually she herself would weary of the clamor and turbulence, and give in. She had always done so. For Lisa was stronger; she knew it, and Lisa knew it. There was always a place where Coralie would weaken and given in. There was in her a lack of hardness, which Lisa never lacked. Therefore Lisa could always triumph when she wearied her antagonist to the limit. No, she must think up some other method. Of course she could threaten to tell Ivor or Errol, but that might involve her with them, and she would rather give up every cent she had than to have anything further to do with either of them. No, she must think this thing out and have a regular plan. Oh, if she only had a wise one to help!

There was her brother, of course, but there was still some pride left in her. She couldn't go to him and tell him everything. She couldn't bear to let him know the sordid life they lived. For she had caught enough vision of what his ideals must be to make her shrink from lowering herself in his esteem. Just why she felt this way she didn't know. She hadn't time now to argue it out with herself, but she couldn't go to Dana except as a last resort. Though it was a comfort to remember that he was in New York, and would in all likelihood do something to help her if she did call for help.

But why should she need help? She had always been sufficient to herself in emergencies. She could carry this through somehow. Only she seemed to have lost interest in life. Why did she want to carry it through? There was nothing that thrilled her any more, nothing that she really cared about.

She drew a deep sigh as she stepped from the train to the platform, and followed the crowd up the stairs.

But in the great station she stared about her aimlessly. She didn't want to go right home. She wanted to come to some decision first, plan some line of action, and go home to carry it out at once, not go home as undecided as she was when she went away last week. Nothing could be decided at home. Lisa dominated everything there, even one's thoughts. She must outline her course and then follow it, no matter what anybody else said.

So she went into the waiting room and sat down, but her thoughts were just as much at sea as they had been all the way down in the train, and at last she got up and began to walk about impatiently, pausing at the news-stand to glance over the magazines with unseeing eyes, drifting on up the marble stairs to the shops on the street floor, stopping at each window and looking at each object displayed, without comprehending anything. Finally she arrived at the flower shop almost next to the street door. Just outside was a taxi. She should take it home, and in a very few minutes be in an atmosphere that would dispel all this doubt and uncertainty and put her right back into the deadly despondency and desperation that had sent her off to that house party. But she didn't want to go back yet. She wasn't ready to face Errol and fight against his attentions. She wasn't ready to meet Lisa's storm of fury when she found out what she had said to Mr. Brewer.

Yet if she turned and went down those stairs again to the waiting room and sat there for hours she wouldn't be any more ready than she was now. Because she hadn't it in her to be ready. She needed something outside of herself to help her face this, but she didn't even know what it was she needed. It was no use! She was destined to be unhappy no matter what, and why did she try to protest against it? This was what Lisa had wished on her when she carried her away with her, carried her out of her natural home and inheritance! If Lisa had only left her with her father she would perhaps have come up like Dana, and had some knowledge of how to deal with the hard things in life.

Suddenly it all came over her how hopeless and forlorn she was and most unexpectedly two great tears burst forth from her lovely eyes and splashed down her cheeks.

She wasn't a crying person, and she was furious at those two tears. What was the matter with her anyway?

She had cried before Dana too. It was too childish! Why, she never used to cry even when she was a child!

Frantically she plunged her hand into a trifling pocket and brought out a handkerchief which she was about to stealthily and delicately apply to the splashes of tears on her cheeks, when suddenly she felt a touch on her arm! She turned startled, indignant, and looked up straight into the eyes of Bruce Carbury!

Then a great light of wonder blazed into her eyes, and she stared at him as if he were not real.

13

"OH!" she said in a pitiful little cry that was wholly involuntary. "Oh, how did you happen to be here?" There was something almost like fright in her voice, and he looked at her with a deep tenderness in his eyes.

"Please excuse me," he said gently. "I shouldn't have intruded perhaps, but I happened to identify you just as those two tears rolled down, and I wondered if you were in trouble and I could be of any assistance? I don't want to annoy you, but I'd greatly like to be counted friend enough to help if there is anything I can do."

"But I don't understand," she said, lifting bewildered eyes to his face. "How could you happen to come along just when I was needing you? Just when I was wishing I could talk to someone who would understand and explain?"

He smiled down at her.

"Were you wishing that?"

"Oh, yes!" she said with a quick little gesture of desperate need. "I was wishing so I could see you or Dana and ask you something. It seems so strange you should have come just now. How did you happen to be here?"

"Why," explained Bruce, "I am on my way to a train, and I looked around and there you were! And then those tears came and I couldn't go by and leave you in trouble. Come! I have at least fifteen minutes before my train leaves, perhaps twenty. Let's walk down to the waiting room and find a quiet corner. One can say a great deal in fifteen minutes."

He took her arm quietly and folded it under his own, turning her away from the window, and fell into pace with her.

"But—I oughtn't to take your time!" she gasped, even while the sound of her voice showed her relief.

"That's all right," said Bruce, "what time there is before my train leaves is at your disposal. Don't waste words protesting. Tell me your trouble as briefly as possible."

He watched her face as he spoke. It was like a child's grasping at a hope in the midst of a bewildering trouble.

"Well," she said, "then tell me how to be what you call 'saved.' I've been thinking about you all, and the faces of the people I saw in that meeting, they looked so happy, and I've figured it out that perhaps being saved is what makes them different from us. You see I've never heard of this being saved before. I've never been happy, though I've always been grasping after happiness."

Bruce's eyes were fine with tenderness, and his voice husky with feeling, as he laid his hand gently over hers and said:

"Poor little girl!"

The tears almost came again at his sympathy, but she was coming back to herself, struggling with this unwonted feeling. Also the time was short before he would leave, and she must get all the information possible to help her to face her own problems.

Then after an instant's thought he spoke.

"The way to be saved is simple," he said, "and you're right, it makes all the difference in the world between sorrow and joy."

"Yes?" she said eagerly. "I wondered. Well, what must I do?"

"Believe on the Lord Jesus Christ and you shall be saved," answered Bruce quietly, speaking very slowly and gently.

Coralie seemed to hang on his words but she still looked bewildered.

"Just what must I believe? I don't know anything about Him. How can I believe?"

"To believe on Him means to put your trust in Him as your Saviour from sin, as the One who took all your sin and sorrow and emptiness and worthlessness on Himself so that you could have His righteousness, His life."

Bruce looked at Coralie to see if she would resent being called a sinner, and worthless. But instead of the indignation and scorn that he feared a wonder and delight suddenly began to dawn in her face.

"Did somebody do that for me?" she cried. "Oh, why didn't I find it out long ago!" She took a deep breath, like one who has been stifled and has just come into fresh air. "Tell me more," she pleaded. "You see, I don't know anything about Him. Why would He do it?"

"He is God. And God so loved the world," explained Bruce, "that He gave His only begotten Son, that whosoever believeth in Him should not perish, but have everlasting life."

Coralie was listening intently as he spoke, and now she interrupted him.

"Will you write that down for me? I'm afraid I can't remember it all."

"I certainly will," said Carbury earnestly. "Have you a Bible?"

Coralie shook her head.

"Then I'll get you one. Meanwhile take this and read the first three or four pages, especially what is printed in red." He handed her his own little leather bound copy of John's gospel.

"But I always thought the Bible was written in the kind of language ordinary people couldn't understand."

Bruce smiled.

"That's where you made a big mistake. Some parts of the Bible are so simple that a little child can understand. Where, for instance, would you find anything simpler than this: 'Come unto me, all ye that labor and are heavy laden, and I will give you rest'? Do you find anything in that hard to be understood? Or this: 'Cast thy burden upon the Lord, and He shall sustain thee.' Or this: 'Fear thou not; for I am with Thee: be not dismayed; for I am thy God: I will strengthen thee; yea, I will help thee; yea, I will uphold thee with the right hand of my righteousness.'"

Coralie was looking up at him, her eyes wide in wonder.

"Are there many things like that in the Bible?" she asked.

"A great many," he answered gravely.

"But who were those things said to? Not to one like me, I'm sure!"

"Yes, to one like you," said Carbury. "Listen to this: 'For I have loved thee with an everlasting love, therefore with loving kindness have I drawn thee.'"

"But I guess you don't know about me," said the girl humbly. "I've never known a thing about God, nor ever thought about Him. I've just gone my own way and tried to have fun. Those things must have been said for good people like you."

"The Bible says, 'there is none good, no not one,' and it says, 'All we like sheep have gone astray. We have turned every one to his own way, and the Lord hath laid on Him the iniquity of us all.' That is the wonder of it. God loved us so much that He laid our sin on His own well-beloved Son, because that was the only way we could go free and be allowed to come Home to dwell with Him forever."

"You are sure there are things in the Bible that are meant for *me?*" she asked, still incredulous.

"Perfectly sure," said Carbury. "God says 'whosoever.'"

They had come to stand in a deserted corner of the wide rotunda not far from the stairs he must go down to his train, and Carbury swept a quick glance at the station clock now and again as he talked, and watched the intent face of the girl who looked as if she were trying to decide whether to believe him or not.

"It's true!" he said. "Read His Word and you'll find it out. And begin to pray."

"I don't know how to pray!" she said with sudden fierce bitterness. "I never was taught. And after all the things I've said, and the way I've lived, I couldn't have the face to pray."

"But after all the things *He* has said, and the way *He* lived, and most of all the way *He died,* why should you hesitate to go to Him with all your perplexities? He knows all about you anyway and understands. It is a great deal easier than coming to me with them, and yet, thank God you did come to me! Can't you go to Him?"

"But—you had been kind! You had said things about all this to me."

"Ah! He has been kind. He died to save you. And just you begin to study that Bible and find out what *He* has said to you about it. I'm sure you'll find out you can trust Him!"

"How do I pray?" she asked after a longer silence than before.

"Lock your door, shut the world out even from your thoughts, and then just tell Him, as you would tell me or Dana, all that troubles you. Tell Him too that you are beginning to understand you are not worthy to come to Him, but you are trusting in His promises. Read the Book and find out more of those promises. Now—I'm sorry—but I've got to leave you. The train goes in one minute. But I'll be praying for you all the way to Boston, and when I get back I'll be seeing you again. Meantime, you talk to God! Good-bye!" He gave her hand a quick warm clasp, sprinted across the space to his gateway, and was gone!

Just a bright look to remember, and that quick warm handclasp!

Coralie stood watching the gateway where he had vanished, till the gateman closed the gate, and then she turned and slowly walked back through the station to the outer world where she could take a taxi home.

Strangely enough her trouble and uncertainty had vanished. She had something definite to do and she was going home to do it. Errol might be there to trouble her, Lisa might rage and storm, but she didn't have to trouble about them any more. She was going to the great God and try to find out if He would have anything to do with her. With that in mind she had no time to worry about what might happen at home.

Coralie did not take a taxi, as was her wont for even a short trip. She walked. She had a strange reluctance to break the drift of her thoughts by getting home too soon, by having to take up the thread of her life again, and meet its problems. She wanted to take a deeper grasp on what had just been said to her, and make it thoroughly hers before she came in contact with anything alien to it. It was as if she had unexpectedly found a precious jewel, and she was afraid she might lose it, afraid someone else would try to snatch it away from her.

Lisa often snatched pleasant thoughts and sensations away from her. She had learned that long ago when she was just a little child, learned to guard anything that was sweet and pleasant, to hide it in her secret thoughts, and cultivate a false brazen front that could not be read at a glance. This had often been her only defense. And now as she walked down the bright crowded street, she steered her going so that she would not be likely to meet any of her acquaintances. She was carrying a precious thought, precious words like a handful of bright jewels that she must con until she knew them by heart. She must remember every word and expression, so that if possible, when she was at home, she could easily recall what had seemed to bring her so much hope.

So, walking through the city, taking unaccustomed byways for deeper more assured privacy, she recalled bit by bit, moment by moment her conversation with Bruce Carbury.

And as she in her soul asked over her own questions, she noted again the light in his eyes, the thrill of her own heart that he took her so in earnest with an answering eagerness of his own. Each turn of phrase, each inflection of his voice, each fleeting expression of his face was reproduced again in her memory without interruption, or disappointment. Yes, the whole interview stayed as it had first seemed. It did not, like so many other hopes and bright rays in her past, fade with reviewing it. It was genuine. It bore the test of thinking over. Nothing had ever done that before for her. They all presented some false note, some weakness that showed up when she looked at them calmly afterward. This was a test to which she put everything. And since this talk with Bruce had not failed under scanning did that not prove that it was worthy to be followed?

So, word by word she went over the directions.

"Lock your door. Shut the world out even from your thoughts! Then just tell Him."

She said it over and over to herself as she arrived finally at the home apartment and went in.

Then her mother's world rushed about her, and fairly seemed to stifle her. Stark furniture of modern build, garish ugly colors flaunting themselves, sophisticated perfume spicing the air, a tang of incense Lisa had been burning. Why did Lisa like incense? It rasped her nerves with its suggestion of mysticism.

Then the butler came down the hall carrying a breakfast tray. A glance showed it had scarcely been touched. Toast, eggs, bacon, even the orange juice untouched. That showed Lisa had had a full night last night and would be in an execrable mood this morning. The thought quickened her footsteps. Best not come into contact with her if possible.

Coralie slid into the music room and escaped the butler, who might not yet have noticed her, and waited until he had vanished kitchenward, then she hurried to her own room and locked the door.

"Lock the door," the directions had been. Well, it was locked. Was God anywhere there? She was going to talk to God. It was supposable that He was near, that locked doors could not keep Him out, though they could keep other people out. She cast a quick, furtive, half-frightened glance about. She had never prayed before. How did she know God was there? Would He know she was going to speak to Him? Bruce Carbury had been so sure He would hear, would know about her.

She flung off her hat and gloves and faced the next thought.

"Shut the world out, even from your thoughts!" That had been the next direction. Then she must not even let her mind wander to think what she would do if Lisa came to the door and demanded to know what she had said down at the bank. She must not worry about anything else. She was to have audience with the King of Heaven. Other things did not matter now. This was not a form, a ceremony that had to be gone through, like an incantation. It was something that might, if she fulfilled the conditions, make a difference in the whole of her life.

She closed her eyes and after an instant, suddenly dropped to her knees, a strange young figure with a little painted lovely face lifted to Heaven.

But over in her own room, Lisa was planning how she could quickly get a certain large sum of money together.

Just about that time Valerie Shannon, passing through the big outer office of the publishing house, chanced to meet Dana Barron on the way to his office adjoining, and the sudden lighting of his eyes at sight of her met an answering light in her own.

"You're rather a busy person around here, aren't you?" he said smiling. "I scarcely ever see you."

"Rather busy yourself, aren't you?" she said with a mischievous twinkle.

"Well, rather," he smiled. "I'm beginning to learn that nobody around this place wastes any time, it isn't being done. It's rather interesting to keep the pace, isn't it? However I haven't forgotten you said I might come over some evening, and I may carry that into effect rather soon now. Bruce has deserted me for a few days, gone on a business trip to Boston."

"Fine!" said Valerie. "Why don't you come over to dinner tonight? Mother would love it, I know. And oh, by the way, what's your sister's address? I forgot to ask her, and I've been wondering if she wouldn't come to us for a week end pretty soon so we could get really acquainted with her."

"That would be wonderful of you," said Dana with sudden gravity, "but—she isn't saved, you know."

Valerie's eyes were full of quick understanding, and a gentle sympathy.

"I wondered," she said.

"She might not come," said Dana sadly. "You see, I don't really know her. But I'll be grateful if you can be a friend to her. I think she needs one."

"I'll try," said Valerie, flashing him a smile. She took the address and was gone to her own desk.

Dana passed on to his own work with a feeling of cheer in his heart. What a thing it would be for his sister if she would get to know this girl well! But probably she wouldn't care for her!

He sighed and stood a moment by the window next his desk looking out with unseeing eyes over the city roofs, wondering if there was anything that he personally could do to further such a friendship.

Presently he sat down at his desk and took up his new work, but there lingered in his heart a brightness of anticipation. He was going to dinner at the Shannons', and he might have opportunity for a few minutes' private talk with Valerie. If so perhaps he would tell her more of his sister, and his mother, and ask her to pray for them; and for him as he tried to help them. The thought gave him comfort and ran like a thread of pure sunshine through the labor of the day.

14

BRUCE Carbury spent the most of the journey to Boston, his head lying back on the chair, his eyes closed, praying for Coralie Barron.

Now and again his prayers were interrupted by the chatter of two girls, whose countenances were highly illuminated, and whose garments showed that they belonged to the wealthy social order. They were seated just across the aisle from him and their conversation was distinctly of the world. Occasionally they took themselves to the club car to smoke, or to drink, and returned to gossip about their parties and their men friends. And as their lively talk continued it came sharply to Bruce that these girls belonged to the same world that Coralie Barron did. The mark was unmistakable. Studying them casually under the fringes of his lashes, he found himself wondering that a girl with such background and traditions should have been stirred to ask the questions about salvation that Coralie had asked. And would she be able to get the real meaning from the Bible he had promised to send her? Wasn't it a sort of hopeless task to try and bring Dana's sister to a true knowledge of salvation in Jesus Christ?

But ah! the Lord had not thought it hopeless! He had given His life for such!

So Bruce prayed on.

And when he reached Boston one of his first acts, after he had made an appointment to meet the man he had come to see, was to go to a book store and purchase a lovely Bible, bound in genuine leather, dark blue, soft and flexible, with India paper and clear print, a Scofield that would give her help with its enlightening notes and references, in case she really wanted to know the truth and search for it. It was indeed a lovely Bible, "deluxe" so far as any book could be, and as he held it in his hand a moment his soul thrilled with the thought that it was his privilege to give it to that little lost lovely sister of his friend. Its whole make-up was beautiful, and seemed fitting for her to have. Of course a common ordinary Bible would have brought the truth as well to any lost soul. But it might well be that the beauty of the binding would hold her to a passing whim to read it, until the matchless words themselves should have reached her soul.

He had the book mailed to her at once, and then went happily about the business that had brought him to Boston. He had done his best, and now he must trust the Holy Spirit to do His work. His own part from now on would be to continue in prayer for this soul, who had so strangely asked his help. She might be genuine, and she might not. His part was to pray.

And while he prayed he included Dana, and his strange unhappy situation with regard to a mother who was not a mother.

And curiously enough, just at that very moment, back

in New York, Dana Barron was in receipt of a rather disturbing letter.

Right into the midst of the pleasant morning and the work that he enjoyed doing, it came. An announcement from a lawyer that he must furnish within the next few days a full statement of his deceased father's financial affairs, accurate knowledge of where his holdings now were, and a copy of his will. The letter ended with a threatening sentence, which might or might not mean much.

Dana was not well enough acquainted in New York to know that the man whose name was signed to the letter was one of the trickiest and most notorious lawyers the city boasted. But he understood the language in which the letter was couched well enough to know that his mother was resorting to extreme means to carry her end. And that end? Well, it was all too evident that it was money. She didn't believe what he had told her, that his father had given her everything except his bare living.

The letter was a most disturbing element and bade fair to get in the way of work that day, till he finally faced the thing in the quiet of his office with closed eyes and asked his Heavenly Father to take command of him, and to work out the matter in the right way.

He looked up from that moment's contact with the Throne with his thoughts at peace, and he began to realize that there was really nothing in the whole matter to worry about. There wasn't any property, and it would be easy to prove that. The shaft that hit him hardest was that the woman he must acknowledge as his own mother was doing this thing. That she was so sordid and material-minded that all she cared for from her son was a few paltry dollars she hoped he would be able to supply to her. He hated to acknowledge that she was such a woman. Of course, he ought to have been prepared to find her so, since she had run away from her husband and baby son to lead her own willful life, yet somehow he had hoped against hope that there would be found in her somewhere something sweet and lovable. He shrank, too, from the thought that perhaps his few acquaintances here in New York might have to know what she was.

But after all, this was no more than he had known he might find, before he came here, and why should he tear his heart out over it? His father had suffered worse, and cheerfully carried on that he might give a life as nearly normal as possible to a son whose mother had deserted him.

So with a quiet mind Dana wrote a brief letter to the lawyer stating that his father had no property whatever when he died, and that he himself had nothing save the little cottage where they had lived; his father had given him that when he came of age. He said that his father had left no will, as there was no property to leave, and that these facts could easily be verified by writing to the following addresses in the west. Then he gave the names of business men, the tax collector, a lawyer friend, their doctor, their pastor, and the president of the bank where his father's accounts had formerly been kept.

After the letter was dispatched Dana felt better. Why should he worry? This matter would straighten itself out. And after all, he was going to Shannons' to dinner tonight! He just couldn't be despondent. The Shannons were not people who would believe he was trying to steal property from his own mother, even if she had deserted him.

So Dana went into the day's work with an absorbing interest that completely shut out unimportant annoyances. Dana's faith in an all-powerful Heavenly Father was too strong for worry or annoyance to get an absorbing hold upon him.

But as the day wore on it began to come to him strongly that he would surely tell Valerie a little of his own story and prepare her to help his sister, in case she finally carried out her suggestion of inviting her to the Shannon home. What a wonderful answer to prayer that would be, to have Coralie become a real friend of Valerie Shannon's! If Coralie only would.

Coralie, meantime, was having troubles of her own.

Her very prayers had been interrupted that morning by a summons from her mother, and with a gasp she went with fear and trembling to meet her. Was this the way her new-found God was going to answer her as yet unspoken petition, just send her into battle unprepared?

Yet though she went defiantly, there was about her a certain soft deference, as if she sensed that one who was yielding to the leadership of God should not go as a worldling. Where she got that idea she did not know, but she carried it with her as she entered her mother's elaborately stark bedroom.

Lisa looked at her with cold unloving eyes.

"Well, so you did decide to come back!" she said cuttingly. "It does seem as if you might have left some word for me, especially when you knew I was having guests and depending on you to help me entertain them. Where in the world have you been?"

Coralie promptly forgot her new resolves and tilted her chin impudently, no longer conscious of a God before whom she must walk softly.

"Does it make any difference where I was?" she returned. "I had an invitation to a house party and I chose to accept it, that's all. As for your having guests, that's a daily happening. If I stopped on that I wouldn't ever go anywhere. Besides, I didn't care for your guests."

"That's it exactly," said Lisa vindictively. "You chose to insult the people I invited. You knew they were coming largely on your account, at least one of them was, and you made a point of being away, and not leaving word where I could call you up."

Coralie assumed a sleepy indifferent attitude.

"You make me tired," she said, "spending time and effort telling me things I already know. You have stated the case quite clearly. I did all that, and I meant to. And what's more I very possibly shall do it again if the same occasion arises."

"You'd better not!" said Lisa bitingly. "I warn you! You'd better not try that thing twice. I have ways of making you suffer if you do that again."

"How sweet of you, Lisa, to remind me of that!" said the girl bitterly. "But of course it wasn't necessary. The past has taught me to remember that well. In fact I considered that matter before I went away, and decided the game was fully worth the candle. Do you understand me? Lisa, I'm not going to be made your cat's-paw any more. Certainly not for those two men! I despise them! I loathe them! And I'm done pretending I'm fond of them any more."

"Indeed!"

"Yes, *indeed!*" went on the angry girl. "I used to wonder why you didn't leave me, too, when you ran away from your home and your obligations and your little boy baby. You chose to take me along. But lately I've been wondering if it wasn't just for this, to be assistant charmer for your various men friends."

"Be still!"

"No, I won't be still! You sent for me and now you've

got to take it! And you might as well know now as later that I'm done going around with that Errol Hunt! Whether you like it or whether you don't like it, I'm done."

"You're a silly girl!" said Lisa contemptuously. "Here's a man who is fabulously rich, and adores the very ground you walk on, and you turn him down." Her voice was cold and hard. "You needn't think I'll support you after you've spent all your own money if you turn down a man like that!"

"After *you've* spent my money, you mean, Lisa!" said the girl bitterly, her eyes suddenly flashing. "Lisa, what's the idea of you writing my name on checks and making out I've written it? I thought they used to call that forgery!"

Lisa's eyes grew strangely dark, her face suddenly very white.

"What do you mean?" she screamed, "talking to me like that? Using such criminal words! As if I wouldn't have a perfect right to write my name on your checks if I chose! The perfect idea! It seems to me you are getting very uppish and independent after all these years when I've been taking care of you. Using money for your foolishness that I might have used for myself."

"It was *my* money!" said Coralie, her chin thrown high. "It wasn't yours. You were only a trustee. It isn't as if you didn't have enough of your own for your own needs."

"Yes, certainly I was a trustee! And now you are objecting to my being a trustee. What kind of a silly idea have you got anyway?"

Coralie looked at her mother coldly but firmly.

"Don't kid yourself," she said. "You aren't a trustee any more. I'm of age. And I've told the bank not to cash any more checks for anybody but me, no matter how well they can imitate my handwriting!"

"You wicked girl!" cried Lisa, springing from her bed and standing slim and lovely in her costly negligee of pale blue chiffon ruffles, her little feet like pink flowers planted angrily far apart on the soft rug like a child in a rage. "Do you mean that you dared to do a thing like that? *You!* After all I've done for you! You whom I might have left behind in the hospital to go on charity if I had chosen! You dare to cast ignominy upon me like that! You shameful child! Do you really mean that you dared do a thing like that?"

"I did!" said Coralie. "And I made them understand that I meant it!" She was fully as angry as her mother now. "You thought I'd stand for your purloining all my rights, and squandering my money on that loathsome Ivor Kavanaugh! You thought you could sell me body and soul to that drunken Errol, and get away with it! And then when those two crooks got away with all the money, who would take care of you, if I had nothing? And who would take care of me?"

Lisa's slender form in its chiffon ruffles was fairly trembling with fury and her eyes were flashing indignantly.

"You poor silly little fool! Don't you know that Ivor and Errol are very rich and fully able to care for those who belong to them? And don't you know that you are in great danger of losing your hold on them if you go on the way you have been doing? Besides, don't you realize that I can as easily as anything declare that you are not yet of age, and take all your money from you, if you continue to act in such an idiotic way? I could even have you committed to an insane asylum if I felt it necessary!"

She paused, her voice growing cooler as she saw the startled look on her daughter's face.

"And I certainly will," she declared firmly, "if I hear of any more such performances! I didn't bring you away with me to have you turn against me and frustrate all my wishes!"

"No!" said Coralie slowly, solemnly, "you didn't intend that, but you are willing to do anything to me now if you don't get your way. Well, I'm not surprised, since you were willing to go off and leave my brother, a mere baby! You'll do *anything!*—If you *can!* But I'll take good care *you can't!*"

She flung the words with a blue flash of her eyes at her mother, defiantly.

But Lisa was almost beside herself.

"Try and stop me!" she flung back. "You little fool you!"

"Watch me!" said Coralie as she turned swiftly toward the door.

"And don't you *dare* have any communication whatever with that contemptible brother of yours, do you hear me?" shouted Lisa, following her to the door. "I won't stand for his interference in our affairs, do you hear me?"

But Coralie went steadily on to her room.

Ten minutes later Coralie was speeding down to the bank as fast as a taxi could take her, and before the morning was over she had placed all her money, capital, interest and everything, in another Trust Company. Returning later in the day, head held high, she found Lisa in one of her most imperious moods. She was on the watch for her and followed her stealthily to her room, slipping in after her before the girl realized she was there, and forestalling any attempt to lock her out.

"Now!" she said turning on her with fire in her eyes and looking as Coralie could remember she looked sometimes when she was a child and had inadvertently transgressed some unguessed law. Inwardly she quailed over the remembered cruel whipping that always came with such a look. There were no looks of love in her memory to make her forget them, and she steeled herself for whatever might be coming, and did not let her eyes even flicker as she steadily faced the woman who had dominated her so many years, a woman whose temper she had fully inherited.

Lisa, after their talk that morning, had tried to get the bank over the telephone and stop whatever her child was perpetrating, but had found that she was already too late to do anything, even if she had had the power. Coralie had done the deed promptly and fully, and had left no traces behind.

"What have you done? Silly, ignorant child, what ridiculous, disgraceful thing have you done that I shall have to humiliate myself to undo?"

"I haven't done anything silly, and I have not done it ignorantly," said Coralie coolly. "I have only done what I had a right to do, so that you couldn't use all my money up pampering that disgusting Ivor."

Her voice was so quiet, and so free from her usual raving and protest, that Lisa was almost awed by her for the instant. Then a frenzy of anger seized the mother again and she stormed on.

"Disgusting! Why should you use that detestable word about a noble and kindly gentleman?"

"Because I don't believe he is noble, and I'm sure he is not kindly, else why should he fawn upon your gullibility and torment you for money. I'm quite sure that the only reason those two keep hanging around here is to get every cent out of you they can possibly extract. If they found that your money was all gone you would see them disappear quickly enough."

"Corinne! I forbid you to speak of my friends in that way. They are wealthy men of noble lineage. I happen to know more about them than you do. I have friends abroad who have enquired into their fortunes for me."

"Oh!" said Coralie, "then you didn't trust them so much yourself at first, did you? But I wouldn't be surprised to hear that these friends abroad were suggested by Ivor himself, and perhaps even introduced by him. You are gullible, you know, in spite of your cleverness in some lines. And I ask you again, Lisa, as I asked you once before, if these gentlemen are so rich and noble, why do they wish to borrow from you whom they have known so short a time? It doesn't hang together, Lisa. Rich noble gentlemen don't borrow large sums of comparatively casual acquaintances, even if they are contemplating marriage, I'm sure they don't."

There was a look in Lisa's eyes like something at bay, as she faced her calm young daughter whose steady eye met her own with a look as battle-sure as ever Lisa had worn. It was almost as if Lisa were desperate. She stood for an instant watching her child, with a look of almost hate growing in her great expressive eyes. Then came a sudden change. Lisa was an accomplished actress. Sudden shame and sorrow swept over the beautiful contours of her face like a veil dropped about her. It was as if she were acknowledging that she had reached the limit of humiliation and could bear no more. Her shapely head drooped and drooped, and her lashes veiled the cunning in her eyes. For an instant she was an angel sheathed tenderly in repentance.

"I shall have to tell you the truth," she murmured finally, in a small but dominating voice. "I cannot let those noble gentlemen bear your misjudgment. It is not true that Ivor has been asking me for money. I told you that once to shield myself. It is to pay my honorable gambling debts I want it, child. I must have it! And who should I come to in my need if not to you, my child for whom I have done so much."

"Just what have you done for me?" Coralie watched her steadily, with a countenance unchanging, hard. "You took me away from what seems to have been a wonderful father. What kind of a mother have you been? And if what you say now is true then it is the fault of those two men that you are in such straits. You never gambled that way before. Not beyond what you could pay. And I will not have that man get possession of the money my father left me."

"What have you done with your money? I demand to know!"

"I shall not tell you."

"Well, there are ways to make you tell me."

"Yes? Well, try them, and see how far you get with them." There was a haughty lift to the girl's head that gave her a strong resemblance to her mother. "I begin to see why my father safeguarded my money."

Lisa's eyes narrowed and a furious anger swept her face, unlike any that Coralie could remember to have seen there before.

"Ah! I see now!" she fairly hissed. "I know where you have got all this rebellion and stubbornness. You have been with your brother. You have been taking counsel together against me. That is where you have been during this week end."

"No," said Coralie quietly, steadily. "I have not been with Dana. I have not even seen him this week end! But when I saw him last he talked to me about Jesus Christ. Lisa, did you ever know God?"

Lisa, checked in the midst of her fury by this most unexpected question, looked at her child in horror, and then suddenly stamped her foot at her and shouted:

"Get out! Get out of my house before I strike you! You are an unnatural, wicked child. Don't ever speak to me again, and get out of my house at once."

A look of almost pity came over Coralie's face.

"No," she said steadily, "I'm not going out of your house. You brought me with you and I have a right to stay. At least until I choose to go. And I am not being wicked when I talk this way. I am asking a question because I want to know the answer. Didn't you ever know God? Didn't you even know *about* God? And if you did, why didn't you ever tell me? You should have told me. I think my father would have told me if you had let him have me. I had a right to know."

Lisa looked at her with eyes that seemed almost insane in their hate and fury, and then she screamed, burst into awful overwhelming tears, and went reeling out of the room and down the hall to her own apartment, weeping wildly, hysterically.

Coralie had never seen her cry before. She stood staring at her as if she could not believe her eyes. And when Lisa's door closed with a slam and the sound of a turning key in the lock followed, the girl stepped back into her own room and locked her door. Then she turned and looked about her.

It was almost as if the shadow of those interrupted prayers of hers stood there, torn and waiting, like a rent robe that had been suddenly cast aside, and she were looking at them sorrowfully, regretfully.

At last she said aloud, with her face lifted up as if her gaze penetrated far beyond the ceiling of her room:

"O God! Could anyone pray, after a scene like that?"

15

THE house was very still. Coralie's room was at the extreme end of the hall. She did not hear when Lisa went away. Her mind had been in too much of a tumult to be on the alert anyway.

She had dropped into a forlorn little heap on her bed, and fallen into a deep exhausted sleep, from which she did not waken until late in the afternoon when the maid tapped at her door.

"There's a special delivery letter for you, Miss Corinne," she called.

Coralie hastened to open her door, with a strange uncanny premonition, as she took the letter that had somehow a familiar look about it.

She glanced at the writing and then she knew. That was the hand of her stepfather, Dinsmore Collette! She knew it at once, though she hadn't seen it since he had left her mother more than three years before.

Her heart contracted with quick fear.

She hadn't ever liked him, though he had been nice to her at first, and had sometimes sought to please her by bringing her expensive presents. She had reluctantly consented to take his name, and had made no objection to it until after Collette went away. Then she had made intermittent protests about it, only to be told that it was all nonsense, she might as well be Collette as anything.

"What's the difference? You'll soon marry somebody and then the name will change without any trouble, so why worry?" had been Lisa's way of dropping the matter, and the girl had been too indifferent to pursue the subject further.

But now as she gazed at the name in that handwriting she was suddenly filled with aversion for it. Every curve of the letters seemed to recall his harsh unkind treatment and selfish language, especially during the last months he was with them.

And now, what could he be writing her for? A cold horror filled her as she tore open the letter. Nothing good she was sure. Was he coming back to them? Had he a right to come? There had been no divorce. The last she had heard of him was that he had gone to Africa to shoot lions. Or was it India, or Siberia? She wasn't quite sure. Lisa had thought him dead, some word like that had come, she was sure. But this letter was postmarked here in the United States. A cold chill went down her spine. Was he going to try to make some trouble for them again? She had felt almost sorry for Lisa the last few weeks of his stay with them, he had been so studiedly hateful to her, so frightfully jealous and coarse in his accusations.

She took a deep breath and tried to steady the hand that held the thin foreign-looking paper on which the scrawl was written.

"My dear little girl;" he addressed her. That was the way he used to address her before Lisa and he were married. She shuddered as she read on.

It is a long time since we have seen each other, and though you may be surprised I have missed you a great deal, since certain distressing circumstances occurred which made my going the only honorable course for me. It was nice to have a pretty child calling me father. I did not realize when I went away how very much I was going to miss you!

In utter disgust Coralie flung the letter from her. She felt as if she could not bear to read another word from his false lips. It sounded so like the way he used to talk when he wanted her to take some offensive message to Lisa. Anger and fear surged in her heart. She cast a frantic look at the letter lying arrogantly on the floor, and knew she must finish reading it. She had got to be prepared for whatever despicable thing the man might try next. She must find out why he had come into their vicinity again.

She stooped and picked up the letter and read on.

And now, my dear, I must tell you that I am in trouble and distress and I have come to you to help me out. Your dear mother would of course help me if she knew my need, but I hesitate to trouble her. And besides the other day I suddenly remembered that you are no longer a child. You are of age, and have come into your own at last. And of course you are the one I should have thought of in the first place. I recall that you were to inherit your money some months ago, and of course by this time you are quite used to making out checks and transacting business for yourself, so it will not be a difficult task I am setting for you.

My dear Corinne, could you lend me a little matter of five hundred dollars for a couple of months until my own money from the sale of my Oriental estate can reach me from the other side of the world?

Of course if you find that five hundred dollars will straiten you too much all at once, I could make out with three hundred now and the other two hundred a month later. But I do hope that your tender heart will see your way clear to letting me have the whole sum at once for it will make my way much easier and assist me in what I am trying to do.

You will be pleased, I know, to hear that I am planning to return to my native land to live, and am thinking strongly of taking an apartment in New York. I find that the separation from your dear beautiful mother is more than I can bear, and I want to come back and see if I cannot win her to myself again. I know that this would make you very happy, you were always such a loving and obedient daughter, therefore I am sure you will help me all that you can. Of course if I have to come out in the open and ask Lisa for that money I loaned her several years ago and which she has never repaid me, it may be more uncomfortable in the end for you. Therefore I am hoping that you will be in a position to lend me this small sum at once, and I assure you that it will be repaid within a short time, and that I shall not forget your kindness, and will repay it with paternal love as well as with money. On the other hand if you fail me it is fair that I warn you, that much suffering for yourself will result.

Your very loving father-in-love,
Dinsmore Collette.

Coralie crumpled the pages viciously into a ball and flung them across the room in her wrath, wishing she could vent her feelings somehow on the innocent paper.

Oh, what a life! Trouble and battle in the morning! Trouble threatening in the evening! And no peace anywhere!

Now! What should she do? Of one thing she was sure, she would never lend a cent to Dinsmore Collette! He was false through and through. Just how he could get revenge upon her she did not know, but she was sure he would find a way if it meant enough to him, and she was afraid. Somehow she knew he was aware she would be afraid.

To think he had ferreted out her little holdings and remembered when she would come into her own. He was daring to count on playing on her weakness! How well he knew how helpless she was, with no friends who would dare to help her!

Ah! But she had a brother! Dinsmore did not know about her brother, and that he had come to her vicinity, and that she could call upon him in need. He did not know that her brother had a friend who was strong and knew God. He did not know that even she could have God for a helper, and that she was in a way to find out how to be saved. Did being saved include things like this which threatened to disrupt one's life on earth as well as in the hereafter?

Softly she slipped upon her knees beside the bed in the dusk of her room and put her face reverently down in her pillow. All day she had been going to seek audience with a great God and had been interrupted, and now here she was face to face with a great need. Could she just tell God about all about it, as Bruce Carbury had said, even without preliminaries? Even though she didn't yet know Him?

Down at the entrance to the apartment the postman and the butler were having a discussion. The butler was shaking his head gravely.

"No sir! No one of that name here. Coralie Barron? No sir. We haven't got any guests just now either, not of that name!"

"But that's your number," said the postman insistently. "Maybe it's somebody that's coming tonight. Why'n't ya go ask?"

"We've had no word of any guest coming," said the butler stiffly. "Coralie Barron. Never heard of her."

"But I think Coralie's Miss Corinne's other name," interpolated the maid who had dropped out in the hall to see if there was any mail for herself. "I'm sure that's her other name. It's Corinne C. you know," she persisted. "And Barron was the name of the madam's first husband, at least something like that. And that was the name of the young man that looked so much like Miss Corinne. Dana Barron. Don't you remember?"

The butler looked at her stupidly.

"It might be so," he said.

"I'll go ask," said the maid eagerly. She was very anxious to know why Miss Corinne was staying all this time in her own room and the madam was out. So she took the letter to Coralie's door, all excited to be bringing another letter although this wasn't a special, and looked only like a note from the city. Maybe only an ad.

So once more Coralie was roused from an attempt at prayer by a letter.

But this time it was only a little note from Valerie Shannon asking Coralie to come and spend the next week end with her, and it came in its quiet simplicity like an answer to her incoherent prayer for help.

"Would that letter be for you, Miss Corinne?" the maid had asked. "The postman insisted it was our number."

Coralie glanced at the address.

"Why, yes, Bella. That's my real name, you know, and I'm going to use it after this, so please tell the postman, and the others," and then she went on reading her letter, a bit breathless because it was so different from other letters she had been used to receiving, and because it was from another world, and seemed a note of calm in the turmoil of her day.

With the balm that came through that little quiet letter, soothing her troubled heart, Coralie went back to her interrupted prayer, and this time it seemed easier to talk to Valerie's God, while she held Valerie's kind friendly little letter in her hand. So she rose at last strengthened in her faith by her few stumbling words, feeling that in a feeble way she belonged to a great company of believers. That gave her more confidence.

It was a new experience to have a little thrill of joy of anticipation in her heart, as she finally rose, and sat down to answer that note of Valerie's. Would she spend the week end with her? Joy! Of course she would. It would give her opportunity to see more of this family and find out if the love they seemed to have for one another was real. It would give her some idea of what life could be when it was lived on a different plane. Perhaps she could find out more about the kind of life her brother had lived as he was growing up. She wanted to see whether she liked such a life. Whether on close observance it would stand the test and appeal to her as something that might bring happiness.

So she wrote her little note of happy acceptance, and mailed it, and then went to investigate what was going on in the apartment. She was getting hungry, and surely it must be late. She wanted to eat dinner and get away somewhere so that she would not have to come into contact with Errol and Ivor that evening. She wished the invitation had been for tonight. She wondered whether there might be another meeting at that mission. It wasn't going to be easy to go out every evening for there weren't many places where she felt she wanted to go just now. She wanted to get away from the old life and get hold of something real.

She summoned Bella.

"Isn't it almost dinner time?" she asked.

"Whenever you say, Miss Corinne," said Bella deferentially. "The madam is away, you know."

"Oh!" said Coralie. "Did she say when she would return?"

Bella gave her a searching glance, but Coralie wore her usual lazy inscrutable look.

"She took luggage with her. She said she would telephone when she got ready to return. She said you would give your own orders."

So! It was to be a new form of punishment, absent treatment. Well, that was a relief, but surely there would be some new found way of torture. Whenever there was mystery there was always punishment.

"Yes," said Coralie. "I should have ordered sooner, but I was asleep. All right. Bring me a tray, please. I won't bother to dress for dinner tonight. Just bring what there is, something hot, and a little fruit. You know how to get me something nice, Bella." She gave an unwonted smile, and the girl hurried away wondering, but Coralie sat trying to puzzle out just what this move of Lisa's might mean. Would she return later in the evening with her own crowd, or had she taken them all away somewhere to one of her favorite haunts? Or was she planning some disagreeable surprise that would spring on her later in the evening? Could it be possible that this letter from Dinsmore had been faked by Lisa, who had used her ability to imitate handwriting to frighten her rebellious daughter? Could it be possible that Dinsmore might arrive later and demand to see her when she was all alone? She shuddered at the thought, and cold fear crept up to her heart. Surely not that. For if he were really here and this was a genuine letter she had received from him, he would surely wait until tomorrow to see if she would answer and offer the demanded five hundred dollars peaceably.

Nevertheless, so real were her fears that she took the precaution to look up the Shannon telephone number. If anything did happen so that she needed help she could call there and one of those boys would surely get her in touch with Dana.

Besides, she had asked the Lord God to help her and guide her and save her. Wouldn't He do it? Bruce had seemed to think He would.

When Bella returned with the tray Coralie had only a soft low light burning, and the rest of the room was in shadow.

"I'd like a fire on the hearth, Bella," she said. "It seems chilly here, and I've a bad headache. Suppose you send the boy with some wood and let him light a fire. And if anyone calls for me this evening you can say I've retired, that I'm not feeling well, but you will come and see if I am awake. But don't let anyone come unannounced."

"Yes, Miss Corinne!" said Bella, and slipped away to give the order to the boy.

So presently there was a pleasant fire on the hearth, and Coralie settled herself to her tray, trying to put away the thought of disturbing things, and take this quiet reprieve that had come to her so unexpectedly.

The supper wasn't bad, considering she hadn't ordered. There was a dainty cup of soup, a bit of the breast of chicken, an attractive salad, hot rolls and a dish of hot-house strawberries, with coffee. Bella had lingered to ask if she would have wine, before she left, but Coralie shook her head. "Just coffee," she said, and the girl went away wondering again.

Coralie herself wondered at her feeling. Somehow it seemed to her as if wine symbolized the things she was up against. She could not get away from the memory of Errol babbling outside her door the evening before, so under the influence of liquor that he could scarcely speak her name.

As she sat there eating she realized that it was the first time in years that she had eaten alone this way with an empty house and no demands upon her, and she really enjoyed the sensation. For these few minutes at least she could call her soul her own, could know what to count on, and have time to think and plan.

After Bella had taken the tray she locked her door securely and luxuriated in the thought that nobody would have the right to interrupt her.

But she grew a bit frightened as time went on, and she heard the distant sound of the elevator, and voices. In a panic she turned out her lights and kept perfectly still when she heard Bella come quietly to her door and listen, and then go away again. The dark transom over the door would make her sure that she was asleep, and after a little she heard the voices again in the distance, and the soft clang of the elevator going down, and then all was still.

The noises of the city night went on, and by and by

it grew dimmer as if the night were weary. She prayed again, with that strange awed feeling that she was not alone, but God had come to company with her and she need not be afraid.

Over on the other side of the city in that plain old-fashioned house, Valerie and Dana were talking in a cosy library lined with wonderful old books. Dana was telling Valerie a little about his strange saddened life, his wonderful father, the sorrowful little sister and unnatural mother. And then they were praying together for Coralie. Was it possible that something of their faith-winged petitions reached across and entered the big dark room where Coralie lay, and brought peace and hope to her frightened young soul? Certainly those prayers must have carried restraining power to the forces of darkness that were striving to form a battalion around that young soul, and give her trouble enough to make her forget a great God about whom she had just been learning.

16

"IT is wonderful of you to take an interest in my sister," said Dana. "If she will only respond and be friendly I shall take new heart of hope. The little contact I've had with her is deeply disappointing, and frankly, I don't see much hope of getting into closer touch with her. My mother resents my coming, and if there is going to be any way to do anything for them besides praying, the Lord will have to open the door, for it is most decidedly closed to me just now."

"He will," said Valerie, "when the right time comes. Remember when it was that the Lord Jesus healed the nobleman's son? 'The seventh hour.' And seven stands for perfect completion. Probably things are not ripe yet for God to work. But the seventh hour may strike at any time, and you may not even be conscious that God has worked. The nobleman didn't *see* any difference at first, you know. He had to go away and believe. And don't you think the Lord usually shuts us up to prayer first, anyway, when we get the idea of working for someone? I do. I've found it so again and again. Perhaps it's because we might begin to think *we* had done something ourselves. And besides, we must be *filled* with the Spirit when we finally have the opportunity to speak."

Dana smiled, and watched the lovely girl with deep appreciation.

"You're right," he said reverently. "I find I always want to get right out on the field and go to work, even before I've taken much time to ask the Lord if that's what He wants me to do. I think sometimes I've covered a good deal of ground and then it suddenly occurs to me that the Lord may not want me meddling in the matter at all, except by prayer."

Valerie smiled.

"I don't think there's much doubt that the Lord wants you on the field in this case," she said gently. "It seems a wonderful testimony that a deserted son should bear the message of God's love to a prodigal mother."

"Well, but that's just it, I haven't," said Dana, dejected. "I really haven't had an opportunity. There hasn't been a particle of opening. Perhaps I didn't try hard enough at the beginning. Perhaps I didn't even intend to try. I went there belligerently, with the intention of carrying out my wonderful father's wishes, and presenting his last letter to her, and as it turned out I had no opportunity to do more."

"You will," said Valerie quietly.

"I don't know," said Dana sadly. "She has made an issue of certain business affairs, for which she has no grounds whatever, and she is determined that I am trying to deceive her. I'm afraid there will never be an opportunity again. I think I didn't pray enough before I went."

"There will be opportunity," said Valerie again very quietly. "When the Lord gets ready He will give you another opportunity to give your witness."

Dana studied her sweet earnest face thoughtfully.

"But you don't believe that everybody is saved, do you?" he asked at last. "It might be that she has sinned away her day of grace."

"That is true of course," said the girl, "but that is something neither you nor I can say. Our business is to witness of the love of God for lost sinners and tell them His way of salvation. We have to leave the rest with God. I'm sure you will have another opportunity, so that your responsibility will be discharged, and you must pray that you'll be ready when it comes."

His face kindled with a heavenly light as she spoke, and in a moment he lifted his eyes to hers and said earnestly:

"I'll be ready."

Just then the boys came in from the outside world where they had been on some errand of mercy, Kirk and Ranald and Kendall, and they all gathered around the piano and sang. It was wonderful singing, and presently the whole family gathered from the different quarters of the great house to listen to it.

"That is a rare young man!" said father later when he and mother were preparing for rest. "And a rare voice!"

"Yes," said the mother quickly. "He's all that. But I do hope Vallie won't get her heart too set on him."

Father Shannon paused in the act of pulling off his shirt and looked at her in astonishment.

"Why, mother!" he said in a startled voice. "Why, mother, what's the matter with him?"

"Oh, nothing's the matter with him at all," she laughed apologetically. "That's it. He's too wonderful, and I don't want our dear wonderful girl's heart broken."

"And why should you think he would break her heart?"

"Oh, I don't mean he would intend to do it of course,

but I could see our girl's face while they were singing. It was all lit up with joy, and father, I'm just afraid she's going to lose her heart to that handsome young fellow before she knows it, and anyone can see he's made for great things and a high place in the world. He's stepped right into a big job at the office, and he'll be in with all the great of the earth."

"But mother, he's a Christian! Quite an unusual one, I heard Kirk say, and he looks it and sounds it too."

"Yes, I know," sighed the mother getting out her little stock of the wisdom-of-this-world and sorting it over. "But there are degrees in social life even for a Christian, father, and you know a man as good-looking as that isn't going to pick out just a plain little nobody with no money at all, to fall in love with!"

"Well, now, mother, I think you do him a wrong judging him that way, making him out a man who would pick a girl because she had money. He doesn't look like that kind of a man to me at all. And besides, mother, I don't know where he could find a prettier, better behaved girl than our Valerie anywhere. There aren't any prettier eyes anywhere than hers, with all those black lashes curling away from the blue of her eyes. They look just like big blue pansies. They look just like your eyes, mamma, when you were Vallie's age, and I'm not going to stand for you thinking there is any better girl for anybody on the face of this whole earth, than our Vallie-girl."

"Oh yes, I know, father, we feel that way about her of course, but she's ours, and we love her. That's not saying every young man is going to fall in love with her. And I don't like the idea of running any risks with our treasure-girl. I don't know as we should invite him here so much."

"But mother, I don't understand. I thought you had just been praying for a number of months that the Lord would protect our dear girl, and would send some worthy strong Christian man to love and shelter her through her life if it was His will, and now when He seems to have done it you want to step in and try to frustrate His plans! How's that, mother, can't you trust your Lord?"

Mother Shannon looked at her husband startled.

"But father, I didn't really expect the Lord to send such a wonderful-looking man, with a voice like that!"

"Oh, mother, mother! Would you presume to dictate to your Lord just how the little girl's lover should look, and have him sing the wrong notes betimes, so you won't be afraid of him? Little mother, just get you down on your knees and tell your Lord you're trusting Him, and ask Him not to let our darlin's heart be broke, and then let come what He shall send."

"Well, I guess you're right, father," said mother Shannon smiling half sheepishly. "I guess I just wasn't trusting fully, was I?"

And then those two sweet old Christians knelt hand in hand and prayed about their dear child.

And Dana Barron went home thanking his heavenly Father that he had found such delightful Christian friends, and especially a girl like Valerie Shannon.

The next morning Coralie's Bible came, quite early before she was up.

The maid brought the package in with her breakfast tray and Coralie was so excited about it she forgot to eat her breakfast until everything was quite cold.

However that didn't matter to her in the least. She sat against her pillows eating, one hand out touching the soft leather of the beautiful book, her eyes shining as they had not shone in years.

She made short work of breakfast and dressed as rapidly as she could. She was in a hurry to get to that Bible.

And then when she finally settled down to investigate it, she had no more idea than a child how to go about reading it. Should she begin at the beginning? She let the pages slide softly through her fingers, catching sentences here and there that seemed intriguing, the clear print standing out alluringly from the India paper.

Then she turned to the beginning and started. A strange sort of fairy tale it was to her, for she had never read before how the world was made. The teachings of science with regard to the beginnings had been so vague that they had scarcely touched her mind as real. They had faded into the unknown as soon as her studies were completed. But now this book stated that God had made out of nothing the heaven and the earth, and incredible as it might be it seemed more sensible as a belief than any of the follies and foibles of so-called science that she had been supposed to study in school.

Coralie belonged to a bridge club that met that morning, with a costly fee for being absent, but she read on regardless, forgetting all about it. The telephone rang insistently after a time and she answered it, annoyed at the interruption. She was wide-eyed at the drama of the world that was opening in the pages before her.

It was Myrtina Dalrymple.

"What in the world is the matter with you, Corinne? Haven't you started yet? Don't you know you're holding us all up! You're the limit! What do you think we are, ladies of leisure? We're all furious at you. Are you just starting? Make it snappy. We haven't a substitute at all today!"

"Oh! The Club! Sorry, Myrt. I completely forgot it.

No, I can't possibly come today. Get Doris Foster. She'll be charmed to pieces to be asked, and they say she plays a perfect game. What's that? A lovely prize? Sorry, but I'm not in line for any kind of a prize this morning. What's that? The fee? Oh, sure! I'll pay up! No, really, I can't possibly come this morning. Sorry I didn't let you know sooner, but I was so busy I completely forgot what day it was. Yes, get anybody in my place you like."

She hung up and went breathlessly back to her Bible, dimly conscious that the story she was reading must be the foundation of all the references one heard and read relating to one Adam, and a Garden of Eden. She had realized long ago that these things were supposed to be common knowledge, but she had always been rather vague about them. Why had she never come on this before?

She had left Adam and Eve hiding from God and she wanted to see how it came out. Of course they could not hope to hide from a God who had made them, and made the universe and everything. And yet perhaps that was just what everybody tried to do when they had sinned.

And while Coralie read on in the sacred Book, Valerie between her multiplicity of duties, and Dana in his office alone working out new problems, and Bruce up in Boston going from place to place making new contacts for his company, were all finding time to pray for her.

Weary at last with her unaccustomed employment, Coralie reached the end of a chapter and closed her book softly, with a touch on its soft flexible covers like a caress, and knelt, herself, to talk to the God about whom she had been reading, and with whom she felt quite a good deal better acquainted than she had the night before.

Late that afternoon after she had been out for a brisk walk in the crisp cold air it occurred to her to wonder where Lisa was.

It was not the first time that Lisa had disappeared without a word, but it had been a long time since she had done it. Not since Dinsmore Collette had finally taken himself away had it happened, Coralie recalled. Always after some terrible clash, it was Lisa's method of punishing people, to disappear, and well Coralie knew that she was the one who was being punished now. Only would Lisa have stayed so long if she had known what a relief this little time of quiet was to the girl just now? And how glad she was to be rid of Errol Hunt as an accompaniment to every evening?

Coralie sighed as she thought how all too brief would the respite probably be. If she had gone to some house party, or up to a mountain resort where winter sports were beginning, they would not last forever, and Lisa would return, either to bleed her somehow for money, or to spring some unpleasant surprise of a new marriage, perhaps. And when she came Coralie would have to be on the alert.

She thought with relief of her invitation to the Shannons's. The week ends were always worst, and if Lisa did not return until then she would have a refuge. Was it supposable that if she stayed away often enough from Lisa's evenings that Errol Hunt might seek other pastures?

But if she should come sooner where should she find haven? She could not bear the thought now of ever companying again with the crowd that frequented her home. Something had happened since Dana had come into her life, and his friend Bruce, that had changed her. She wanted to get away from all that had gone before.

"I would tell you how He changed my life completely," sang the words of Dana's song as if in answer to her thoughts. Was it that that had come to her? No, she had no right yet, surely, to count herself among those who felt the confidence of having Jesus Christ as their friend. Bruce had said God loved her, and was ready to save her, and she had only to believe, but she wasn't sure she knew yet what believing was. It all seemed too simple!

Still something had come to her that had made her utterly dissatisfied with her former way of living, and she could not settle down even for a morning or an evening to amuse herself as she used to do. What was it?

There was another letter there from Dinsmore Collette when she returned from her walk. A short threatening letter. It sounded so like himself that it fairly made her tremble.

> So, you are hiding behind silence! If you do not answer within the next day or two I will find a way to make you answer.
>
> I understand that you are alone in the apartment while your mother is enjoying herself with her friends. If you prefer I will come to you while you are alone there and find a way to make you hand over what money I need. If, however, you choose to send me your check for five hundred at the above address by Friday afternoon I will say no more about it, and will see that you have no further trouble in the matter. These are not idle words. Remember I always keep my promises.
>
> Your loving stepfather,
> Dinsmore.

Horror of horrors, the address was nearby. She could not, she simply *could not* remain here!

Well, he would not come tonight. He would likely wait till Friday, and if Lisa had not come then what should she do? She would not dare to stay here alone. Should she call on Dana to help? Tell him all about it? How she shrank from that!

And how did Dinsmore find out that Lisa was gone? There must be something in the papers that gave him the clue. He was never one who let anything get by. He always found out the things he wanted to know.

She rang for the papers to be brought her, yesterday's and today's, and searched them carefully. Lisa never did anything quietly. No move, however trivial, was allowed to pass without a dramatic touch to it. Yes, here it was! Lisa's picture in the midst of a sporty group on skis. Coralie hadn't realized that it was late enough for skiing, but in Canada, of course. That was a two-year-old picture but that wouldn't bother Lisa. The descriptive column that followed the picture noted a dozen or more of Lisa's friends who were in the party, and of course Errol and Ivor were of the number.

She turned from the paper with a sneer of scorn on her lips. Lisa, her mother, hurrying around to sport her beauty everywhere in the limelight. Poor Lisa! No! She couldn't tell Dana all about their mother. Dana who loved his father so much would feel it too keenly. No, she must avoid telling Dana if possible all about this terrible stepfather, who had disappeared and now had come back, unwanted and unheralded. Oh, how terrible life could be!

Still, it would always be possible to call to Dana for help. She must think out some plan and get ready in case she got too frightened.

But the next morning as she contemplated another grim silent day full of horrible possibilities her heart shrank and at times she was almost ready to call up some of her old friends and go a-pleasuring. Not that there was any particular thrill in anything she knew the rest of her erstwhile group would be doing, but anything, anything would be better than waiting here alone for Dinsmore, or Errol.

But no, she dared not go out alone now, for fear that man would be on the lookout for her. Then her eye would fall on her new Bible and her look would soften and lose its desperation, and she would settle to read once more.

Not that she understood all of what she read of course. The brief explanations at the foot of the pages were in such unknown phrases that she scarcely comprehended what they were meant to convey sometimes. Yet through it all she gathered the thought of a God who had made people because He wanted them, and loved them, bad as they had become, and wanted them to be good. And somehow it kept her reminded of her new brother, and his friend.

So she kept herself indoors that day, reading, idling about, putting her small affairs in order, and her private papers in such shape that no stepfather, or even mother could find them and gain any inkling of how much she had, or where it was kept. She arranged matters so that if she was called upon by circumstances to go away suddenly she would leave no telltale papers behind, and would not find them too bulky to carry. She hunted out a suitable little innocent-looking leather handkerchief case in which to carry them, and camouflaged the whole with collars and handkerchiefs in such a way that no searcher would suspect they were there. All this occupied several hours of a day that in spite of her prolonged reading began to hang heavy on her hands.

So it was with great joy that late in the afternoon she

heard Bruce's voice over the telephone, calm, assured, friendly.

"Hello! Are you all right? And could you possibly spare time to take dinner and give me at least a part of your evening tonight?"

Could she? Oh, how joyously she would accept that invitation. Fear suddenly fled from her, and a new kind of joy took its place. She was going to see Bruce again, and could ask him a great many questions. He had come back to New York, and New York suddenly seemed safe and sane again.

"Oh, yes. I'll love to accept," she said eagerly.

"You're sure I'm not interfering with any plans of your own?"

"Oh, no!" she said with a great relief in her voice. "I had no plans. Lisa is away, and annoying things have happened. I'll be so glad to come. And I want to thank you for the beautiful Bible. I love it. I never had one before."

"Oh, did it reach you? I'm glad you like it."

"May I bring it along and ask you some questions?"

"I wish you would. I'll find a quiet place somewhere where we can talk after dinner. How soon may I call for you? Is six o'clock too early?"

"No indeed. I'll be ready."

After that there was no more loneliness. Her heart was fairly singing with pleasure. She was glad he was coming early and they could get away before there was danger of someone calling. Or there was always the possibility of Lisa's return, and then there would be questionings. Somehow she didn't want this first call of Bruce's spoiled by anything like that. Lisa could be so disagreeable when she chose, and she would surely choose this time, if she came and discovered him there. Coralie had no illusions about the unpleasant scene that would surely take place when Lisa returned. She had probably thought it out carefully in every detail, with a purpose of breaking her daughter's will, as she had always been able to break it before this. Coralie knew that Lisa had by no means given up the idea of getting what money she needed from her. And there would be more gambling debts probably, added to the old ones. Lisa would not have been away these days with her special crowd without new gambling debts, and expenses for travel and hotel bills. She sighed as she hurried about her room getting ready to go out with Bruce. Money! What a trouble it was. Both mother and disowned stepfather trying to make her give up what her own father had been able to save for her! Oh! But they never should. It was not worth so much trouble except that it was precious because her father had left it to her, and never, never would she let them have it. It was a sacred trust that she must keep. If Lisa was ever in need she would care for her, but it should not go for dishonorable debts.

Joyously she prepared for the simple outing. She dressed in a plain brown suit with a short brown fur jacket to match, and never stopped to notice how exquisitely the fur collar brought out the soft tinting of her cheeks, the color of her eyes and hair, nor knew what a pretty picture she had made of herself.

The Bible had a case of leather like its cover. Simple, plain, like any handbag of soft leather. It would not be conspicuous anywhere. She tucked her purse and handkerchief inside the case, and laid her gloves close at hand, ready at a moment's notice.

She had packed her bag to go to Valerie's that morning, and the case with her valuable papers was well hidden under her garments. She took the precaution to put the bag far back in her closet, behind more elaborate suitcases. In case Lisa returned during her absence it would not be where she would be likely to look for it. Then she was ready, and she kept a close watch from her window.

She met him shining-eyed, and greeted his smile with one as radiant. Bella eyed them and wondered. Now who was this young man with the brilliant hair and the look of gladness in his eyes? Was Miss Corinne putting something over while her mother was away? The young man wasn't exactly shabby, yet he wasn't arrayed in quite the garb of the usual guests of the house. Well, it was none of her business, and he certainly was a good-looker. Besides, Miss Corinne had a hard time of it sometimes, and Bella herself wasn't keen on Errol Hunt. Why shouldn't the young lady play around with some-one interesting now and then?

So Bella watched the two away with satisfaction.

Bruce took her to a nice place he knew where the food was good and the people were of the quiet type. There was a large pleasant reception room which they had almost to themselves after dinner, and they took possession of two comfortable chairs near a lighted table and studied the new Bible to their hearts' content.

It was when they were on their way back to the apartment that Bruce spoke about the meeting Friday evening and asked if she would like to go again, saying that he knew Dana was to sing, and he would be glad to call for her unless she had some other escort.

"I certainly would!" she said eagerly. "I—there is something—someone I would like to avoid Friday eve-ning—and that will give me a good excuse to be away. You see, Lisa is away, and I'm not just sure when she is returning, and—I'm rather afraid of this person who might turn up. I suppose it's silly, but I'll be glad to be out."

He gave her a quick anxious glance and wondered.

"How about Saturday morning? Would he come then?"

"Oh, I think not, not in the morning. But anyhow I am spending the week end with Valerie Shannon so that is all taken care of."

"Yes?" he said questioningly, but smiled over the lilt in her voice. "You like Valerie?" he asked.

"Oh, I do!" said Coralie fervently. "She's not like any of the other girls I know. I would have liked to be born into a home like that."

"Yes," said Bruce, a gentle look coming into his eyes. "That is a wonderful home!"

After that he insisted on going up in the elevator with her, and lingered a minute or two at the door of the apartment, although he wouldn't come in.

"You're quite sure you are all right tonight?" he asked a bit anxiously as he heard the elevator coming.

"Oh yes, quite all right tonight," she said brightly, "and thank you so much for the lovely evening, and the instruction."

He smiled.

"All right! I'll see you Friday evening then," and he was gone.

Coralie went into her room and glanced about with a shrinking feeling. Bella had said that no one had called, so she felt fairly safe, but she would not light the lamp. If it should be that Dinsmore was keeping watch of the apartment, at least he should have no clue to knowing she was at home, unless perchance he had seen her enter down at the street door.

So she locked her door and then moved a heavy piece

of furniture in front of it. Of course that was silly, but she would sleep better for it.

Before eight o'clock the next morning she was awakened by the telephone at her bedside, and in quick alarm she answered it.

Then she recognized the voice.

"This is Valerie Shannon," it said blithely. "Excuse me for calling so early, but I wanted to get you before I leave for the office. You see, I met Bruce Carbury last night and he told me that you were going to be at our meeting Friday evening. I wonder why you couldn't just bring your overnight bag along to the meeting and then come on home with us afterward? It will be that much longer to have fun together. Can't you?"

"Oh, that will be wonderful!" said Coralie in wonder. "I'd love to come."

"Of course I'll have to be at the office Saturday morning for a little while, but you won't mind staying around the house with mother and the girls till I get home, will you?"

"Not a bit. I'll love it," she said eagerly, like a little girl.

Coralie lay there thinking it over after she had hung up. Now wasn't that beautiful? Was it the Lord who was working things out for her that way so that she needn't be afraid, or was it just Bruce Carbury? Perhaps the Lord working through Bruce, she thought shyly.

She drew a deep breath of relief and let her heart thrill with a real joy.

17

WHEN Bruce Carbury got back to his room he found Dana there ahead of him, ready to welcome him heartily.

"Well, Dana," said Bruce hanging up his hat and coat and dropping into a chair, "I don't know what you'll say to me. I've been out with your sister all the evening. Had dinner and a good long talk afterward. If you don't like it you'd better say so, because I'm tremendously interested in her, and I'm liable to go out with her again. In fact she's promised me to go to the meeting tomorrow night. So speak your mind."

"Hop to it, Bruce my lad," said Dana fervently. "There's nobody I'd sooner trust her with. Only I must in conscience warn you. I don't believe she's very dependable, and if she's anything like her mother she's got ways with her. I wouldn't like to see you get your heart broke, old man." He gave his friend a comical look, with a keen question behind it.

Bruce smiled.

"It hasn't gone that far yet, fella," he said, "but I wouldn't be surprised if you are going to be very much mistaken about that girl, Dana. To tell you the truth, I believe she's *saved!*"

"Bruce! You don't mean it! So soon!"

"Man, it doesn't take long for the Lord to save a soul, you know."

"But—does she understand? Is it real?"

"She understands," said Bruce solemnly, with a lovely light in his eyes. "We've been talking all the evening, and if I ever saw a soul accept the Lord and be born again, it was tonight."

"Praise the Lord!" said Dana in amazement. "I've been praying for this but I guess I had a very weak faith. I certainly didn't expect an answer to my prayers very soon. I thought the Lord had a long way to go to bring my sister to Himself. Well, Valerie told me last night it was going to be a case of the nobleman's son being healed at the seventh hour."

Bruce smiled understandingly. "Probably it's always the seventh hour when God does wonders."

"I guess so, brother. I sure am glad you went after my sister, and the Lord used you to save her. Now perhaps I can have a little faith to pray for my mother. It has almost seemed as if it wasn't worth while, as if it might be a waste of time. Well, now, fella, tell me all about it!"

So they sat and talked, those two, going over every bit of the story, from the time when Bruce had come on Coralie weeping in the Pennsylvania Station, and she had asked him how to be saved. And as they talked they seemed to feel the presence of their Master in the room, and to grow nearer to Him and to one another.

As they rose from their knees Dana took his friend by the hand warmly.

"I shall never cease to thank God that He sent you along to New York at this time. If I'd come alone I should probably have gone on my way back the next day and left my mother and sister to their own devices, concluding that they were beyond saving. I'm just beginning to learn what a bounder I've been. Thank the Lord He sent you with me! If my people are saved I'll have you to thank for it, under God."

"Don't kid yourself, Dana. You wouldn't have left this little old town, not even if you'd been here alone, till you'd turned every stick and stone to do all you could to get hold of your folks! For it was God's seventh hour, you know, and He was guiding you. But I'm glad God let me have a hand in it; for it's been wonderful. Come now, let's get some sleep or we'll be all haywire tomorrow."

And on the other side of the city across the street from Lisa's apartment, there lurked her erstwhile husband, Dinsmore Collette, taking careful note of every light on every floor of the great building.

Not that Lisa was living in the same apartment where he had left her. She had moved almost at once after his departure. But he knew her habits. In fact he knew one of her servants, the butler, who had been with her for years, and who was one of those who liked to keep in an attitude favorable to receiving occasional tips from anybody.

Dinsmore Collette had not understood before his marriage that Lisa's fortune was forfeit if she married. She had carefully guarded that fact even for some time after their marriage, but in due time, of course it had come out, and he discovered the truth, that on their wedding day practically all of her money had automatically passed into the trust fund belonging to her daughter. Of course until the daughter should come of age, there was a fair amount of the money held in trust by her mother for the child's expenses, as well as an allowance for her own maintenance as guardian. And at first Lisa had cleverly made it appear to Collette that these monies were from her own fortune. So it was a good many months before Collette discovered that he had not married a wealthy woman, and by that time Lisa had also been disillusioned about her husband. After that there were continual battles about money. They always ended in Lisa going to her child and advising her to purchase some new and delightful luxury, the price of which Lisa enlarged to suit her own needs.

But Dinsmore Collette wanted money and he wanted plenty of it. He wasn't going to be satisfied with the mere pittance that could be bullied and deceitfully purloined from a little girl's plentiful allowance. He wanted the bountiful fortune that Lisa used to have before she married him, so he had sought it in the form of a richer woman, not quite so handsome as Lisa, but far wealthier, and taken himself to far lands, quite out of the picture for the time being.

But having heard by some underworld wireless system of his own that Jerrold Barron had left this world, and knowing well that there were crooked ways a-many and crooked lawyers to walk those ways, and since the oriental lady had not turned out to be so easily won as he had hoped, he had returned to see what he could make out of his step-child's fortune.

He had taken a room in a great building across the street from the apartment house where Lisa lived, and from time to time that evening he took his way around the block; taking into account the lighted windows on each floor, and interpreting signs that he knew well, which told him whether the dwellers over there were at home or away, and whether there were guests making revelry.

Finally he walked into the building and took the elevator up to the apartment. Bella met him with her mistress' carefully directed word, and returned from down the hall with the report that Miss Corinne was asleep. He thought a moment and then decided he would do better to wait until the time he had set, and departed without leaving his name.

Several times since he came to New York he had entered into discreet conversation with the butler, but as yet he had not been able to discover whether the rumors concerning a new foreign admirer of noble lineage were true or not. If they were he meant to make Lisa sweat blood for daring, while he was still alive, to smile on anyone else. Not that he still had illusions about Lisa, either financially or sentimentally, but he had a bitter jealous nature that would not brook an insult. It was the cause of his frequently, during his eventful life, being sought after by a much-feared long-eluded justice.

Now that he had come back to see what could be done about the Barron fortune, he knew that he must go cautiously and understand fully the situation about Lisa, his former wife, or he might make some mistake and ruin the whole thing. As he remembered it the girl, Corinne, would come in for something pretty handsome in the way of property, especially if the decree about the bulk of her mother's former portion going to her still held. Of course it might just be that Lisa had succeeded in getting back that property since he had been away. In which case he must move very carefully, so that if possible there would be no further financial losses.

But having concluded that the time was not ripe for him to make himself known at the apartment, and noting that the hour was late for any likelihood of further developments, he at last betook himself to sleep.

Tomorrow night was the time he had set in his letter to Corinne. It might be that even as late as the afternoon mail a check might come from the girl, and it would be so much safer and better to get at least that much money first, for he really was in need of it at once.

So he repaired to his own apartment, taking the precaution to have a goodly assortment of liquors sent up, and prepared to bide his time and give his step-daughter plenty of opportunity to respond to his request.

But Coralie, unaware of the net that was being cautiously spread in the way of her young feet, slept happily through the night, and awoke when the day was young, filled with pleasure over the visit she was to make, and the company she was to be in over the week end.

Quite early she went out to a nearby flower shop and pleased herself by selecting a box of flowers to send to Mrs. Shannon. She had a good time choosing them. She didn't simply order by the dozen, a dozen roses or carnations. She picked them out individually. First a layer of spicy carnations, pink and white and a very deep crimson; then a layer of tea rose buds like coffee and cream; a handful of African daisies in pastel shades peering tropically from the midst of them; then, nestling at the foot of the longer stems a mass of deep purple sweet violets and three gardenias. The whole was breath-taking in its loveliness. Coralie felt that she had never enjoyed buying flowers so much before in her life, and she paused to look at them and think of the sweet old lady who would open them. Not an old lady, really, just elderly, with soft gray hair in a plain old-fashioned knot in her neck, and a look of sweet motherliness about her. Oh, if Lisa could have been like that, and she could have called her "Mother" the way Valerie did her mother. "Mother dear!"

But if Lisa had been like that she wouldn't have had

that smooth baby complexion, and that hard glint in her eyes. One couldn't have motherliness without any mother-lines in her face. What would it have been to have had a mother like that?

And then there came a passing wonder about what Lisa was doing now, off in the Canadian snowy regions. Having a good time of course. Lisa never went anywhere without that. But how did she get the money to go? Lisa simply could not get along without plenty of money to throw around as she pleased, even if she took it away from her own child, and Coralie had made certain she could not do that this time.

Then suddenly as she looked around her, walking through the empty rooms of the apartment, Coralie noticed a lack. Something was gone that made the place look strange. Something that had been a part of the place so long that she hadn't realized it was gone except for the emptiness. What was it that had stood there—and there—each side of the tall mirror that dropped irregularly and erratically in zigzag blocks at one end of the big reception room? Ah! She knew now! Two heathen gods, hammered priceless creatures of old silver, set with strange winking lights done in jewels. Had Lisa parted with those? She had often heard her say that they were her costliest possession! Ugly distorted countenances, with wide screaming mouths, and forked jewel-tipped tongues. Wild wicked jeweled demon eyes and frenzied limbs twisted in the anguish of the lost. Coralie had always hated them, and turned away from them.

But Lisa had rejoiced in them. She had called them her gods, and said she would never part from them.

She had won them in some kind of a wild orgy-like contest, and boasted of how many had given almost all they had for them and lost. As a child Coralie had wept at sight of them, and shuddered always when she passed them. They had symbolized for her that something in her mother that the child could never understand, an utter devotion to a kind of satanic influence that prevented and circumvented anything like love, or gentleness, or devotion.

Coralie paused as she stared at the empty spaces where these heathen creatures had been so long, appalled. What did it mean? Had Lisa sold them? Was it possible that she had found something greater than these her gods to worship? Or perhaps she had merely loaned them somewhere for a good sum, for the time being, intending to redeem them.

But it appalled her, because it made her see how determined Lisa was to get money.

In the midst of her meditations came Lisa's lawyer, wanting Lisa. He glared at Coralie when she assured him that Lisa wasn't there, and she wasn't sure just when she would return. He said that she had written demanding instant service, and now she was away and he had many questions to ask. He wanted to know where Dana was.

This was the first intimation that Coralie had that Lisa was about to put Dana through the third degree to get more money from him. She suddenly felt a great pity for him. What must he think of a mother who would descend to such things? And yet, it had never come to her mind to criticize Lisa in this way before. She had no idealism concerning mothers to judge from.

The lawyer was standing grimly surveying her.

"Where is this son, then?" he questioned. "Won't you call him in? I would like to talk to him."

"He does not live here," said Coralie quietly. She got rid of the lawyer at last, telling him she knew nothing about Lisa's affairs and he would have to wait till her return.

When he was gone she went and read her new Bible awhile, but underneath the attention she was giving to the Book she found a constant clamor of questions. What was going to happen next? If Lisa made trouble with Dana did she want to be mixed up in it? Could she get away somewhere out of it all? It was unthinkable that Lisa would strike Dana for more money that she might marry Ivor. Oh, Lisa was heartless of course! She would not have been Lisa if she weren't. She would have stayed with her husband and brought up her children as other women did. Coralie sighed. Oh, if she only had! She would have had a normal home like other girls, and a wonderful father such as Dana had. She wouldn't have had a lot of bad habits that must be broken if she wanted to make herself fit to associate with her brother and his friends. Now here she was hampered by gnawing desires. Drinking and smoking were not compatible with the new life she was considering. She could not help seeing that girls like Valerie Shannon did not do such things. Since that evening she had gone to church with Dana and Bruce she had smoked very little, only when her nerves grew frantic for it, and she had not drank at all. But it was not easy, and she sensed that the future held for her a terrible struggle if she really decided to be different. Perhaps one could be saved and still smoke, or even drink a little now and then, but those things just didn't belong in a saved life. She could see that without being told, and she wished with all her heart that she had grown up without them.

The morning was a disturbing one, and in spite of her pleasant anticipations of the evening, and the week end that was to follow, she found an uneasiness creeping into her thoughts continually, until as the time drew near for Bruce to come for her, she was almost too restless to sit down. She kept wandering from one room to another, starting at every sound, fearful lest Lisa would arrive just as she was leaving and try to hinder her. If she had known how to reach Bruce she would have gone somewhere else and told him to meet her there.

She had given careful directions to the servants to be expecting Lisa home that week end, for she felt intuitively that that would be Lisa's next move, and glad indeed she was to be away when she arrived.

So she hovered anxiously about until Bruce arrived, and the glad lighting of relief in her eyes made his own heartbeats quicken, and almost frightened him. He mustn't let his personal interest be caught. She was lovely, but she was not the kind of girl who would be interested in him, even if he were sure of her. Yet it warmed his heart which had often been lonely, to have her glad to see him.

They went out into the pleasant evening, he carrying her overnight bag, she regulating her steps to his, and as he drew her hand within his arm he looked down, and she looked up, and a smile passed between them that bore something of a great gladness and promise in spite of all reason or thought, just gladness and a sense of both belonging to God in a special way.

It was pleasant to get back to the mission and see some of the same faces she remembered from the week before, to give an answering smile to shy greetings from this one and that, to be recognized as belonging to the young preacher's crowd, to sit up near the front this time and be able to watch Dana's face as he sang. To get that thrill of belonging to him, his sister! To hear Bruce sing and realize that he had a great deep voice too, and to catch his glance as he came down from the platform.

Maybe some of her erstwhile companions would wonder that she could get a thrill just from a religious service. But it was true! She was having a good time, with not a dance nor a drink nor a smoke in sight the whole evening.

Of course, she admitted to herself, it was a new experience. But somehow she couldn't imagine it palling upon her as the amusements of her crowd had been doing of late. She felt as if she had waked up suddenly and found that life was interesting, though she had been thinking for some time now that the sooner she was done with it the better.

The meeting was even more fascinating than the week before, the message about salvation was very clear and helpful, and she watched with amazement as a poor old sodden woman of the baser sort came forward of her own accord and accepted Christ as her Saviour. It was a tremendous experience, watching her contrition, her overpowering joy that God loved her, a poor fallen sinful creature. Coralie had never been where thoughts and feelings were analyzed and called by their true names, where sin was sin and not a laughing matter. It made her feel akin to the old sinner kneeling there with Valerie beside her, pointing the way. It showed her many things in her own heart just like those things in the older sinner's life. She listened and rejoiced that the old woman had found her Lord at last after all the sorrowful years.

And then a strange thought came to her. Suppose this were Lisa kneeling here, weeping over her sins! She had no doubt that Lisa's heart, and her own, held things as sinful as ever the old woman had harbored. But suppose Lisa could be changed, "saved" as they called it. Would it make a difference in her? But, would Lisa ever be willing to acknowledge she had sinned? She turned from the question perplexedly, with a kind of queer little longing such as she had never felt before, and a hopelessness, too, for Lisa never had been willing to acknowledge herself in the wrong. She probably would take that attitude with God, also.

After the meeting they had a happy evening at the house, Dana and Bruce coming back with them of course. They sang and later made Welsh rarebit, and had a jolly time generally. If the group with which she usually companioned could have looked in on her they would have been surprised to see how well Coralie fitted in. For it seemed to her that this atmosphere of love and simple cheer was something for which she had always been longing.

It was late when they broke up that night and the two young men went home, Kirk and Ranald walking part way with them for company.

It was a new experience to Coralie to room with a Christian girl who knelt to pray at night before lying down to sleep. Coralie watched her for a moment kneeling there so sweetly in her simple white robe, and then she slipped softly out of bed and knelt beside her. Valerie put out a loving hand and clasped hers as they knelt there side by side. Then after some minutes, Valerie broke the silence with a soft petition.

"Dear Father in Heaven, I thank Thee for this new friend. May our coming together be to Thy glory, and may our fellowship be blest. Grant that Coralie may find great joy in the Lord Jesus. We ask it in His name."

And Coralie breathed softly "Amen" as she had heard people in the meeting do. Amen had never meant a thing to her before, but now it seemed to mean a great deal.

Morning came all too soon, and Coralie woke up to the unusual excitement of seeing that big loving family come awake and start each other off for the day.

Valerie did not have to go until nine o'clock, so they had a pleasant time together for a little while, washing and wiping the pretty old delicate china, some of which had come from Scotland, and some from Ireland. Then they put it up in its places in the quaint old corner cupboards, which a beloved grandfather, a skilled cabinet maker, had made. The Shannons were very proud of these ancestral pieces.

When Valerie went away to the office Coralie donned a borrowed apron and went into the kitchen to be taught how to get lunch. They were going to make real old Scotch scones, and oatmeal bannock. Coralie hadn't the slightest idea what they were but she was greatly intrigued to learn.

The morning went swiftly, Coralie watching everything that went on. She had never realized before that cooking could be a fine art. At least Mrs. Shannon made it appear so. There was bread set, and during the course of the morning it was flipped out in a springy mass onto a marble topped table and molded into smooth loaves, then set to rise again in nice shiny sheet-iron pans. There was pot roast slowly simmering in the great kettle on the back of the stove, getting itself ready for the dinner that night. And there were pies, a whole row of them ready to go in the oven, apple pies and pumpkin pies. It fascinated her to see how they were made.

And all the time that Mrs. Shannon was skillfully building them and fashioning fragile covers with little slits in them where the cinnamon could look through, and pinching lovely flutes in the crust-rims, they were talking. Mrs. Shannon knew so well how to bring out what was in a young heart. So many years she had guided young feet along slippery ways, and so tenderly did her heart yearn over dear girls with life all before them, that she soon understood all about Coralie, although Coralie didn't dream how much she was telling in her few little revealing sentences.

So they got on beautifully together, and Coralie wished more and more that Lisa had been a mother like this one. (How Lisa would have sneered at the thought.) She couldn't help wondering whether if Lisa hadn't had any money at all, she wouldn't have settled down to do nice pleasant things for her family, like making pies and setting pretty tables. How nice and cosy that would have been!

Then the family began to drift in from everywhere, getting back from work and study and conferences and music lessons and basket ball practice and all the various things that the Shannons engaged in, coming home to Saturday lunch! How pleasant!

Last of all Valerie came hurrying in apologizing for being late. Mr. Burney had asked her to take an important letter that had to get off at once.

Coralie sat down with the rest, a smudge of flour on one cheek, and a little flush of triumph on both of them, because she had achieved the baking of a set of scones all by herself.

Her flowers were on the table, glorifying it. And the family all took her in just as if she were one of them. Even Turla and Leith demanded to know if she could play basket ball, and offered to get her tickets for the high school game.

After the lunch dishes were out of the way, at which they all helped, Valerie whipped up a luscious caramel cake for the evening, when she said Dana and Bruce were coming to practice a song for the Sunday service. And then the two girls went upstairs and Valerie gave Coralie a lesson in knitting, with the idea of making a sweater she very much admired. After which they took a brisk walk downtown to purchase needles and wool.

Coralie had a feeling as she came back with her fat bundle under her arm, as if she were really beginning to amount to something at last. She was determined to knit a whole dress like Valerie's. It might take her years but she knew it was going to be fun.

At dinner the pot roast was good, tender as could be, and tasting so much better because Coralie felt that she knew just how it had been brought to perfection. Mrs. Shannon had let her stir the thickening up and make the gravy. She felt as if she had accomplished a great feat, something like making the world, or fashioning a dress. There was a wonderful thrill to her in finding out how common everyday things were done and being able to say she had helped. She told it to Dana triumphantly that evening when he came.

"I've learned how to make scones and thicken gravy," she said joyously. She looked up at Dana sweetly as if she were glad he belonged to her, and she had a right to boast to him. Dana too felt a thrill as he watched her sweet young beauty, and thought how proud and glad his father would have been if he could see her now.

"And perhaps he does," he said softly to himself with a tender look coming over his face and touching the smile on his lips, till suddenly Coralie leaned over and grasped his hand with a quick little clasp.

So! After all, was he going to have a sister?

18

CORALIE went back to the apartment after lunch Monday.

She had lingered a little while to help Mrs. Shannon, watching the process of the Monday wash, being initiated into the mysteries of washing machines and ironing machines, partly because it fascinated her, but more than that because she dreaded to go back.

She was very sure that Lisa would be home by this time and she dreaded meeting her.

It was a very sweet talk she had with Mrs. Shannon. She asked her questions that she would have asked Lisa long ago if Lisa had been the kind of woman who was wise. Then she asked her wistful questions about God and prayer. There was something so gentle and tender in this good woman's way of explaining life that she sat at her feet and enjoyed every word she said. Coralie felt as if her soul had got home after a stormy voyage, and it was great to be able to trust and ask unafraid.

So she lingered and ate of the delicious soup that had been simmering on the stove all the morning, and proudly washed the few dishes herself, putting them away carefully, feeling that she had done something worth while for the first time in her life.

Then wistfully she said good-bye, cherished the warm hug and kiss that came from a loving mother-heart, and went back to what she called home, though she had now learned it never had been a home at all.

She took a long way around, and stopped on the way to make a few trifling purchases, putting off her arrival at the apartment until late in the afternoon.

She knew as soon as she got out of the elevator that Lisa was back and that she had brought guests with her. Both guest rooms seemed to be occupied.

Encountering Bella on her way to her room she found that Lisa had returned on Sunday with several guests and had held revelry until after daylight that morning, but was now still asleep.

Coralie's heart sank. This was what she had feared. It was not the first time this had happened and the girl dreaded the evening when the revelers would waken and begin again. She knew it would be a great contrast to the last few days, and she shuddered at the thought.

Bella did not know just who were the guests, though she admitted that Mr. Kavanaugh had been there till dawn, and she thought he was returning to dinner. The ladies in the guest rooms were strangers who had come down from Canada with the party.

Coralie paused at her door, giving uncertain glances up the hall, but all was quiet so far. She wondered whether she ought not to slip away again somewhere and get out of all this, but where could she go? Not back to Shannons' after such a prolonged stay, even after all their kindly hospitality. That would never do so soon again. Of course she might go to a hotel, but since her stepfather had arrived in the city in such a mood she was afraid to take refuge in a hotel where he might trace her. It was really Dinsmore's threatening notes, two more of which she found on her desk, that frightened her beyond anything. Perhaps she ought to send some word to Dana. He had a telephone now, and that was a comfort. She could call him up if she needed him.

So she ordered a tray early, before dinner was anywhere near ready, and before any of the people were stirring about. She told Bella she was tired and did not want to be disturbed during the evening, and did not want it known that she had returned, unless Lisa should ask for her.

There was this difference between the Coralie who had come home this Monday evening and the girl who had gone out Friday evening. She had learned how to pray in the meantime.

So now after Bella had left her she locked her door and knelt down for guidance and help. And she prayed for Lisa too. For the first time it occurred to her that she could pray for Lisa, and just put the whole matter in the hands of her Heavenly Father.

She had taken the precaution to pull the shades down, covering the window completely before she lighted a single lamp, for the address Dinsmore Collette had given was too near at hand for her to run any risks, and her experience with the man had taught her that he would not stop at anything to carry his point. Therefore she searched her room and closets most carefully before she settled down to eat the supper Bella brought, and locked her door again. She would take no more chances than were necessary. Would she have to tell Lisa about those letters Dinsmore had written? Perhaps that would bring Lisa to her senses, to discover that he was not dead as she had been told. Perhaps it would cause her to send away Ivor Kavanaugh for the present at least.

But there would be no opportunity to tell her tonight since there were guests in the house, and more returning to dinner. There would be more festivity tonight. It was no time to tell Lisa of danger and trouble when she was drinking.

So Coralie finished her brief supper, and putting on a severely plain black satin so that she might be fit to go out in case it became necessary, gave Bella the tray, and then locked herself into her room again, turning out even the little bedside light. Perhaps she could get through the evening without their knowing she was at home.

She threw herself down on her bed. The noises of the city drifted in the window which she had opened a few inches, a radio droned not far away, gay voices floated up from the street, a fire siren screamed, the engine tore past, and so the whirl of life went on, while Coralie lay and thought out all that had been happening to her the past few days, trying to think her life through from its beginning, to a wider fuller way with Heaven at the end. Was it thinkable that Lisa would ever find God?

Over and over it all she went, and back to the same question again.

The sounds in the street changed. Hurrying feet and languid voices passed on and there came lighter footsteps, and laughter. People seeking rest and amusement, people going home to rest.

Then there came distinct though subdued sounds from the other side of the apartment. Footsteps toward the dining room. Elevators rumbling. A light laugh now and then. There! That was Lisa's voice! Was she coming down the corridor? No, she had gone on to the dining room. But there was her voice again, from farther away. Talking in that high excited unnatural tone that always succeeded a night of drinking. Oh, well did Coralie know the shades of contempt, of scorn, of even hatred that could sound in that voice, that should have been dearer to her than any other earthly voice, and was not. She would not dare approach her in such mood to tell her of Dinsmore Collette's presence in the city, his threatenings. She knew such approach could only bring the worst possible reaction and forestall any possible precaution.

So she lay and suffered through the hours.

She knew just when they left the dining room, and went to the reception room. She held her breath lest any would come her way, hoping against hope that Bella had not told them she had returned.

But no one came, and by and by between fear and prayer she drifted off to sleep.

Sometime in the night, she did not know how late it was, she heard a piercing scream.

She started up and stared around in the dark room, wondering if it had been a dream.

And then it came again, louder, more fraught with crazy terror. It was Lisa!

Coralie sprang to her feet and dashed toward the door, snapping back the bolt and flinging the door wide. Something awful must have happened. Lisa was in some terrible trouble!

She fled down the corridor toward the main hall, and then the scream came again, more terrific, more blood-curdling than before. Someone must be doing something terrible to Lisa!

The great reception room ran the full length of the hall. It had originally been two rooms, but Lisa who

loved palatial mansions had had the partition taken out
and made one mammoth room of it. The door to the
back part which had originally been a library, stood open
now, and was nearest her as she sped breathlessly along.
Before she reached it she could catch a glimpse of Lisa
through the door, standing in huddled fright, looking
with terror toward the far end of the room. Her hands
gripping one another were pressed to her breast and her
eyes were wide with fear. Just a step beyond her Ivor
Kavanaugh stood holding out with uncertain hand a
wine glass filled with wine, but he too was looking with
suddenly startled eyes toward the other end of the room.

Coralie swung close to the door now, where she
could see what they were looking at, and with quick
constriction of her heart she recognized the man who
stood there as her stepfather, Dinsmore Collette. Then
with horror she saw that in his hand he held a pistol,
pointed straight at Lisa. His eyes were dark with a look
of jealousy and hatred so great that it almost looked like
insanity. In that instant he fired, and it seemed to Coralie
that the sound of that shot went through her very being,
as she saw Lisa fall with another scream that died away
into a sudden awful silence. And then, too quick almost
for comprehension, she saw Ivor drop the glass of wine
and flash out another pistol.

The two reports of the guns were almost simultaneous. Ivor fired and suddenly slumped, his body sway-
ing, tottering, and falling away toward a little table filled
with bottles and glasses, bringing it down with him and
about him in dreadful confusion.

And when her frightened eyes caught a glimpse of the
other end of the room she saw Dinsmore lying prone
with a scarlet spot rapidly widening above his heart.
Then the scattering guests hid the view and she flew into

the room toward Lisa, lying there so still and white and beautiful.

Someone made a wild dash to the door as she entered, and shoved her rudely aside in his madness, cursing under his breath as he passed her. A long time afterward, or so it seemed, she recognized that cursing voice as Errol's, but when she looked about for him later he was nowhere in sight. He had made good his escape, leaving Ivor, his supposed uncle, lying still as death upon the floor. But Coralie, with white face, was kneeling on the floor beside Lisa, searching with trembling hand for sign of a heartbeat, and these things passed her mind as ugly dreams that did not fully register.

Afterwards she discovered that Bella, terribly frightened, had taken things in her own hands and telephoned for her brother who was a policeman, and presently the room was swarming with grim-faced men in uniform, asking questions of the guests who still remained, who had been startled into semi-soberness.

She saw them kneel beside Dinsmore and shake their heads, but when she looked again they were carrying him away, whether dead or alive she did not know. It was enough for the present that he was gone.

She was wildly trying to lift Lisa in her arms now, for somehow the sight of her helpless loveliness reached something in her heart that Lisa in her scornful blithesomeness had never touched. This was her mother, lying here, with blood spreading slowly out over the white brocade of her delicate frock, and her golden beautiful hair that had always been arranged so carefully, mussed and lying low on the floor. Oh, was Lisa dead?

She remembered how they had prayed for Lisa that Sunday night at Shannons', and how she had let her mind picture what it would be if Lisa could be saved, and change her way of living, could perhaps grow loving and motherlike. While they were praying it had all seemed too impossible ever to happen. But now the thought came to her with a great throb of regret. Oh, was it too late forever? Was Lisa dead?

Yet she did not seem dead. Her body was warm. Oh, was there nothing she could do to save her life, to have a chance perhaps even yet to tell her about Jesus who would save to the uttermost, who had saved even herself?

Then came Bella with the doctor. Coralie looked at her with a wan smile of gratitude. Good Bella.

The doctor knelt beside Lisa and examined her, and then looked up.

"No, she is not dead," he said in answer to the question in Coralie's frightened eyes. "Not yet."

He opened his case, and put something in a teaspoon, administering it drop by drop, till Lisa drew a brief breath and moaned.

"We must get her to her bed," said the doctor quickly. "Where is that maid?"

Then to Bella:

"Call my office and tell my nurse to come at once."

Coralie knelt beside Lisa and held her hand until the butler and the doctor lifted her and carried her to her room. Then she arose and looked wanly around her.

There lay Ivor, huddled in that ghastly heap on the rug only a few steps away! She gave him one frightened glance and hurried after Lisa, Lisa being carried so carefully, and lying limp and white with one beautiful arm falling down inertly at her side.

She was aware of men with measured tread coming after Ivor. She did not wait to look back. It was all a stark awful happening, shooting in their apartment! Three concerned in it. Lisa the cause of it all. Or was it Lisa?

Could it be that Dinsmore had truly cared for her, and to see her drinking intimately with Ivor had stirred his jealousy to all lengths? Perhaps Ivor was the cause. Oh, it was a terrible mess, and her heart sickened at it all.

Then it came to her sharply that she might have been concerned in it too, as definitely as Lisa, if Dana had never come. If she had never gone to the meeting, and if she had not talked with Bruce and found another way of life! She might, she probably would have been a part of it all!

But—ah—these were not real thoughts she was thinking. It was as if her mind had strayed away and snatched up this thought and that and tossed them into the dreadful vacancy of the moment. Perhaps she was to blame too. And Errol! What had become of him? Drunk, probably! Suppose she had been in that room drinking with the rest! Suppose she had been stupid with liquor!

She hurried to Lisa's room but Lisa was lying there like a broken lily in her sheath of white satin, with the awful crimson streak down the side that was blood, and that strange blank look on her face.

Lisa, her mother, who had run away from her home and her motherhood, and had made an imperious court for herself where she might have her own way! Now it had all ended by her lying broken and the room as still as death.

The nurse had come. She was going swiftly about making quiet preparations for the doctor, slitting down the costly dress that Lisa had been so pleased with when it came from the shop! Flinging the pieces in a heap on a paper on the floor, a discarded froth of white with that terrible crimson staining it!

Coralie stood at one side watching, shivering, in her little plain black satin frock, the tears running down unbeknownst to her, her hands gripping one another, her lips quivering.

Another nurse came in presently. The first nurse spoke to her in a low tone and then she came over to Coralie.

"They think if you would go in the other room and lie down it would be better," she said gently.

"No," said Coralie. "I must stay with Lisa till I know. Is she—"

"Yes, she's living," said the nurse and her voice was grave and dependable, "but—we can't tell the outcome yet until the doctor has made an examination. Can't I take you to your room?"

"No!" said Coralie. "No! I can't lie down! I must go and telephone someone. Then I will come back."

The nurse watched her go unsteadily out of the door. She turned and gave a sad little twisted smile toward the other nurse.

There were officers out in the hall but Coralie did not notice them as she went by. They were alien like the walls and the furniture. They did not mean anything to her yet except as something that had to be endured with all the rest.

As she stood in the hall by the telephone booth one of the officers walked behind her, hovered near her, but she was not noticing him. The door of the booth was propped open, but she did not trouble to release it. What difference did it make?

"Is that you, Dana? Oh, Dana! Something awful has just happened! Dinsmore Collette has shot Lisa! No, they say she isn't dead yet, but they don't know whether she will live or not. And there were two more. Dinsmore shot Ivor Kavanaugh, and Ivor shot Dinsmore. No, I don't know whether they were killed or not. They both fell down and lay very still. Yes, I saw it all! I had been asleep in my room when I heard Lisa scream, and I ran out and saw it all. . . . Oh, Dana! Can't you come? I'm so frightened. . . . What? . . . Yes, there are policemen here! . . . Yes, there is a doctor and two nurses. I don't know who sent for them, perhaps the butler, or the maid. . . . Yes, there were other people here, guests of Lisa's. They all seem to have gone."

She lifted tear-filled eyes and looked across the hall through the open doorway and noticed that Ivor was no longer lying on the floor. Where had they taken him?

The officer stepped closer as she hung up the receiver.

"You saw the shooting?" he asked severely.

"Yes," said Coralie.

"You knew the man? The men?"

"Yes, I knew who they were."

"Well, the chief will want to talk with you when he gets back."

She gave him a sad helpless look and went back to Lisa's room, but she found that the doctor had given orders that nobody should come in until he gave permission. So she stood sorrowfully leaning against the wall outside the door until Bella, passing that way, brought her a chair, and asked if there was anything she could do. Bella was frightened and tearful, and gave her a compassionate look.

"Tell me, Bella, when did Mr. Collette come in?" she asked in a low tone.

"I ain't just sure," said Bella. "I think he came up just a few minutes before the shooting. The butler would know. He saw him come in. Shall I ask him?"

"No," said Coralie with a weary sigh, leaning her head back against the wall, and partly closing her eyes. Then suddenly she opened them again.

"Are the guests all gone, Bella?"

"Yes, every one," said the girl with satisfaction. "And high time it was, too. Some of 'em went so fast they didn't take their overnight bags nor their wraps."

"And—what of the two—who—were shot?"

Bella gave her a startled, hard look.

"Oh, *them!*" she said with a shrug. "They've took them away."

"Away?" said Coralie with a strange puzzled look. "You mean—mean—?"

"They took that Mr. Kavanaugh to the morgue, but they took the other one to the hospital in the jail!" There was a kind of grim satisfaction in Bella's tone.

"Then—is—he still living?" There was shock in her voice.

"Oh, sure! He's a tough one, he is! Though they do say he won't likely last till morning. Still they weren't taking any chances!"

"But—how did they know—who did it?"

"Oh, the butler and we all told the chief, and anyhow the officer that stood behind you when you telephoned heard what you said. Besides, those officers ain't so dumb. There was the guns and there was the bullets, and the finger-prints and all. It didn't take much brains to see what had happened, even if the butler hadn't told them about his hanging round the place these several days. There! There's the elevator. I gotta go."

"Listen, Bella, if Mr. Barron or Mr. Carbury come, bring them right here to me, please."

It seemed ages before Dana arrived, and Bruce with him, and got through the cordon of police who seemed like a hedge about the apartment. As Dana put his arm comfortingly about her shoulder and gave her a tender sympathetic look, Coralie suddenly felt that she could not keep the tears back any longer.

Then Bruce's warm handclasp and earnest solicitude nearly broke her down again.

"Oh, it's so good to have you both here!" she sobbed softly. "It's been so dreadful!"

"You poor little girl!" said Bruce warmly.

"Dear little sister!" murmured Dana gently. "It must have been awful. But—how is she? Is there any hope at all?"

"Oh, I don't know yet," she quivered. "The doctor won't let anyone in the room yet. He has two nurses with him."

"Oh! Then they'll be doing everything possible!" said Dana with relief. "We've been praying all the way down. And now, hadn't you better tell us in just a few words how it all happened? Because if we're to hang around here we probably ought to understand. Will that be too hard for you?"

"Oh, no," said Coralie. "I'd rather tell you. It seems that the whole thing is locked up in my mind somewhere, and perhaps if I tell it I can get away from it a little. It seems as if my head is going to burst."

She pressed her hands frantically on her temples.

Dana drew her arm within his own, and Bruce walked on the other side, and together they went down the hall to the door where Coralie had first looked into the reception room.

The tears were coursing down her cheeks now and her face was very white, her eyes bright with excitement. She told the story vividly as they stood in the doorway, and she pointed out where Lisa had stood as she screamed, and where Dinsmore had stood with the pistol, and Ivor, unsteadily with his glass.

They sat down together on a handsome formal couch, Dana pushing aside a low table littered with half-filled glasses. The couch was large enough for them all. Coralie sat in the middle, and Dana and Bruce one on each side giving utmost attention, deep sympathy in their eyes. From time to time a policeman would stroll past the door, keeping careful watch without seeming to do so. The butler presently entered and began to gather up the clutter from the hasty exit of the frightened guests, taking away overturned tables and trays of glasses, and brushing up broken glass. But the three talked on in low sad tones, waiting, as death hovered in the offing.

Then all at once the nurse came quietly among them.

"It is over," she said quietly. "He has found the bullet. It was a very delicate operation. The shot had gone so near to the heart that it was a question if the bullet could be removed, but it is out at last, and she is resting. No, she has not regained consciousness, and of course it is a serious question whether she will be able to hold out. The next few days will decide that. It is a miracle that she was not killed instantly. And now the doctor says there is no reason why you should not go to bed and get a good sleep," she said turning to Coralie. "You look as if you needed it. Would you like me to go and help you get into your bed?"

"Oh, no, thank you," said Coralie. "I don't think I could sleep now."

"You'll have to," said the nurse calmly. "You'll need your strength later, and you must be ready. And there is no reason whatever why you should sit up now. You know there is no immediate danger, since she seems to have come through the operation well. Her pulse is all that could be desired, and we will of course watch her every minute, so you need not worry. I will have you called at once should there be the slightest change."

She looked with an appealing glance at the two young men for a seconding, and Dana spoke up at once.

"Of course you will go and rest, at least, Coralie, even if you cannot get to sleep," he said earnestly. "And we'll stay here tonight, anyway."

"Of course," said Bruce. "Something might be needed."

"I don't think that will be in the least necessary," said the nurse rather stiffly, eyeing the two severely. "The servants are here, you know."

Dana smiled sadly.

"I should say that the servants had had rather a strenuous night of it," he said, "and besides," he gave another wan little smile, "the woman who was hurt is my mother!" He looked the nurse in the eyes steadily.

"Oh!" she said, changing her severity into graciousness, "that makes it quite different, of course."

"Yes," said Dana. "Now, Coralie, go and rest at once. I'll have you called if there is the slightest necessity. I'll stay till I have to go to the office in the morning, and even then, if there is any reason why I am needed here I'll arrange to stay of course."

"Yes," said Bruce quietly, "and any time when he can't come I'll arrange to be here, so there will always be someone for you to call on if there is need."

"Oh!" said Coralie, her lip trembling into a ghost of a smile, "that will be wonderful of you both! I won't feel so lost if one of you is here."

So Coralie went back to her room, and the nurse to the sick room. The doctor presently left, and Bruce and Dana settled down in the great room, each finding a comfortable couch and turning the lights out till the room was lighted only by a distant hall lamp.

Perhaps neither of the two young men slept at all the

rest of the night, and Dana at least lay thinking of his beautiful mother. Would she live? And would God somehow speak to her heart?

Coralie lay in her bed staring at the night and thinking what a change had come in the little time since she had lain there before. She did not dare to sleep. She was fearful of the morning and what might come then, even though Dinsmore Collette was lodged in a prison hospital, and Ivor Kavanaugh, the other man of whom she had been so afraid, was lying dead. She shivered as she remembered him huddled on the floor, a broken wine glass by his side! How unready he had been to go from this world! How unready all of them were, for the matter of that!

If Dinsmore lived there would likely be a trial, and they would all have to testify. Perhaps there would be anyway. She knew so little about the law! How frightful it all was! Why did Dinsmore want to shoot Lisa? Did he really care enough about her to be jealous of Ivor drinking there beside her? Surely not that. Perhaps this was the revenge he had threatened if she did not send him the money! Oh, should she have sent it? Was all this awful happening her fault? And if Lisa died would she have killed her?

Then she remembered what Bruce had whispered to her as she left them for the night. Dana had been asking the nurse a few questions about Lisa's condition, and Bruce had taken her hand in a brief clasp and whispered:

"Remember the Lord knows all about it and is caring for you every minute. Remember He is close beside you through it all!"

Well, since that was so, she would just trust God for all the days that were to follow and rest back on that! Whatever was coming tomorrow could only come through His permission. Bruce had told her that the other day, and it came to her now with startling comfort, as if she heard his voice again speaking the words. How good it was to have a friend like Bruce Carbury who seemed to know just what was troubling her, and just what would comfort! How good it was to have a brother like Dana! And what would it have been to have had a father such as her own must have been?

Suddenly a new thought came. How good it was to have a God like their God, like *her* God, who loved her no matter what she had been!

The thought enfolded her like loving arms that held her close, and thus she drifted into sleep.

19

THE two young men were gone in the morning when Coralie woke up. They had talked with the nurse and found that Lisa was at least holding her own. They had left their telephone numbers so that they might be called at their offices if needed, and had promised to return, one of them at least, as soon as they could arrange matters.

Coralie was wan and white when she came on the scene. It had been hard for her to believe when she awoke that the happenings of the night before had been real, but when she met the nurse and heard the report from Lisa everything stood out vividly in her mind again, and she was suddenly sure of details she had not noticed last night. She could visualize where each person had sat as she had entered the room the night before, and now she went and looked in the door again. Then she turned away with a shudder as she remembered Ivor so utterly unalive as he lay on the floor, as if life must have been extinguished in him the instant that bullet touched him. How terrible! Murder right before her eyes. She had been afraid of him, she had dreaded him, but she had never wanted such an awful fate for him! Oh, he wasn't fit to die!

And then she thought of Dinsmore and wondered how it was with him this morning. Would he live? And would there have to be a lot of publicity, and a murder trial? Oh how fearful to think about. Poor Dana! And his friend Bruce. They had been so kind. And now if she got them into a thing like this! Oh, why had she called them while the police officers were here? She ought to have thought of them, to have protected them. Of course Dana's name wouldn't be known in New York, and most people knew her as Corinne Collette. They wouldn't connect her with the name of Barron, not unless some reporter got hold of it. Even then the few friends Dana had here in New York would understand. But Dana was so fine and sensitive he couldn't help but hate all that publicity, if the matter went to trial.

She was standing there sadly looking over that big empty tragic room when a hand was laid on her shoulder, and there stood Bruce beside her!

"Are you all right?" he asked anxiously, and suddenly her heart thrilled with his gentleness, his care for her.

She turned eagerly.

"Oh, yes, I'm all right," she answered with a catch in her voice. "I'm only thinking what a fool I was to get you and Dana into this terrible thing. I should have had my head about me."

"You did perfectly right," said Bruce warmly. "We wouldn't have wanted to remain out of it for anything. We would have chosen to be called at once, and to be here for at least a show of being your natural protectors."

"How sweet of you!" said Coralie, trying to stop the trembling of her lips. "But—I shouldn't have done it. And you mustn't feel that you must stay here all the time. It wouldn't be right at all. The nurse has been telling me that Lisa may be a long time hovering in this state, even if she rallies. She says her pulse is still very good, but there are so many complications that may follow a wound like this, and it depends so much on her own physical state, that it may be even weeks before we know whether she will live or die. Oh! Poor Lisa! How she would have hated all this. She never liked to be dependent. She wanted her own proud way. She liked to dominate every situation. But I hope you and Dana won't feel tied down to dance attendance on me till this is over. I couldn't bear to feel I was hampering you."

"You mustn't feel that way," said Bruce looking tenderly into her face with his nice brown eyes. "This is our trouble, not yours alone. We want to bear it with you. And Dana at least has a right to. She is his mother, no matter if she did not stay with him. He has a right to look out for her as much as possible, and to look out for you. And I, because he is my beloved friend, and because you are—well, because you are a child of my Father God, I claim the right to look out for you too, and to help in bearing all that this means to you." He suddenly took both of her little cold hands into his own and held them warmly, his eyes upon her face with a great lovely gentleness in them such as she had never seen in any face before.

"Oh!" she said. "Oh!" and suddenly laid her face down upon his hands that held hers, her warm lips softly upon them like a caress, her tears splashing hotly over them.

Bruce bowed his head and looked down at her bright head there before him, and suddenly wanted to take her into his arms and hold her fast, but instead he stood perfectly still, looking down, and said very softly:

"Dear!" and then after an instant, *"dear* little girl!"

There were steps coming down the long hall, and the beauty of the moment was held in abeyance as they both realized that someone was coming. Bruce's clasp was quick and sudden as he released her hands, and Coralie, dashing the tears away from her eyes, turned toward the door, in time to see it was the doctor going toward Lisa's room, with a specialist following him.

When the door had closed again Coralie was standing a step or two away from Bruce, but she turned to him with a look which answered him in a way she could not have brought herself to speak in words, and the brightness, the wonder of that look was like sunshine as it touched the bright drops on her lashes. Bruce answered it with a smile that was almost blinding, and thrilled her for days afterward whenever she dared let herself think about it.

The words they spoke after that were very commonplace, about everyday matters.

"Dana will be here as soon as possible. He found a few letters he felt he must dictate before he left, but he'll be coming. He wanted to be here and talk with the doctor when he came. He ought to be here any minute now," said Bruce.

And then presently came Dana, looking tired and responsible, and Coralie had a sudden realization of how much dignity her brother and his friend added to the terrible situation.

The detective and chief of police came while Dana was there, and they had a long session with them. It seemed there was nothing much for the police to do. Ivor was dead, and Dinsmore was probably dying. He had not rallied sufficiently to talk with them. Coralie felt that it would be just as well if he were not able to talk, for his tongue could twist a glib story and leave an impression that would live behind him, even if he died afterward. And it was altogether thinkable that even if Dinsmore were dying he would want revenge on Lisa for failing him financially before he went away.

The detective asked questions of Coralie. Did she know the man who shot her mother? Yes, he was her stepfather who went away quite a while ago, and they thought he was dead. A few days ago she had received a letter from him asking her to send him money.

Coralie brought the letters and let him read them, and from them the officers took the address of the hotel where he had been staying.

"Was he drunk, do you know?" one of them asked as they got up to leave.

"I don't know," said Coralie. "I was in my room asleep. I did not know he was here till I heard Lisa scream, and then when I got to the door I saw him, but just then he shot, and I saw Lisa fall. I did not think any more about him till I heard the other shots and saw him fall."

"Who made that other shot?" asked the detective.

"There were two shots, almost simultaneous. Ivor Kavanaugh shot Dinsmore, and Dinsmore shot Ivor."

"And you don't know whether this Dinsmore was drunk or not? You don't know whether either of them were drunk?"

"I think very likely they both were," said Coralie sorrowfully. "When he lived here Dinsmore was always more or less drunk in the evening, and I'm sure Ivor was drunk. He got drunk every time he came here."

Dana's face was very white when this interview closed at last. He had never realized before just what his sister's life had been.

"Will this thing come to trial?" asked the girl fearfully.

"If both men are dead, who would there be to try?" asked the officer sharply. "I understand there's no question of the lady having shot anybody?" He looked sharply at Coralie. "How about it? Has she got a gun?"

"Oh, no!" said Coralie. "She was fearfully afraid of guns. It was about the only thing she did fear."

"Have you got a gun?"

"Oh, no!" she said. "Lisa would never have allowed me to have one even if I had wanted it, and I never did."

"Mind if we search?"

"Of course not," she said.

"How about your servants? Do they have guns?"

"I wouldn't know. But not likely."

"Well, we'll look around, and then we'll run over to this fellow's hotel and see what else we find. It seems a pretty clear case."

The other officer nodded and they took their leave.

Then Dana turned compassionate eyes to his sister.

"You poor child!" he said gently. "What a life you've been through. If our father had known it he would have felt that he should save you from all this at any cost. I think he wanted me to come out here to find out that he was justified in letting our mother go. He must have wanted me to see that it wasn't just that she was hard to live with. But now I see he didn't dream what he had left you to face."

"But it was Lisa's fault," said the girl sorrowfully. "She took me with her. I wonder why?"

"I think my father thought it was to hurt him that she did it, though he never said so. But he could have got you back if he had known all. The law would have given you to him."

"Oh," said Coralie, like a little terrible groan, "how I wish he had. I would have loved him, I know."

Dana went over and put his arm around his sister.

"Thank you for saying that, sister. I'm sure you would have if you had known him. But I used to have a feeling that you sided with your mother. I didn't realize that you were too young when it all happened to have a say in the matter, and of course you didn't know."

"No, I didn't know," she said sorrowfully, "and what could I have done if I had known? Lisa would never have let me go, not if she had a reason like that."

"Well, perhaps she didn't," said the son sorrowfully. "Poor little soul, she's come about to the end of her willfulness. If she only could know the Lord before she has to meet him!"

Then he gave a startled look at his sister. Would she understand what he meant? But she nodded sadly and answered:

"Oh, yes. But would He take her? Would He save her when she's lived her whole life without Him?"

"Of course," said Dana with a radiant look. "Don't you know about the thief on the cross beside the Lord Jesus, how he confessed his sin, and the Lord said: '*Today* thou shalt be with me in Paradise!'"

"No," said Coralie seriously, "I've heard about a thief on the cross but I never knew what it meant. I didn't know Christ could save like that!"

"Yes, He can save like that!" said Dana in a triumphant voice. "He can save to the uttermost, them that come unto God by Him."

"Oh!" said Coralie. "Then we will pray. Will that help?"

"Yes, we will pray, little sister! Thank God that you have found our Saviour and are willing to pray with us!"

Dana could not stay much longer then, but Valerie came in about an hour after he left and stayed with Coralie for a little while. The two girls got very near in heart, as Coralie told her a little about her childhood, and what had been going on in her home of late.

"I wish you could see Lisa. She is beautiful, you know. In spite of all she has done she is very beautiful. Almost you forgive her everything, sometimes."

"Yes?" said Valerie. "If she looks like you I can well believe it. You are very beautiful."

Coralie gave a wan little smile.

"That's nice of you," she said sadly, "But you wouldn't say so if you knew me inside my heart. I've been very ugly toward God, I think. Though of course I didn't know much about Him. I never really knew anything only just words that didn't mean a thing, until Dana came. And now, oh, I wish Lisa could know!"

"We will all pray!" said Valerie softly. "There is great power in prayer."

That night the two young men came again and established themselves in the big room, prepared to stay all night, for the doctor had said Lisa was very weak, and might go at any time.

"But I'm all right," declared Coralie. "I really don't need you. The two nurses and the servants will be enough."

"You are to have somebody of your own," smiled Dana gently. "Besides, I have a right to stay. She is my mother too."

"Well, then you shall have a guest room," said Coralie and gave orders to have a room made ready.

What Lisa would have said if she could have known that her abandoned son was sleeping in her house, keeping watch over her, praying for her half the night, it is hard to think. But Lisa was lying on her bed moaning feebly and did not know. Lisa was very near the borderland that night.

But morning came and Lisa was still there.

Two days went by and still she was living, but the doctor shook his head and said it was only a question of time, a few hours at most. He had been afraid from the start. She had used up her vitality. She had lived on her nerves. There was fever. There might be infection, although he had done his best. The shock—! He said a great many words, but they did not explain. The brother and sister who stood near and listened felt that he knew nothing. The beautiful woman who was their mother was in God's hands, and even death could not conquer Him. Death had *been* conquered. Not until God decreed it would she stop breathing, and go from them. For they had prayed, and their friends had prayed, and even yet the "seventh hour" might come when the fever would leave her.

That night Dinsmore Collette died. Word was brought to them the next morning. But still Lisa was breathing.

The doctor stood over her, touched her pulse lightly, shook his head. The temperature? Yes, there was still fever. Strange! It worried the doctor who had his reputation to sustain.

The detectives had gone to Dinsmore Collette's hotel and searched his room. They had found in the waste basket fragments of another letter to Coralie, never finished. They had found other things that corroborated her story. But now he was dead. And Ivor Kavanaugh was dead. There was no point to working up a case. Likely the woman they had both brought low would be dead by another day. The two men had gone into the other world and taken their evidence with them. They could not be brought to punishment here any more, not even to answer each his charge of murder. They would have to answer to a Higher Court.

They ferreted out the place where Ivor Kavanaugh

and Errol Hunt had had an abode together, a miserable little forgotten hole, whose meagre rent had been unpaid for some time. But Errol Hunt had not been seen in those parts since the night of the shooting. So there was no one to question but a poor complaining landlady who knew nothing of the men at all except that they were always out of funds. She was keeping their effects in place of rent, and she complained bitterly that the police forced her to show them all there was.

But though they searched through everything, for Errol had not paused to go back and gather up anything, they found no evidence of where the two belonged in the scheme of this world. There were only a few bits of paper that hinted possible criminal complications in their past.

They buried Ivor Kavanaugh in an obscure corner of a country potter's field because they had no other place; and not far away in another burying ground belonging to the state they laid Dinsmore Collette, unmourned, and unattended save by officers of the law.

But still the woman who had caused the strife and the crime and in the end their death, lay tossing on a bed of fever, her heart keeping determinedly on as if she clung to life in spite of all.

Her children had been expecting all that day to be told at any moment that it was over and she was gone, but after the doctor had told them he did not see how she could live through the night, the young people gathered toward evening in a little room across the hall, where Lisa had kept her household accounts and interviewed her servants. There they knelt and prayed.

"A friend is dying," they had told their employers, and promised to do all in their power to make up for lost time afterward. So they were all there, Dana and Bruce, and Valerie and two of her brothers. And they knelt there that last hour quietly praying. Till as dusk came down, and the room grew darker, and the hush of evening was in the place, as if God had come into the room, Dana began to pray aloud for his mother, to plead with tender words, as if he were not only pleading on his own account, but on behalf of the father who was with the Lord already. Pleading that if the Lord must take her, that He would somehow save her first. Then one and another of the little group prayed, pleading the promises of God sealed by His blood. Till in turn it came to Coralie, the little newly saved daughter who had been so sinned against.

Nobody expected her to take up the petition except in her heart. She had never prayed in public. She had only just begun to pray in secret, like a babe stumbling with the first syllables of a language. But Coralie's voice, clear and shy and sweet, took up the petition:

"Please, dear God, give Lisa one more chance to be saved. She doesn't know. I don't think she understands. Give her one more chance and save her. Amen!"

And then Bruce's voice took up the prayer with a petition that must have reached the heart of God because it was so fraught with precious promises straight from His own word.

And as he came to an end there came a tap at the door.

They rose from their knees and Dana opened the door.

There stood the nurse, a look of wonder on her conventional face.

"The doctor told me to inform you that an unexpected change has come to the patient. The fever has left her, and the heart seems to be steadier. It may be that there is still some hope."

"Perhaps it is the seventh hour," said Dana with a sweet quick look at Valerie.

20

INCREDIBLE as it seemed to be, the fever was gone. The patient, though exceedingly weak, was gaining a little day by day.

She hadn't come back to their world yet, to know them, or to speak. Her murmurings were feeble plaints, mere syllables of suffering, of weakness, of protest against her strait.

"You don't think, Dana, do you, that maybe she'll come back to life and be the same as she was before; unsaved, unhappy, unloving?" There was a horror upon Coralie's face as she asked the question, and Bruce watched her as she spoke. She had the look of one who had passed beyond the place where mere petition for earthly life was enough. "Why, Dana, we'd be sorry we prayed if that was all," she went on. "Perhaps we had no right to insist on her living. Do you think that may be so?"

"Oh, no," said Dana quickly. "That doesn't seem like God's way. We did not pray merely that she might get well. We prayed that she might have a chance to be saved. You know it is not His desire that anyone shall perish. He has brought her back that she may have the chance to accept her Saviour. I believe that He will do it!"

The days went by and Lisa slowly improved, though she seemed still to be existing apart from them, in a world of her own. She did not seem to recognize them nor try to talk.

Coralie had been in to see her, had touched her hand and called her by her name, but she only looked silently at her an instant and then turned her eyes away. Restless eyes, that always seemed to be searching for something. Even Dana had been in, had sat beside her for a few minutes several times, and her eyes had lingered on him for an instant with a puzzled glint, and then closed as if she were weary.

But one evening the night nurse wanted to go out, the day nurse was asleep, and Coralie seemed very tired. She was lying on a couch in the big room, with Bruce and Kirk and Valerie sitting near talking quietly to her, but she told the nurse she would come and sit with Lisa until she returned.

"No," said Dana, "let me go."

"All right," said the nurse, "you go. Your sister is all worn out with those folks calling on her this afternoon. The patient is asleep and she won't be any trouble to you. If she should waken you can call your sister. Leave the door open and she will hear you."

So Dana went and sat beside his sleeping mother. The room was very still, with only a low night lamp burning. He could just see the halo of Lisa's beautiful gold hair, and delicate face. Strange that all her strenuous night life had not brought lines into her face nor spoiled her baby complexion.

Dana sat there for a few minutes watching her, trying

to realize that that was his mother. Wondering about their answered prayer. Was she really going to get better? The fever was gone, but she was creeping up to life very slowly. She had not taken hold of living again. It was as if her mind were somewhere else, busy, but not noticing the things of earth.

And while he was thinking these things he was praying.

Suddenly she spoke, and looking down he saw that her big lovely eyes were open and looking full at him.

"Jerrold! That is you, isn't it? I thought I saw you once before, but I wasn't sure, because they had told me you were dead. But you're not dead, are you?"

Dana sat breathless. He put his hand out and touched her hand softly.

"Yes, that is your hand. I would know its touch anywhere, though it was thousands of years since I had felt it. So smooth and tender! I have missed your hands, Jerrold."

His heart almost stood still. Should he tell her it was not Jerrold, only Jerrold's son? Should he spoil her vision, and perhaps lose the only touch he had ever had with her? Or should he humor her dream—perhaps it was only a dream—and let her go on thinking her husband was here, the husband from whom she had run away so long ago?

Her voice went on sweetly, gently:

"You don't believe that, do you, Jerrold? But I have missed your hands on mine. I have missed you too. I have sometimes wanted to come back to you, but I couldn't live the life you lived. I couldn't give up the world."

It was very still in the room. Dana could hear the soft murmur of the voices in the other room. He hoped they would not hear her talking and think they must come. Not yet, till he had heard all she had to say. It was as if he were permitted to hear a conversation between his long estranged father and mother.

"You don't answer, Jerrold," she said. "Perhaps you are dead after all, as they said! Or perhaps I am, and this is only dreaming."

Her eyes slowly closed and for a long time she did not speak again. He thought she was asleep.

Then suddenly she drew a deeper breath and turning, looked sharply across the room, then back to him.

"You are there yet, aren't you, Jerrold?"

He pressed her fingers softly.

There was another long pause and she said:

"I'm glad you came. I don't like to be alone. I thought I heard God walking over there. Did you see Him anywhere?"

"God is always here," said Dana very quietly.

"Oh, you are alive then! I'm glad. Because I'm afraid of God! And now you've come I suppose He'll be coming all the time. He's been in here several times, looking at me, usually in the night when no one else was awake. I don't like to be alone with God. He is not pleased with me. He did not like it when I went away and left you and my baby boy."

He pressed her fingers softly again, but did not speak. He must not frighten her. The fever might return.

Her eyes closed and she was still so long he was sure she was asleep again, and thought perhaps it would be well for him to slip away and send Coralie to her. But then she spoke again.

"I always knew that if I ever went back to you I would have to say yes to God," she said. "You knew I said 'no' to Him, didn't you? Well, I did. I couldn't bear to give up and be good like you, and just settle down and be solemn all the time. I wanted good times. I wanted to do as I pleased."

"But you know you were not happy, doing that," he said. His tone was very low and gentle. He did not know how startlingly like his father's it had grown.

Out of the silence of the room there came an answer presently.

"No, I was not happy, but I was too stubborn to let you know it. And I was too stubborn to give up to God. I thought sometime He would give up and go away. But He never did. Sometimes He would come and stand by my bed and hold my baby boy in His arms, and look at me till I thought my heart would break, and say 'What shall I do with this little child I gave you?' and then I couldn't get away from His look, and I would go and get a drink to forget. But I never could forget for more than a little while. And now God has come again, and I cannot stand it! I hate my life and all the things I have done, and I know God must hate me too!"

"No," said Dana gently. "He says 'I have loved thee with an everlasting love, therefore with loving-kindness have I drawn thee.' He wants you to take Him as your Saviour from all the things you have done that you despise. Won't you take Him now?"

"What would I have to do?"

"Just say, Jesus, I have sinned."

"Jesus, I have sinned," repeated the clear musical voice, and Dana held her hand softly, praying that the Holy Spirit would guide.

"But You have died and taken my sin upon Yourself," said Dana slowly, distinctly.

"But You have died and taken my sin upon Yourself," repeated Lisa.

"And I take You for my Saviour."

Word by word Lisa repeated the rest of the prayer, reverently, and then lifted her eyes.

"I'm tired now. Sing to me, Jerrold, I want to go to sleep."

And softly Dana began to sing:

> "Just as I am without one plea,
> But that Thy blood was shed for me,
> And that Thou bidst me come to Thee,
> O Lamb of God, I come, I come!"

Her eyes closed, and her hand lay quietly in his, as he sang on tenderly, till the nurse came back and took her place.

It seemed almost a desecration to see her move the chairs around and get everything in order for the night, there in that room where God had been, where perhaps angels had been listening while a soul that long had wandered came to God and was born again.

Dana slipped out of the room and met Bruce and Coralie a little down the hall waiting for him, a light in their faces that flashed joy to his heart.

"We came to see how you were getting on," said Coralie eagerly. "We thought you might need help. And then we heard her voice, and listened. Oh Dana, isn't God wonderful!"

"He is!" said Dana with a glad triumphant ring to his voice.

"And we heard you singing, Dana! That was the greatest gospel you ever sang, fella!" said Bruce with a sparkle in his eyes.

"I think we'd better all go into the little room and sing hallelujah, don't you?" said Dana with a look like glory in his face.

"Yes, and man, you're the one that said, not so long ago, that you didn't know as you ought to have come, and ought to stay in New York, and here you were the one the Lord chose to show the way to the Light!"

Dana smiled wonderingly.

"Well, I'm glad I came, brother. I didn't know how good the Lord could be to me. I just thought it had to be my planning that would work things out, and I hadn't any plans. But now I see God had. I hope I never do forget what He has done for me this night. Now, come on, let's go home and let this little sister of mine get some rest, or we'll have her sick on our hands."

So they left her and Coralie went to her room to lie in the dark and rejoice over all that the Lord was doing for her. It was all working out so wonderfully!

As the four walked home together there was great happiness among them. Bruce and Kirk had fallen into step together, just behind Valerie and Dana, and for a few blocks they walked very near to each other talking like one big happy family. Then Kirk and Bruce stopped to get a paper, and Valerie and Dana walked on ahead.

"I feel as if I ought to thank you under God, Valerie, for this wonderful thing that has come to my family," said Dana, drawing her arm a little closer through his and looking down at her sweet surprised face.

"Me?" said Valerie. "What in the world have I done?"

"You've helped me pray," said Dana, "and you've done a lot for my sister. You've encouraged me when I was about down and out, ready to run back west and try to forget them all."

"Oh, but I loved your sister from the start. I have enjoyed every minute of her that I could get. And of course I'd pray for anyone who needed a Saviour. As for encouraging you, why you great big silly *un*conceited fellow, if you'd had any sense at all you'd have known God wouldn't have sent you to New York if He hadn't had something for you to do here, so why get excited about me?"

Valerie was laughing as she spoke, looking up with her lovely pansy-eyes. Dana thought how sweet and dear and unaffected she was. Then suddenly he spoke from his heart, laying a loving hand upon hers and looking deep into her laughing face.

"Well, I can't help getting excited about you because I love you, Valerie. I know you've known me too short a time for me to begin to tell you that, but somehow I'm so happy tonight that I can't keep from telling you, even if it is too soon. Can you ever forgive me, and try to think well of me, and give me a chance for the future? Or will you always think I'm a big blunderbuss you want nothing to do with? I love you, Valerie, and I've loved you since ever I first saw you. It seems as if you are the answer to all that I shall ever want on earth."

"Oh, Dana!" cried Valerie eagerly, "but I've loved you longer than you have loved me."

"Oh no," said Dana. "I tell you I've loved you since the first minute my eyes met yours."

"Ah! But I saw you before you ever saw me!" said Valerie. "Yes, I did. I saw you and your sister walking on Fifth Avenue and I came home and told the folks at night about you. You ask them if I didn't. If I were a painter I could paint you just as you looked. You seemed that night to me the most wonderful person I had ever seen. And then you walked into the mission and sang with such a heavenly voice, and I *knew* you were. And the next day when I came into the office and saw you there with Mr. Burney I couldn't believe my eyes! But I never, never thought you'd ever look at plain little me!

Oh, I wouldn't have dared think such a thought as that! But I knew in my heart you were the man I could love if I ever had the chance."

"Plain little *you!* What do you mean?" cried Dana. "You with your pansy-eyes, and your sweet little mouth, and that look of trust and utter selflessness, and the holy look that tells you belong to God! You think you are *plain?* Don't ever let me hear you call yourself plain again, little lady! Not if you love me!"

They were walking slower and slower now and presently the two boys caught up with them.

"Say, are you two expecting to reach anywhere tonight at that rate of speed?" demanded Bruce genially.

"Well, we got to talking," explained Dana elaborately.

"I should say you did!" laughed Kirk, glancing significantly at the two hands clasped so closely. "But say, what time do you expect to get up in the morning at this rate?"

They laughed it off, but when they reached the Shannon house Dana declared he was going in for just a minute. "I want to get something," he said as he vanished into the hall and followed Valerie to a little room beyond the living room where her mother kept a desk and sometimes wrote letters while she was baking pies or bread and didn't want to run upstairs.

"Well, make it snappy," yelled Bruce. "I've got something myself I want to consult you about, and I'm not going to wait for you all night either."

But it was hard to tear himself away from that first opportunity to take Valerie in his arms and lay his lips upon hers. That first tender precious moment when they felt that they belonged to one another.

It was Valerie who first came to her senses.

"You must go, dearest. You can't keep Bruce waiting. There are other days coming for us, you know, and besides isn't it enough tonight just to know we love one another?"

And so at last with shining eyes he came forth and announced himself ready to go. He had wanted very much to tell Valerie's father and mother about it, only it was really quite late and they had retired an hour and a half ago, so that wasn't practicable.

"Now you have to be very circumspect tomorrow, you know, Dana. I can't have the official head of the department trying to kiss me on the sly," she warned him in an aside.

"Look out, young lady. If you say another word I'll kiss you right here and now, no matter who sees."

"Well," said Valerie with a twinkle, "I don't know that I should mind that so very much."

"Oh, you wouldn't, would you?" said Dana, and suddenly stooped and kissed her.

"Oh-h-h-*yes?*" cried Bruce in sudden comprehension. "How do you get that way? Is this fact I see before me, or fiction?"

"It's not fiction," said Dana with shining face. "Come along fella, let's get home. I thought you were in a hurry."

"Well," said Bruce as they walked briskly toward their quarters, "I've seen that coming in the distance, that is, I hoped I saw it, but I certainly didn't expect it to get here so soon."

"Nor I," said Dana in joyous abandon. "I didn't think I'd ever dare ask her to marry me, a girl like that! Why she's a wonder, Bruce! I'm only amazed she'll look at me. I just expected you'd cut me out before I got my nerve up to ask her. Having seen you, you giant, with your flaming red banner of hair, I wouldn't have supposed she'd even look at me."

"Cut that out, fella," said Bruce. "As if you didn't have hair like an angel yourself, that you hafta make game of mine. And as for your girl, she's all right I guess, but I've got one that counts more with me than ever she would."

"You don't say!" said Dana stopping short in the street and whirling his friend around so that the light they were passing would shine full in his face. "Is this true, or is it just a come-back because you're jealous?"

Bruce grinned and then suddenly sobered and gave Dana a searching look.

"Dana, what would you say if I told you I've fallen in love with your sister, and I want to marry her if she'll have me?"

Dana's face lightened up.

"I'd say it was great news, Bruce. The best news I could think of for my little sister. I haven't done much for her myself, but I haven't been blind to what you've done, and I couldn't think of anybody in the world I'd rather see marry Coralie than you. I know it would have pleased father, too. Oh, *boy!* What have I ever done to deserve so many glorious surprises all in one night? Nothing! But I have a wonderful Lord! But Bruce, about this surprise of yours. Does my sister know about it yet?"

"Well, I sort of think she has an inkling," said Bruce with a grin. "Of course I didn't just exactly feel like going ahead *too* far till I'd asked permission of her brother. I didn't know whether I would qualify in your eyes or not."

"Fella, it's not question of *your* qualifying," said Dana joyously, slapping Bruce happily on the shoulders, "it's a question of whether my sister can qualify. Remember she's never had a bringing up, and you may find that out to your sorrow some day."

"We'll work it out together with the help of the Lord, praise be!" said Bruce solemnly.

"And under those circumstances," said Dana, suddenly sobering too, "I can't think of any more ideal prospect. If you both feel that way, you'll succeed. And I believe in my heart she feels so too. I wouldn't have felt sure a month ago, but I do now, and it was you the Lord used to bring that about, too. Bruce, I hope my father knows what a night this is for us all. And I'm glad he knew you before he left us. It makes us all seem so much more like a real family."

"Yes, I'd thought of that," said Bruce.

"Fella, it's going to be great, to be real brothers!" said Dana. "There's no fellow in the world I'd rather be brother to than you."

"Same here!" said Bruce as he fitted the latchkey into the lock.

Two days later Lisa died.

Quite quietly, in her sleep.

She had seemed to be doing nicely all day, had asked to see Coralie, and wanted to know who was the man with the gorgeous red hair who came to the door with her. When Coralie told her "just a friend of Dana's," she demanded to see him.

So Bruce came in for a minute and smiled at her, as she looked him over with almost something of her old-time keenness.

"He's better looking than Errol," she said after a minute. "I can see he's a good man, too. I'm glad you've got such a friend, child. It doesn't pay to do as I did."

Then she closed her eyes and they went out. Bruce

led Coralie away to the far end of the hall where they stood at the window looking out on the fire escape framing the view of the great city. But they were not interested in the view.

Bruce turned suddenly and looked down at Coralie, drawing her close to his side.

"I love you, Coralie," he breathed softly with his lips against her forehead. "I *love* you!" and his lips stole down to her.

She nestled closer to him and gave her lips to his. It seemed to her that Heaven had come down and met her in that kiss. Such wonder that a love like that should come to her in place of what the world had offered.

And after a little, with his arm about her, and her head resting against his shoulder, her hand in his, they walked slowly back and forth together for a little and talked.

"I'm glad you took me in to see your mother," he said. "I am glad she seemed to like me."

"She liked you a great deal or she wouldn't have said what she did. It was so like her to speak of your hair. She loves beautiful things."

"Beautiful things! My *hair!*" he said in wonder, running his fingers through the brilliant waves. "What could you find in red hair to be beautiful? Dana is always teasing me about it. Take Dana's now, I'll admit that is as beautiful as an angel's mane, but not mine. I'm only an old red-top."

"Oh, but your hair *is* beautiful!" said Coralie lifting adoring eyes. "I love it!"

"Oh, all right," grinned Bruce. "If you say so, it's beautiful, my beloved! Whatever you say goes," and he stooped with a look of deep reverence, and drawing her close to his heart kissed her tenderly again.

The thrill of that kiss was still in her heart that night when she went in to say good night to Lisa.

It was most unwonted for her to lean and drop a kiss like a butterfly's touch on Lisa's cheek before she left, and Lisa looked up startled, almost as if she recognized something that she must have missed all her life.

Then she spoke:

"He's all right!" she said. "Now go! Good night!"

The nurse came to her then as Coralie left and arranged her for the night. Lisa suffered the service without notice till the nurse was about to turn the light low, and then she said:

"Well, good night, nurse. I shan't be here in the morning!"

The nurse gave her a quick scrutinizing glance, and thought she saw a dreamy look on the face of her patient.

"Is that so?" she said idly, to humor her notion.

"Yes," said Lisa as if announcing a journey, "I'm going back to my husband, you know. You can tell them in the morning when I'm gone! Just say I've gone home at last. Say God wanted me to come. My husband's over there with God, you know."

Then she closed her eyes and drifted off to sleep, and the nurse, a trifle puzzled, took her temperature to make sure, but all seemed well. Could it be there was to be a return of the delirium? She tried to call the doctor and tell him, but he was out on a case, so she settled down to rest. She watched the patient occasionally during the night, but did not notice any particular change. She seemed to be sleeping quietly.

But in the morning she was gone!

A little later they stood about her, and Dana, looking down upon that lovely face which death had only made more beautiful in its quietness, said:

"It was 'the seventh hour,' when our mother went Home, but she has gone Home *saved,* thank the Lord! And father will be so glad! Their meeting will be wonderful!"

Then he stooped and kissed his sister tenderly.

About the Author

Grace Livingston Hill is well known as one of the most prolific writers of romantic fiction. Her personal life was fraught with joys and sorrows not unlike those experienced by many of her fictional heroines.

Born in Wellsville, New York, Grace nearly died during the first hours of life. But her loving parents and friends turned to God in prayer. She survived miraculously, thus her thankful father named her Grace.

Grace was always close to her father, a Presbyterian minister, and her mother, a published writer. It was from them that she learned the art of storytelling. When Grace was twelve, a close aunt surprised her with a hardbound, illustrated copy of one of Grace's stories. This was the beginning of Grace's journey into being a published author.

In 1892 Grace married Fred Hill, a young minister, and they soon had two lovely young daughters. Then came 1901, a difficult year for Grace—the year when, within months of each other, both her father and husband died. Suddenly Grace had to find a new place to live (her home was owned by the church where her husband had been pastor). It was a struggle for Grace to raise her young daughters alone, but through everything she kept writing. In 1902 she produced *The Angel of His Presence, The Story of a Whim,* and *An Unwilling Guest.* In 1903 her two books *According to the Pattern* and *Because of Stephen* were published.

It wasn't long before Grace was a well-known author, but she wanted to go beyond just entertaining her readers. She soon included the message of God's salvation through Jesus Christ in each of her books. For Grace, the most important thing she did was not write books but share the message of salvation, a message she felt God wanted her to share through the abilities he had given her.

In all, Grace Livingston Hill wrote more than one hundred books, all of which have sold thousands of copies and have touched the lives of readers around the world with their message of "enduring love" and the true way to lasting happiness: a relationship with God through his Son, Jesus Christ.

In an interview shortly before her death, Grace's devotion to her Lord still shone clear. She commented that whatever she had accomplished had been God's doing. She was only his servant, one who had tried to follow his teaching in all her thoughts and writing.

Don't miss these Grace Livingston Hill romance novels!

VOL.	TITLE	ORDER NUM.	PRICE
84	Cloudy Jewel	07-0474-6-HILC	4.95
85	Crimson Mountain	07-0472-X-HILC	4.95
86	The Mystery of Mary	07-4632-5-HILC	3.95
87	Out of the Storm	07-4778-X-HILC	3.95
88	Phoebe Deane	07-5033-0-HILC	4.95
89	Re-Creations	07-5334-8-HILC	4.95
90	Sound of the Trumpet	07-6107-3-HILC	4.95
91	A Voice in the Wilderness	07-7908-8-HILC	4.95
92	Honeymoon House	07-1366-4-HILC	3.95
93	Katharine's Yesterday	07-2030-X-HILC	3.95

Mail your order with check or money order for the price of the book(s) plus $2.00 for postage and handling to: **Tyndale Family Products, P.O. Box 448, Wheaton, IL 60189-0448.** Allow 4-6 weeks for delivery. Prices subject to change.

The Grace Livingston Hill romance novels are available at your local bookstore, or you may order by mail (U.S. and territories only). For your convenience, use this page to place your order or write the information on a separate sheet of paper, including the order number for each book.